I0738780

Red And the Big Bad... Wolf?

Also Available From Elizabeth Lee Sorrell

Wrong Turn Fairy Tales

Exclusively available on
Barnes & Nobles for Nook Book.

More Than Instinct

Black & White

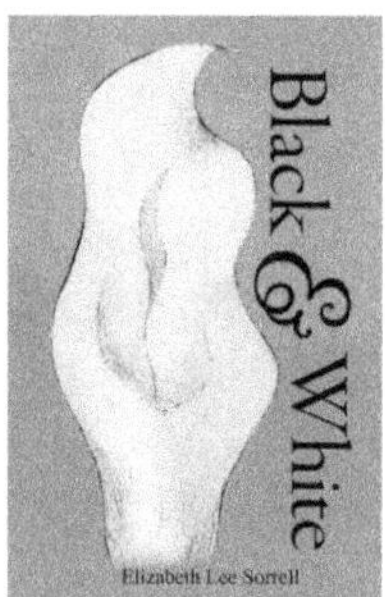

Available from your favorite bookstores.

The Clause Rebellion

Attack On the Clause

Red and the Big Bad... Wolf?

Elizabeth Lee Sorrell

trading as

Yarbrough House Publishing, Inc.

Acknowledgements

I'd like to thank my family who really do all the hard work. While I sit back and make up fanciful stories, my family stays busy proofing, formatting, illustrating, crunching numbers, and taking care of all the "business stuff." All I do is play with my imagination, but my family works hard to bring life to my stories.

Chapter One

Sallee Roxanne Gardner was ready to spit fire as she walked out of the board members meeting. The board members were all pompous windbags that didn't believe a woman should be running a multimillion dollar company. The board was comprised mainly of retired businessmen with an outdated way of thinking. They were hand chosen to sit back and exist in name only, to let others hold all the control of running the company. They had regular meetings, but all that was ever discussed in meetings was Roxie's short comings, not that all they discussed was true. They were old men who just wanted something to sit around and gripe about, so Roxie kept quiet and let them run their mouths as long as they never actually tried to do anything that could undermine her or risk the company. The men had been especially vocal today, but that was not what had Roxie so frustrated.

Everything had gone wrong since she got out of bed that morning. She had reached groggily toward her alarm to cut it off and inadvertently knocked a glass of water off the night stand. Water had gone everywhere, all down the wooden night stand, soaking into the carpet, and splattered across her bed.

She slipped in the tub, almost falling, and when she was trying to make it out the door with a cold, plain bagel and a glass of orange juice in hand, the glass slid from her hand. It shattered on the floor sending glass and orange juice in a five foot radius. Orange juice was dripping from her suit, forcing her to turn back to change clothes as well as clean the mess, and she had a small nick on her right ankle caused by flying glass.

Just in case she was not running late enough already, there had been a wreck on the interstate that Roxie had barely missed but had not managed to miss the traffic back up. The only good thing that Roxie could find that morning was that she had not been involved in the wreck; she had barely missed it.

All the little things that had made her morning so irritating was still not what had upset her the most today. Only one thing could frustrate her this much, her family.

Roxie loved her family very, very much. For the most part, they were a close knit family, but sometimes they could be the most irritating people in her life. She was the youngest of three. Michael and Kris, her two older brothers, were both the big, strong, overprotective type. Michael was eight years older and Kris six years older than Roxie. Their dad had died when Roxie was only two, and both brothers had tried to step in to play daddy.

Michael still lived in the small town they grew up in where he practiced dentistry and helped take care of their mother who had never remarried. Although, he lived on the opposite side of town, which technically put him out of the way in either direction. Kris bounced around from job to job since returning home from a twelve year military career.

Today, Kris was the object of Roxie's frustration. She had not been in the meeting for two hours total, and he had called her cell at least four times. He knew she was at work, and he knew that her job is taxing. She really did not have time for interruptions especially today when her whole day had been thrown off. Because he knew this, Roxie was scared not to return his call. What if something was wrong? There could be some sort of emergency.

Roxie slid into the desk behind her chair and pulled up Kris's number.

"Hey, Red!" Kris's voice came over the line.

Roxie scowled at the phone. Her family had called her Red for as long as she could remember, because she was born with fire red hair and never really looked like a Sallee. She later chose to go by Roxie on her own.

"Hey, Kris, what's up?"

"Remember that friend I've been telling you about?"

Roxie remembered. Kris had been hounding her to get a friend of his a job. It was someone he had met during his time in the military; Roxie had never met him.

"I told you I don't have any openings, and even if I did I don't just hand out jobs."

"I'm not asking you to either. Interview him. He's worked in almost every level of business. He's smart, thinks on the fly. Red, he really needs this. I wouldn't ask you if it weren't important. You know that right."

"Kris, this isn't going to happen. I'm sorry. I've had a rough morning, and I'm running behind. I've really got to go I've got a lot of work to do."

"You've got to take a lunch break right... because I told him to drop by your office around noon."

"Kris!"

"Just interview him. You may change your mind."

"I've got to go, Kris."

Roxie sighed as she ended their call. She couldn't help but wonder if Kris ever bugged Michael at work like this, or tried to coerce him into handing out jobs. Probably not. Michael would not allow it, but Roxie had always been a push over outside of work. She could be a shark at work when the situation called for it, but that simply was not a genuine part of her personality. She thanked her brothers for that attribute, teaching her that in some situations she had to strike back or be taken under someone else's rule.

Roxie glanced at the clock, 11:39. Great. She had not planned on taking a lunch. With everything that happened, Roxie figured that if she worked through lunch, she could catch up. So much for that idea. There was no hope for it. She would have to work late, unless Kris's friend was a no show. Roxie hated working late. This business district was deserted after dark, and the last thing she wanted to do was walk the block and a half to the parking deck alone in the dark.

"Roxie," came Lucy, Roxie's secretary's, voice through the intercom. Roxie had insisted that she call her by her first name. "There is a man out here to see you; he says your brother sent him."

Not a no show then. "It's ok, Lucy. Send him in." Better to get it over with so that she could get on with work.

Roxie stood up to greet the man entering her office. Halfway across the small room, she tried to hide her shock as he strode through the door with a confidant gait. He was not at all what she had expected. This man had been in the military with Kris and had supposedly worked jobs at every level of business. She was expecting someone a little older, but this man didn't look any older than her own thirty-one years. He was huge. He wasn't a giant or anything, but he was tall and muscular. He was built like he was still in the military.

Kris had bulked up a lot while in the military. Kris wasn't a small man before or now, but he had lost some of his bulk since quitting the military. If this man had been any larger or stronger, Roxie would have been rightly scared just to be in his presence.

Roxie could see the muscles through his nice fitting shirt bunch in his shoulder and chest as he lifted his hand to shake hers. "Hi, I'm Patrick Miller."

His handshake was firm, his skin calloused, and his touch warm. Roxie got caught in his gaze, mesmerized by his glassy, dark eyes. They looked almost black; they were so dark that she couldn't tell what color they really were.

"Hi, Roxie Gardner. I'm sorry. I tried to tell Kris I really don't have any openings right now." Roxie forced herself to look away from his eyes. He had a dark tan like he spent most of his time outside. It was a far cry from Roxie's porcelain, pale skin that almost never saw sun. She couldn't tan anyway even if she did have time to get more sun.

"That's ok. I understand. I'm sorry to have taken up your time." Patrick turned back around toward the door.

"Wait, come in and have a seat." Roxie didn't know what she was thinking. The man was willing to turn back around and walk back out the door. She could get her work done, but she was asking him to stay. The smart thing would have been to encourage him to leave, but Roxie just couldn't bring herself to watch him walk away so soon. It was weird, but she wanted to talk to this man. "You took the time to come in today. You might as well interview while you're here."

"But you don't have any openings."

"That doesn't mean that none will open up. You never know when getting your foot in the door could help, right?"

"Sure." Patrick didn't look sure, but he took a seat anyway.

"So, Kris tells me you have some experience in business?" Roxie asked.

"Yes, it's been a while, but it's like riding a bike."

"How long has it been?"

"Years."

"You and Kris met in the military, right?"

"Yes."

"When did you work in business?" This man's story was unraveling right before Roxie's eyes. He was far too young to have worked every level of business before entering the military.

"It was before I met Kris."

"Aren't you a little too young for that?"

"I'm older than I look."

"Exactly how old are you? Did you bring a resume or anything?"

Patrick held up a folder but did not hand it to Roxie instead he stood up and said, "Look, this was a bad idea. I'm going to go. I appreciate your time. Tell Kris that I appreciate his concern, but I can take care of myself."

He had to get out of that office fast. He had met the rest of Kris' family, and his baby sister looked nothing like them. She had red hair that hung in loose curls around her face. It was as bright as a flame in the night, shinning like a beacon, and it was calling to him. Hair like that is definitely an attention grabber.

That short dress showed off her long sexy legs and did little to hide the curves that drove all reason from his mind. She had smooth, flawless, creamy white skin with a scattering of light brown freckles. More than anything right now, Patrick wanted to play connect the dots like some preschooler. Whatever it took to get his hands on her skin to see for himself if it was nearly as soft as it looked.

Even her voice was appealing like perfectly tuned bells ringing through her every word. Patrick wouldn't mind sitting here all week listening to her talk. Responsibilities could wait, couldn't they? That wasn't right. Her sweet voice did funny things to his brain. He couldn't think around her. He had walked himself right into a corner without even thinking about it. Patrick never let anyone get that close to confirming suspicions. He didn't know what she suspected as of right now, but he wasn't sticking around to find out or to give her long enough to draw more theories.

He had enough on his plate anyway, too much to be focusing on a new job. He hated that he was forced to look for one in the first place, but people were beginning to talk. It didn't make sense that a man could go years without steady work and not run low on funds. If only he could have stayed with the military. He fit in better there, and he could more easily do what he had been born to do. It wouldn't have been long before his lack of deterioration caused questions, and he was needed more here, no matter the complications.

Kris wouldn't be happy with him, but that was just too bad. He had never made it his goal to keep Kris happy. Kris was a good friend, but he could take care of himself.

He flew past the front desk and security. He was going to find something to eat and maybe do a little checking around before dark, but he couldn't seem to get Kris' baby sister off his mind. What did she say her name was? Roxie? That wasn't what Kris called her. He closed his eyes and saw her in his mind as he listened to her voice chiming through his head. That bright red hair was lighting up his whole world right now. Red, that was it. That was what Kris had called her, and it suited her well.

◆ ◆ ◆

Roxie had not wasted much time with Patrick, not as much time as she could have wasted if he hadn't shot out of there like a man on fire. Let's face it, she didn't waste as much time as she had wanted after getting an eyeful of that man. What had gotten into her? Her brothers were big, muscled men. She did not usually go gaga like that over a beefy man. That man was built of pure muscle and masculinity, and Roxie could have, wanted to, spend a lot more time talking with him. Still, she had wasted enough time that she would have to work over just a little.

Roxie pushed herself and left only forty-five minutes late, but that little bit of time had been enough for not only the building to empty out but the whole district too. Dusk had fallen, and it was already difficult to see. Roxie knew the way well enough that she could make the trek easily in the dark.

She picked up her pace wanting to get out of there as fast as possible. It wasn't like the business district was a "bad" part of town. Break in's were rare and usually by teenagers easily caught. She hadn't heard of any trouble, but that didn't mean that she wanted to hang around alone in the dark either. There was something in the air tonight creeping Roxie out.

As further proof that any danger out there tonight was in her head, Roxie made it all the way back to the parking deck and her car without anything happening. She remotely unlocked her doors and reached for the handle as something cylinder and relatively small pressed against her back.

Roxie's head began to spin when she realized the danger too late. There was a gun pressed into her back, and a raspy voice whispered, "Get in the car. We're going to take a little ride."

Everything seemed to be moving in slow motion, yet Roxie couldn't process it all. She tried to get her body moving to just do what the guy said, but her body wouldn't cooperate. She needed to breathe and remain calm; there was no one around to hear her scream if she did try. Before she could drag in her first breath, something large and hairy flew over her left shoulder.

This time Roxie did scream as she sucked in a sharp breath and collapsed to the ground and covered her head with her arms. It was a useless gesture, she knew, but she didn't know what else to do. She wasn't a fighter. Her brothers had always fought her battles for her. She had always taken it for granted before that they protected her the way they did, but it was doing her little good now.

Roxie stayed pooled on the concrete next to her car door with her eyes shut tight. Sounds of a scuffle filled her ears, drowning out all other noise. She could hear crashes and bangs. Grunting and... growls? It wasn't growling from a human; it was more animal.

When the racket finally quieted down, Roxie eased her arms away from her head and slowly pushed herself back to her feet. Her attacker was lying behind her car bloody, maimed, and unconscious. To the right of the body, stood a large wolf with a bloody muzzle.

The wolf was dark brown, nearly black. It had long fur and eyes equally as dark as it's fur, and it was staring straight at her.

Roxie made eye contact with the wolf. Then it turned and ran off. Roxie let out the breath that she had not realized she'd been holding and started scrambling to find her purse and her phone.

The 911 dispatcher stayed on the line with Roxie until the paramedics arrived. One of the paramedics checked to see that she was okay then moved her away from the gore. The police arrived soon after and asked a million questions. It was late by the time they let her leave. She was relieved when she turned back to her car and saw Kris leaned against the driver's door.

"How did you know?" she asked.

"Friend on the force," Kris answered briefly.

"You just have friends everywhere, don't you?"

"Pretty much. How you holding up, kid?"

Roxie buried her head against Kris's chest and let go of all the tears she had not allowed herself to cry during the police questioning. "It was so horrible." Kris held her close and did not say a word while he let her cry it out of her system.

"Let me drive you home," Kris suggested leading her to the passenger's side.

"What about your car?" Roxie protested.

"I'll get somebody to bring me back for it tomorrow. Like you said, I have friends everywhere, so stop arguing and get in the car."

Kris drove her back to her apartment and did not leave until she was safely tucked into bed. Sure, he was treating her like a child, but thank heaven for overprotective brothers who would baby you after a night like tonight.

The next morning, Roxie shouldn't have gone to work. She shouldn't have gone anywhere, but she did. She got up, got dressed, and went on as normal. She moved like she was in a trance, going through the motions without much notice. The only thing out of routine was calling Lucy for a ride.

Lucy was great! The way she stepped up to keep Roxie going was tremendous. Lucy has to be by far the best secretary ever, and she proved herself a good friend in the process. She kept Roxie moving through the remainder of the week.

Roxie knew if she could make it through the week, that she could go home this weekend to be with her family. They were planning a get together Saturday. It wasn't much; all they were doing was going to Mom's for lunch, but being surrounded by family just now was exactly what the doctor ordered.

Friday was long and excruciatingly boring. All Roxie wanted to do was to get out of there and try to put everything behind her. Now, she was regretting her decision to continue as usual. Specifically she was regretting her decision to come in to work today.

"Lucy, I'm waiting on a report from... uh" Roxie started scanning through her email looking for the name of the smaller location she was looking for. She was going to have to see to it that they got brought up to date with technology. Every other location emailed their reports, but this location was still printing them out and using snail mail.

"I've got it. It got here a few minutes ago. Would you like me to bring it in?"

"Please."

Lucy walked into the office wearing a big smile. "Phillip, from the mail room, laughs every time he delivers these things." She tossed the large manila envelope on the desk and plopped into a chair opposite Roxie.

"I know, I was just thinking I need to make sure that location becomes a bit more tech savvy."

"Maybe you could go down there yourself. Take a little time off and teach them what they need to know."

"You know I have too much to do here," Roxie reminded.

"Okay, I just thought it might give you a chance to focus your mind on something else for a while. You could really use some time off. I'm really worried about you. You're here in body, but you haven't been yourself since it happened."

Lucy didn't have to say aloud what it was. No one mentioned it out loud, but it was all Roxie could think about. She swore she could still feel the hard steel of a gun pressed into the middle of her back, and each time she closed her eyes she saw the wolf's dark eyes as if they had seared into the back of her eye lids.

"I know, Luc. I'm going to have lunch with my mom and brothers tomorrow. I just need to take the weekend to calm my nerves. Having my family around me will help."

"Yeah... Hey, whatever happened to that friend of your brother," Lucy asked with a waggle of her eyebrows then added. "That one was cute."

"It wasn't like that. He was looking for a job. Kris sent him here. I told Kris it wasn't going to happen, but that's Kris. He doesn't ever give up."

"Any chance he might send that guy back again? I wouldn't mind having him around to look at every day."

"I honestly don't think that guy would come back here if Kris paid him to. He shot out of here in a big enough hurry to set his heels on fire."

"Yeah, what did you do to him? You're usually so nice to everyone."

"I didn't do anything. We were just talking, sort of interview style... Something about that guy doesn't add up. I asked to see his resume, and he took off instead."

"Too bad." Lucy's face had a faraway look. She was daydreaming about something or somebody, Patrick no doubt.

"He was nice looking, wasn't he?" Roxie offered in a whisper.

Lucy looked at Roxie with a knowing smile before that smile turned sympathetic. "Girl, why don't you get out of here? That report will be here on Monday, and no one is going to begrudge you taking a half day after what you went through."

"I might do that. Are you sure you don't mind?"

"You're the boss; don't ask me."

"Thanks, Luc! I'll see you Monday!" Roxie grabbed her purse and still emptied briefcase and practically ran outside and all the way to her car.

There was still a large blood stain in the parking deck. Roxie started parking five spots away, but it did nothing to block out the discoloration. Seeing the blotch was like seeing the bloodied body sprawled out again. Roxie had heard that the guy had recovered and would be getting released from the hospital soon; however, she had also heard that he was not going to be released "scott free". He was under arrest for several counts of armed burglary. Roxie was apparently not his first victim. For some reason, none of that was nearly as comforting as it should have been.

Roxie had an uncomfortable feeling of being watched. It was just nerves after everything that had happened. That had to be it, right? Either way, Roxie fished her phone out of her purse and called Kris.

"Hey, everything okay?" Kris answered the phone.

"Yeah, I'm taking half a day. I'm on my way back to my car, and I just needed someone to talk to me for a while, kinda calm my nerves."

"You want me to come pick you up?"

"No, I'm fine, really. I'm just a little... jittery. Just talk to me."

"Okay, you still coming tomorrow?"

"Yes."

"Mom's been talking about it nonstop all day. I tagged along to help her out with some shopping today."

"That's nice."

"Yeah, I think she's milking it, having me around again. How did she ever survive while I was gone?" Roxie could literally hear the smirk in Kris's voice.

"Michael and I were still here for her."

"Sure, here but busy with work."

"Mom's not as helpless as she'd have you believe either."

"It's a symbiotic relationship. Mom wants the company, and I like feeling needed... Hey, with all the excitement, I forgot to ask you the other day. How did it go with Miller?"

"Kris," Roxie practically whined, "I told you that I didn't have any openings and don't give away jobs... I talked to him. He took off though. I don't know if I offended him or something. I didn't mean to if I did. I don't know what happened. He just left. Fast."

"Strange. I may check on him later see what's up. He's sort of an independent sort. He won't like me checking on him like some kid."

"An independent sort? I'm starting to think that is a prerequisite for the military."

"Right, because you know so many former or current military. How many of us do you know?"

"I know you, and... I met your friend the other day."

"Two, yeah, you're the military personality expert alright."

"Fine, you made your point. I'm almost home now. Thanks, Kris."

"Anytime, Red, anytime. See you tomorrow."

"Bye."

Roxie tried futilely for the rest of the day to relax. She couldn't calm her tattered nerves no matter what she tried. She attempted taking a nap, but when she closed her eyes, the whole gruesome scene replayed repeatedly in her mind. So instead, she got up and trudged to the bathroom for a steaming, soothing bubble bath.

The water was hot, giving her skin a rosy flush. A thin layer of sweat formed over her face and rolled down the sides of her head.

The bubble scent was supposed to have a calming effect on the mind and body, but it had no effect on Roxie today. She laid in the tub watching the bubbles pop and waited for the hot water to ease her tense muscles. Unfortunately, the water had as little effect as the bubble scent.

Next, Roxie tried some double fudge, chocolate chip ice cream. That was always one of her favorite go to stress foods. Today, not even chocolate could help her. What she really needed was a way to forget. Forget the way the hard barrel of the gun felt pressed menacingly into her back, the way chills ran up and down her spine radiating from the point of the gun. Forget her attacker's scratchy, husky voice so close behind her, in her personal space, the way it sounded when he threatened her. Forget the way that wolf came lunging out of nowhere, the color of its fur, the gloss of its eyes. Forget the fact that a wild un-tamable wolf had bypassed her and gone for her attacker, how it calmly walked away leaving her standing and unharmed. Forget the way she felt looking into the wolf's eyes, scared, helpless, excited, and something else that she couldn't put her finger on.

Yeah right. Roxie was sure that the night of her attack was a night she would never forget. Finally she curled up on the couch to watch TV eventually slipping off to sleep.

Chapter Two

Roxie woke late the next morning and had to rush to get dressed and on the road. Mom's house wasn't far, a little over an hour and a half, but there was no way her brothers would wait for her. She wouldn't want them to; it wasn't a safe thing to come between her brothers and food.

When she pulled up to the house, Michael was waiting in the front yard. He was already at her car door before she could even put the car in park. He opened the door and pulled her out of the car and into a crushing bear hug. Her face smashed against his chest making escape impossible even if she had desired to run. "Red! I've missed you so much. Are you okay?"

"I'm fine."

"Kris said you called yesterday."

"Kris is a tattle tale. I'm fine, honest, just a little jumpy."

"That's understandable."

Michael loosened his grip, and Mom was standing in wait. "Red, baby!" Mom scooped Roxie up and cradled her close the same as they used to do after Roxie would get hurt as a child. "Are you sure you're okay? You can stay here until you are feeling more yourself, or I could send Kris to stay with you for a while."

Roxie forced a smile. "Mom, don't be silly. My nerves are shot, but it's only been a couple of days. Give me a little time. I'm going to be fine."

"Of course you will, sweetie. But, in the meantime, Kris can stay until you are ready."

"No, really, I'm fine."

"Hey, y'all give the kid some space. No wonder her nerves are shot," Kris called from the doorway. It was rare that he was the voice of reason. "Now, get in here, Red."

"I'm sorry I'm running late this morning. Y'all aren't waiting on me, are you?"

"Nah, we're waiting on Kris's friend," Michael said. Irritation was clear in his voice.

"Hey, lay off. I told him 12:30; it's not even noon yet. Look, I told you, Michael; he's never late." Kris's friends stopping by for a meal was nothing new. Anywhere Kris stayed had a revolving door policy. People were in and out all the time.

"Never mind. Come inside, sweetheart," Mom said ushering Roxie past the boys. "You can help me ice the cake."

"You made a cake? What's the occasion?"

"I've had the urge to bake lately. I think Kris has enjoyed it."

"I just bet he has," Roxie leered.

Icing a cake with Mom was always a treat; they had a tendency to get carried away when they got together, but it was fun nonetheless. It allowed Roxie the opportunity to relax for the first time all week.

Michael walked into the kitchen silently. He opened the fridge then shut it again without removing anything. He did the same to the freezer and the pantry.

"Michael, what's up?" Roxie questioned.

"Want to tell me what happened?" he responded.

"It's killing you, isn't it?"

"Yeah, I'd kinda' like to know what my baby sister went through so that I know what to do to help. You told Kris what happened."

"The police told Kris what happened," she rebuffed.

"You called Kris for help yesterday." Now he just sounded jealous.

"You were working. I can't help it that Kris is the family bum."

"He's not a bum," Mom rebuked with a grimace.

"I understand if you aren't ready to talk about it. Just don't forget I'm here for you too."

"I know you are." Roxie buried her face in Michael's chest, wrapped her arms around him, and gave him every detail she could remember from her attack.

"Red? Are you sure of what you saw? A wolf is not likely to be in the middle of the business district. It could have been a stray."

"It was a wolf, Michael. It was too big to be a stray dog."

"Think about it. It's far more sensible that it was a stray."

"Michael, do you remember the report that Kris did on wolves for school? Because, I do. Kris used me as his guinea pig. I listened to his speech over and over. I'm telling you that was a wolf. It was taller than a dog with shaggier hair and an arched spine. It had a wider head and pointed ears. The only thing was the eyes..."

"What about the eyes," Michael pushed.

"A wolf's eyes are usually yellow. This one had dark eyes. They were almost black, void of all color."

"See there you go it wasn't a wolf."

"Michael, I know what I saw! You weren't there! It was a wolf!" He was making her mad now. Why wouldn't he believe her? She was upset, sure; who wouldn't be? That didn't make her stupid. She knew what she saw, and she knew a wolf when she saw one.

◆◆◆

Kris was sitting out on the porch drinking a cold beer when Zeke pulled up. The house was larger than he had imagined. Pristine brown paint was trimmed with red shutters. The long front porch went across the front of the house. A swing hung at one end, and at the other end sat two wooden rockers. Kris was lolled in one rocker with his feet propped up on the banister. After returning from the military, he moved back in with his mom, but now it was just him and his mom. The house was too big for only two people; it was no wonder his mom liked having him around. She probably needed all the help she could get.

Kris had suggested that Zeke come for lunch today to meet Michael. Michael was giving Zane a job, and Kris thought it would help things flow easier Monday if they met.

When Zeke stepped out of the car he was assaulted by the sweet smell of apple blossoms from a tall tree to the right of the house and figs from a bush out front. Not as strong he smelt the scent of food wafting from inside the house.

"About time you got here. Everyone is starved," Kris called.

"Am I late?"

"Nah, we're just a hungry crew is all. Come on." Following Kris through the house, Zeke could hear chatter coming from the kitchen. Two people were arguing. One was a male voice, and the other was a familiar female voice. It was a voice that was instinctively drawing him in although he couldn't guess why it would. Zeke had no idea that Roxie would be here today. Kris had not mentioned it. It was a sorry thing to admit, but Zeke probably would not have shown today if he had known that she would be here. He wasn't scared of one little girl. No one would ever get him to say that, but he wasn't necessarily ready to face her again either, not with the things she may or may not have been putting together.

As they got closer, Zeke focused in more on the argument taking place in the kitchen. It wasn't the fact that Roxie was arguing with someone or even that she sounded upset that was the most disturbing, although that was unsettling. What bothered Zeke most was that what he heard was not a promising conversation. "What was a wolf," he asked as they walked into the kitchen. Roxie turned to look at him; her face was riddled with uncovered shock. She was as ravishing as the other day. Every detail was brandished into his mind.

"It's a long story; I'll fill you in later," Kris offered. "You met Red the other day. This is my mom and my brother, Michael. Michael, this is Zeke, your new employee."

"I thought you said your name was Patrick," Roxie accused.

"It is, Patrick Zeke, most people call me Zeke."

Roxie's face fell. Zeke couldn't tell what it was that made her face fall like it did, but whatever it was, he wanted more than his next breath to wipe the fallen look from her face.

"You hired him?" Roxie asked Michael.

"I needed some extra help around the office. He needed a job. What's the big deal?"

"None, I guess."

"What's the deal, Red? You couldn't hire him, so now you don't want Michael to either? When did you turn so petty?"

"I didn't mean it like that. I was just curious."

"Of course you didn't mean anything. She's been through a lot this week, Kris," her mom came to her rescue. Now she looked ashamed, and that Zeke simply could not stand.

"It's cool, Kris. I didn't take any offense. I took it as curiosity," he said and gave Roxie a wink. A lovely flush covered her face a lighter shade than her fire red hair. Red, he would never be able to think of her by any other name from this point forward. From her becoming flush to her enticing hair, she was Red.

Red cleared her throat and said, "Kris, back me up here. Tell Michael there was a wolf in the parking deck the other night."

"Red... I didn't see it."

"You saw the body. You know that no human did that kind of damage. It was a wolf."

"You're right. It was definitely an animal attack, but a wolf?"

"You don't believe me either!" It was not a question. It was an accusation. Her voice was laced with indignation and betrayal.

Zeke knew that he was walking a fine line, but he couldn't help but come to her rescue. "What happened?"

"Red was attacked earlier this week on her way to her car after dark. Some animal attacked and killed her attacker," Kris explained.

"Red has some crazy notion that it was a wolf," Michael added.

"And, there is proof that it wasn't?" Zeke asked.

"No!" Red responded quickly, almost violently. "There is no proof that it wasn't a wolf. No one else saw it, and I do know a wolf when I see one. Despite what these two Neanderthals think, I haven't lost my mind."

"You sound coherent enough. What makes you think it was a wolf?"

"The better question is what makes you doubt your own story?" Michael butted in. "Why could it not have been a wolf?"

"It was a wolf, Michael."

"What's he talking about?" Kris asked.

"The wolf's eyes weren't yellow," Red admitted with defeat.

"Red," Kris said softly, soothingly, "if it didn't have yellow eyes, it was probably a stray dog or something."

"A stray dog that was that violent?" Red challenged.

"It probably thought it was protecting you. Dogs are affectionate with humans; they feel a bond."

"That canine was violent. It never made a sound, not a growl, not a bark."

"Not a howl."

"The wolf never approached me. There was no affection."

"In the middle of the business district?"

"There's no proof that there wasn't a wolf," Zeke pointed out.

"You believe it was a wolf that attacked her attacker?" Kris asked him.

Here came the thin ice. It wasn't necessarily safe to convince everyone that it was a wolf, but he couldn't let them eat Red alive either. "I didn't say it was a wolf or not, but I wasn't there. Red was there. I don't see a reason not to take her word for it."

"Thank you," Red said in a barely audible whisper.

"That's very reasonable of you, Zeke," Ms. Gardner complimented. "Kris, this one may be the smartest one of your friends I've met. You could learn a thing or two. Zeke, you are welcome here anytime. Are you hungry?"

"Yes, ma'am."

"Good, I've cooked a big meal," she said carrying a large casserole dish.

"Here, let me help you with that." Zeke took the dish and followed Ms. Gardner to the dining room with Red hot on his heels carrying a basket of biscuits.

"Come on, boys. Let's eat," Mrs. Gardner called over her shoulder.

Laughing Red teased, "That's the first time she's ever had to tell the two of you twice."

"Bet she won't have to a third time," Kris shot back.

The dinner looked like a Thanksgiving layout. It reminded Zeke just how long it had been since he had a Thanksgiving with his own family. He had been alone a long time now.

Michael and Kris fell silent as they dug into their meals. Ms. Gardner and Red carried on conversation, but did not attempt to involve the guys in their conversation. Zeke had seen wild animals dine with more elegance than Michael and Kris were showing now.

"Was anyone else hurt during your attack?" Zeke asked Red. He wanted to warn her to stay away, but the last thing he needed her to know was that he had been there.

"There was no one else there."

"Do you always walk to your car alone?"

"I had worked late. It was the day we met. It was already dark and deserted. I don't usually like to stay that late, but I had not had much of a choice."

"You might want to be more careful, keep your eyes open. I heard that there is a new gang moving in that area."

"Where'd you hear that? I thought it was a fairly safe neighborhood."

"Zeke lives out that way," Kris provided around a mouthful of food. "You know that historical block with the really old house? That's it, right Zeke?"

"Yeah, it's an old family home."

"You live in the business district?" Red was clearly astonished but trying to hide it. She probably did not want Kris to accuse her of anything.

"Yeah, my family has been there since it was all farmland. We were the only family who wouldn't sell when the county decided to build there."

"I didn't think anyone lived there... I mean... I'm sorry. I didn't mean to be rude."

"It wasn't rude at all. The house was empty for years while I was in the military. I'm the only one left to carry on tradition."

"I'm so sorry," Ms. Gardner condoled.

"It's been a long time."

"Were you young?" Red wondered.

That was a loaded question. He had been young at the time that his family was slaughtered but not by her standards. "Not all that young, but it was before I left for the military."

"I'm sorry," Red breathed before looking down at her plate. Zeke suddenly wished he could take it back. He could no longer see her face, and anything that hid her beautiful face from his view was not worth being said.

"This is very good, Ms. Gardner. I can't remember the last time I had such a delicious home cooked meal."

"Thank you," Ms. Gardner smiled like he had just paid her the most potent compliment she had ever heard. "Do you think you could teach my sons those wonderful manners?"

Zeke smiled and chuckled unsure of how to answer. One does not usually declare intent to teach his new boss manners.

"So, you'll be driving two hours to work every day?" Red asked.

"It beats being jobless."

Red gave him a guilty half smile. "I'm sorry. I really didn't have any openings and I can't afford to create jobs."

"Oh, Red, don't you have anything around the office he could do? It would be so much closer for him," Ms. Gardner begged on Zeke's behalf.

"No, but if Lucy had her way…" Red dropped her head quickly as if catching herself and a flush rushed over her features. She stuffed a piece of biscuit in her mouth obviously to prevent herself from saying anything else.

"Who's Lucy?" Michael asked between bites.

"Her secretary," Ms. Gardner answered without a second thought. Red was close to her mother then, close enough that they talked about work quite a bit if her mother remembered the name of her secretary.

"What did you mean if Lucy had her way?" Kris pursued. "What did Lucy want?"

"Nothing, don't worry about it," Red replied a little too quickly.

"It's fine. I understand. I never expected you to create a job. If Kris had told me you didn't have any openings, I wouldn't have wasted your time."

"Yeah, yeah, what did Lucy want to see happen?" Kris continued to push.

"It's nothing; I'll tell you later," Red tried to brush him off.

Whatever it was that Lucy had wanted, Red didn't want to tell everyone in the room. Zeke wondered if it was her mom she didn't want to tell, or maybe it was him. More likely it was him. She had nothing to fret over; he had heard it all.

"We're all adults in here just spill it. What did Lucy have against Zeke?"

"I never said she had anything against Zeke," Red shot back. "She thought it was too bad that I couldn't hire him around the office so that she could look at him every day. Are you sure we're all adults around here, Kris, because sometimes I swear you are so childish!"

"Lay off. He didn't know where you were going with it," Michael tried to gloss over.

"May I be excused?" Red asked in her mom's direction not waiting for a response. She gave her chair a violent shove backwards and stormed out of the dining room.

"Boys, the whole point of this weekend was to help Red not upset her more," Ms. Gardner scolded.

"She'll be fine," Michael said with a nonchalant air. "It's better for her to get back to normal as soon as possible. What could be more normal than me and Kris giving her a hard time?"

"Oh, I don't know, maybe her older brothers protecting her."

"Sure, I'll apologize later," Kris relented. Zeke couldn't keep the smile off his face. They interacted as if they were still children who their mom was threatening with grounding. It was great! Zeke loved the family dynamic. It had been so long, he had almost forgotten what it was like to be treated like the child of the family no matter how old you get. He remembered complaining once upon a time that his own mom still treated him like a child. He'd give almost anything to have her treat him like a child now.

"So, Zeke, you don't have any experience in a dentist office?" Michael questioned.

Oh, here it comes. Kris forced him on his brother like he tried to do to Red. "No, is that going to be a problem?"

"No, no, you won't be doing anything like that. It's all paperwork, filing, finances, that kind of thing. Do you have any experience with that sort of thing?"

"I spent a lot of long years in business. I think I'll pick it up quick." He also ran the finances for the family farm, but he wasn't about to tell these people that he ran finances for a farm that was shut down before they were born. Of course, that had been before the age of computers, but he had done enough work with computers since then.

"Good, good. Finance isn't really my thing. I've been thinking I needed to get help with that for some time. It's a small town, small town dentist, but I'm a decent dentist. It doesn't hurt that my only local competition retired last year either. You'll never get rich, but it pays the bills."

"That's all I'm looking for."

"I think we are going to get along just fine."

After everyone was finished eating Zeke, Kris, and Michael helped Ms. Gardner clear the dishes off the table and carry them back to the kitchen where Red was already waiting to get started on the dishes.

"Here, let me help with those," Zeke offered.

"Oh, that's very nice of you," Ms. Gardner gushed, "but there really isn't room for more than two people to work comfortably in here at a time."

"Let me take your place then. You cooked all that delicious food. Take a break; you've earned it."

"That's sweet."

It was plain by the look in her eyes that she was going to continue to argue, but Zeke didn't give her the chance. "I insist. I won't take no for an answer."

"Well... ok."

Ms. Gardner followed her boys out of the kitchen, and the room fell quiet as the others all cleared out. Zeke was left standing alone in the kitchen with Red. Insisting on doing dishes didn't sound like such a good idea anymore even if part of him was rejoicing at the idea of being alone with Red. The more practical side of him knew it was a bad idea. Years of self preservation skills were screaming a red alert in his brain.

The room was thick with an awkwardness borne of their silence. Zeke could feel his body literally getting twitchy. Beside him he could feel Red avoiding looking his direction as easily as if they were his own intentions. "I'm sorry you were attacked the other day."

"I was lucky."

"I feel responsible."

That got her attention. She looked up at him with a confused look, and he was struck by the intensity of her eyes. Green eyes were typical with redheads, but Zeke had never seen green eyes so...

amazing. They sparkled in a glittery kind of way, and they bored through his skull like she could read every thought he had ever had. They were the kind of eyes that he had heard people talk about getting lost in but had never understood before now. There really was no end to their depths.

"You weren't the one who attacked me."

"If you hadn't worked late, you wouldn't have been out there alone or after dark, and if I hadn't wasted your time..."

"Don't blame yourself. I had a bad morning that day and had gotten to work late. I was going to have to work late anyway. You really weren't there for very long. If anything, I got out of there earlier because you were so quick... Did I offend you somehow?"

Zeke's relief was cut short when she asked that. "Of course not. Why would you think that?"

"I thought... you left in such a hurry that day. I thought maybe..."

"You didn't do anything. I just realized what a mistake going that day had been. I'm sorry that you thought otherwise."

"While we are apologizing, I should apologize for that whole tantrum at lunch and the... Lucy thing," Red said, the last two words trailing off in a whisper.

"Don't worry about it. I would have given Kris a lot worse if he had done that to me, and I was kinda' flattered by the Lucy thing."

"Don't go and get a big head."

"I don't think we have to worry about that. Now, if you were to say I am pleasant to look at, my head might swell to bursting." Why did he just say that out lout? Exactly what kind of mess was he trying to create for himself? Then again, there was that beautiful blush again. Her face lit up like a delicate pink rose.

"Um... that goes in the cabinet to your left."

Zeke looked down at the plate in his hand that he had dried three times. He turned and put it up, both embarrassed and irritated that he had let himself get so distracted by a girl.

Roxie's body was overheating. None of Kris's friends had ever talked to her that way before. Probably because they would not have been friends for much longer; Kris would have killed them. Roxie was an adult now, yet she wasn't sure if Kris still wouldn't kill him. That was the last thing she wanted to see happen. Zeke was off limits, being Kris's friend, but that didn't mean that Roxie couldn't enjoy the friendship.

After they finished the dishes, Zeke disappeared outside with Michael and Kris. They were playing some game. Roxie did not pay much attention to what they were playing since it had always been far too dangerous to play sports of any kind with her very bigger brothers.

For the most part Zeke and Michael seemed to be getting along wonderfully, which was good since they'd be working together. Roxie could hear Michael's laugh from all the way outside. He had always had a booming laugh like a giant, or maybe it was that she had always seen him as somewhat of a giant.

By mid-afternoon Mom said, "I think I'm ready for cake. I'll get the cake you go get the boys in the dining room."

Roxie stopped on the back porch and watched for a minute. The guys had some kind of three man game of football going on. She couldn't tell who had the upper hand if anyone.

"Hey, Mom is getting the cake. Let's go; move it."

Michael, Kris, and Zeke walked into the dining room dripping and reeking of sweat. Michael and Kris looked disgusting as usual after a game, but Zeke... On Zeke, it looked good. Roxie tried to shake the arrant thought away. She had never had a thing for a sweaty man. Zeke, however, was sweating in a very masculine, very alluring way. It seemed to draw attention to many of his more delightful features. Moisture rolled down his face from temple to chin showing off a strong jaw line that she had failed to notice before. His shirt was wet and clinging. Roxie had only seen the tip of the iceberg before. She knew that Zeke was muscular, but she had not known the half of it. The man was much bigger than he appeared when his clothes hung loose. Even Michael looked smaller next to Zeke.

"Wow, you made that?" Zeke asked Mom as he gawked at the cake.

"Red helped but yes. It's a hobby. I hope you like chocolate; it's Red's favorite."

"Oh, I like chocolate in moderation."

The way the guys maneuvered around to sit at the table, Zeke ended up sitting next to Roxie. From the looks of it, she wasn't sure if it hadn't been done on purpose. It was subtle if it had. No one else seemed to notice anything out of the ordinary, so Roxie assumed it was merely wishful thinking on her own part.

Mom cut everyone a piece of cake and passed them around. Michael and Kris finished first and had a second slice which they were finishing up by the time Roxie was finishing her first piece. Roxie looked at Zeke and noticed that he had only half finished the piece on his plate, and he was picking at it more than eating it.

Mom was occupied in conversation with Michael and Kris when Roxie leaned close to Zeke's ear and whispered, "If you don't like chocolate, you should have said so. You wouldn't have hurt her feelings. She's more resilient than she looks." She dug her fork deep into what was left of Zeke's cake and took a big bite.

Zeke gave Roxie an appreciative smile as she finished off his piece of cake before anyone looked their way. His teeth were gleaming white but not perfectly straight. They were almost sharp looking. Zeke had better watch it around Michael's office or Michael was going to get it into his head to make straightening Zeke's teeth his pet project.

"That's not a bad idea, Red," Michael said. It wasn't until that point that Roxie realized she had been so wrapped up in Zeke's smile and interesting teeth that she had no idea what they were talking about.

"What's that?" she asked.

"Next time you have to work late and you leave after dark like that, call Zeke," Kris instructed in his most brotherly voice. "You don't mind, do you, Zeke?"

"Ah, no, not at all."

Roxie was sure she had heard a hesitation before Zeke answered. "I'm sure Zeke has better things to do than come out simply to walk me to my car."

"No, it wouldn't be a problem. I'm close. I really don't mind. It would be my pleasure." The way he said that last part, Roxie was almost certain that the pleasure would be all hers. What was she thinking? That kind of thinking was only going to get her into trouble.

"Ok, sure, but I don't work late that often. It's very rare." It didn't seem to matter to anyone else that it was rare that Roxie left work late, so Zeke left his cell number with her before he left.

Chapter Three

Part of Zeke felt better having left Red his cell number for emergencies. Another part of him wondered how he was going to be able to keep his phone on him or answer it while making rounds. Of course, there was still another part of him that thrilled at the idea that Red had his number for any reason at all. While he was thinking about making rounds, though, he needed to get out of there before dark. He had work to do, and he was the only one left to do it.

He thanked Ms. Gardner for the delicious food and company then slipped away. Zeke barely got home in time after cutting it so close. He really did have to keep a better eye on the time from here on out, not that he would be seeing Red on a regular basis. And, if he were perfectly honest with himself it wasn't the food or the game with the guys where he had lost track of time; it was sitting at the table over cake watching Red.

Enough. Zeke did not have time to think about Red all night. In an attempt to clear his mind, he took a deep, calming breath before shedding his clothes and letting the shift take over him. Slowly his body morphed from human to canine, a very large wolf. His dark fur was perfect for slipping through the shadows unnoticed.

There was a lot of activity tonight. Seems there's always more activity on Saturday nights. Why did these jerks have to pick Saturday nights to make the most trouble? Tonight they looked like they were gearing up for a drive by. Very original, that would make them stupid jerks.

Zeke had to be careful how he handled them. If he went in and took them all out, it would raise too many questions about wild animal attacks or maybe even start an all out war. He would have to take out a few at a time, but in the meantime the least he could do was stop their planned drive by.

There was a black SUV out back of the building. Zeke stood in the shadows watching as two men loaded the vehicle with weapons. Each and every time they went back for another load, they were leaving the truck unguarded. A vehicle to drive is certainly a necessity for a drive by, and if there is one thing that Zeke has learned over the years, it is to go for the simple. People usually have contingency plans in place for the big stuff, but when the simple stuff goes wrong, people tend to panic, don't know what to do.

Zeke ran over to the SUV on silent paws, slashed the first tire he got to, the driver's side front wheel, then he slunk low underneath the tall truck just as the men were returning. Getting beneath the vehicle was a tight squeeze no matter how tall it was; werewolves have always been known for their size. He waited in the cramp space while the two men loaded their next load and laughed at something. Zeke couldn't imagine finding anything funny while preparing to go kill some random people. Of course, they were aiming at a specific area, but they had no idea who their bullets were hitting when it was all said and done.

The two men went for another load still laughing. This time Zeke sliced his razor sharp claws through both back tires before squeezing under the SUV for the second time. The SUV was sitting at a funny angle now with three flattened tires, but the men did not seem to notice. They were too wrapped up in their banter that kept one another laughing.

Again the men went inside. Zeke scored the last tire and slipped back into the shadows to lie in wait. The men did not return right away, so they must have finished loading weapons while Zeke was busy rendering the vehicle useless.

Zeke had to wait another forty-five minutes before anything more happened. Finally the whole group filed outside together ready to leave. The first one to spot the tires froze mid-step and began to stutter.

"Wh- wh-... what happened?"

After the first initial shock, there were many choice words uttered from more than one mouth. The man who was apparently the leader started barking orders and basically just barking. He was mad to say the least and flabbergasted.

As soon as Zeke was sure the drive by had been postponed, he made his way in the opposite direction. He still had a couple more things he wanted to check out before the sun came up.

Monday morning at work, Lucy spent half the morning in Roxie's office not because Roxie was keeping her that busy but because Roxie was spilling her guts. The urge to tell Lucy all about lunch with her family and, more interestingly, Zeke was too irresistible to be ignored. She walked in and on the way to her own office said, "Lucy, when you get a chance, could you come to my office?" The big goofy grin on her face gave away that what she really wanted was to share some juicy gossip, and it did not take Lucy five minutes to finish up what she was doing and get to Roxie's office.

"What's up?" Lucy asked eagerly.

"You'll never believe who showed up at lunch Saturday."

"Probably not, I thought it was just you and your family."

"It was supposed to be originally, but Kris invited a friend."

"A friend?" Lucy pondered with palpable implications in her tone. "Would this be a friend of the very hot variety?"

"Yes."

"The guy from last week?"

"Yes, he goes by his middle name, Zeke, instead of Patrick."

"I like it. It suits him, but you have more to tell. I can see it on your face, so spill."

Roxie leapt into her tale without any more encouragement.

"I can't believe he said that," Lucy said when Roxie recounted what had been said over dishes in the kitchen. "Rox, he was practically begging you to make a move. What did you do?"

"What do you think I did? I didn't do anything. What could I do? He's Kris's friend, and he's going to be working with Michael."

"So what? Make that man your friend too, your special friend."

"I can't do that to Kris. I can't even count how many guys my brothers have run off over the years for getting a little too friendly with their baby sister. Something like that could break up their friendship. Not to mention the trouble it could cause for Michael and Zeke at the office."

"You are going to have to stand up to your brothers."

"They mean well."

"That may be, but Rox, you aren't living your life."

"I've made a great life for myself."

"That's not what I meant. A really hot guy is showing interest in you, and you are too scared to acknowledge him because he is friends with your brothers."

"There's more to it than that. I don't know anything about him, and there is something... strange about him."

"Strange how?" Lucy demanded.

"I don't know. I can't put my finger on it, but when I figure it out, I'll let you know."

"Okay, fair enough. You have your own reasons for not pursuing Mr. Hottie. Finish your story, and don't leave out any details."

Roxie went through the rest of the details careful to not leave anything out.

"Girl, I would be working late everyday just for an excuse to see that man again."

"Yeah, I know you would. Come on; we've got to get to work before we really are working late."

"And, that would be bad why?"

"Get out of here," Roxie laughed.

The rest of the week flew by in a haze of normalcy as did the following week. It seemed like everything was back to normal except for the can of mace in Roxie's purse and her obsessive need to get out of the office each day on time or early.

Mom called late one Thursday night with an offer more appealing than it should have been. "I just found out that Zeke is coming over with Michael tomorrow night after work. It might be nice if you come too. What do you say?"

Roxie had been counting on getting some stuff done around the apartment over the weekend, but the idea of spending time with Zeke was too intriguing not to cause hesitation.

Finally, Roxie was able to answer, "Mom, I don't know. I was going to try to catch up on some housework that I've been putting off."

"So you put it off another day; what will it hurt? It's just Friday night; you'll have more time on Saturday anyway. I'm going to cook a big meal. Michael found out that Zeke is basically living off of frozen dinners at home, and he invited Zeke to come over after work."

"He didn't ask you first?"

"You know I don't mind. I think it is a great idea. I liked Zeke, and I don't like the idea of him not eating well. I want you to come. A big meal just isn't complete without the whole family."

"I guess so."

"Good, I'll see you then."

The next day, Lucy was psyched enough for both of them. She giggled like a school girl and gushed over the opportunity. "You've got to be kidding me! You get a redo? Girl, don't you mess it up this time, Rox. If that man makes another comment like the last time, you don't hesitate. Go for it. Don't let what you think your brothers won't like stop you."

"It would ruin their relationships," Roxie argued.

"You don't know that for sure. He sounds like a great guy. He's already friends with Kris. It's not that farfetched to think that your brothers may like him and even approve of the two of you together."

"Sure, Luc, but that doesn't change the fact that there was something off, remember?"

"Oh, you're paranoid; too much happened that first day for you to remember it clearly, what with the attack and all. If you don't take a chance, you'll never know."

"I don't know."

"Tell me you'll think about it."

"I'll think about it."

"Fair enough. Now, I've got to get to work. There's a lot I want to get done before I leave today, and there is no way that I'm crazy enough to leave late and alone.

"Hardy har har," Roxie mumbled as Lucy exited the office. It may not have been a good idea to get too close to Zeke, but Roxie still found herself keyed up and eager to get there. She rushed through her work, pausing only long enough to make sure everything was done correctly. She didn't take any breaks and worked straight through lunch; she would be having a big dinner to make up for it later.

It was all Roxie could do not to speed the whole way to her mom's house, but she eventually got there. Now if she could only relax. Her muscles were tense, and her mind was racing with delicious thoughts, most of which Roxie would never admit were not about the food waiting inside.

Mom's and Kris's cars were there. Michael's was pulled in behind as well as a black Celica that Roxie was less familiar with. She was the last to arrive, which meant everyone was waiting for her inside, including... Zeke.

◆ ◆ ◆

Zeke was all but pacing. This whole thing had been a bad idea. Zeke needed to be working. He didn't have time to be here at a dinner party, but apparently Michael was worried. Now, he had his mom worried too. Zeke had reluctantly given in. One night off wouldn't be the end of the world. It wasn't necessarily good, but it wouldn't destroy everything, just set him back several days. All that would have been distracting enough, but now Red was coming.

Neither Zeke nor Michael had known that Red was coming until they got to Ms. Gardner's house. "I talked to Red last night, and she should be here any minute," she announced.

Michael nodded his head, but of course it didn't surprise him for his sister to be coming to his mom's house. Zeke, on the other hand, had immediate butterflies in his stomach. Conflicted, the term didn't feel strong enough to describe Zeke in that moment. He had a job to do, but he tended to get distracted from that job whenever Red was around. His logical side didn't want that distraction, didn't want to have anything more to do with Red Gardner. His more emotional, irrational side... Well, he was thrilled to see her again. It was the best news he had heard since the last time he saw her. He could hardly wait for her to arrive, but he wouldn't have to wait long, he thought with trepidation, as he heard a car turn onto the drive.

Zeke's heart did a flip inside his chest when he watched Red walk in through the front door.

"Hi, guys," Red greeted casually as she walked through the foyer.

Michael gave a nod of his head, and Kris gave an acknowledging grunt. Ms. Gardner said, "Hey, sweet pea, how was your day?"

"Good, quiet. Can I give you a hand?"

"Yeah, could you get ice for the glasses please? Kris get up off that couch and offer to help your sister."

With a roll of his eyes, Kris complained, "How is it offering help, if I've been ordered to help."

Kris was already lurching off the couch to follow Red to the kitchen, but Ms. Gardner still scolded, "Just get up and do what I asked. You should have done the gentlemanly thing in the first place. I shouldn't have to remind you."

Red had not looked Zeke's way yet, and he could literally feel his spirits dropping. She left the room without a single glance, and Kris was hot on her heels.

"Is there anything I can do to help?" Zeke offered.

"No, I think that will do it. As soon as those two get in here with the glasses, we are ready to eat. Come on into the dining room and let's have a seat."

Red sashayed into the dining room with three glasses, and Kris sauntered in with two more. They sat the glasses down on the table one in front of each person. Then Red sat down next to Zeke. He tried to hide his joy at her decision.

Red was hot in more ways than one. Zeke could actually feel the heat radiating out from her body. There was so much heat hitting him in the side it was like her skin was fevered.

"So, how is the job working out?" she asked.

It took Zeke a moment to realize that she was speaking to him. He recovered quickly and answered, "Everything is great on my end."

"Mine too. It is amazing how much more I can get done with Zeke around to do all the harder stuff, and it all comes so easy to him. I don't know how we ever got along without him," Michael piped in.

"I'm glad to hear it," Red responded.

"You know what I wasn't glad to hear?" Ms. Gardner started off. "Apparently, Zeke cannot cook so much as a grilled cheese sandwich."

"Well, that may be pushing it. I'm sure I could nuke a cheese sandwich," Zeke tried to defend.

"Exactly, just like you cook those microwave dinners that Michael was telling me about. Red is an excellent cook."

Red froze her fork in mid-path toward her mouth. She looked up at her mom, and even as incredulousness was obvious in her eyes a blush crept down her cheeks. "Mom," Red squeaked voice ringing with accusation.

"I'm just saying it is a shame that Zeke is trying to live off of frozen dinners when you live roughly fifteen minutes away."

That was when Zeke caught on to Ms. Gardner's plot to invite him over to Red's for dinner on a regular basis. "The frozen dinners really aren't as bad as you think. They beat that ready-made stuff we had back in the day, right Kris?"

"You got that right!" Kris agreed enthusiastically.

"Still, it's a shame," Ms. Gardner continued. "I mean you would just be sitting down to dinner by the time Zeke got back home each day. I just think it is a shame that the two of you can't work something out."

"Okay, Mom, she gets it. It's a crying shame, but it is still her decision. For that matter, Zeke never said that he wanted to start eating with Red," Michael interrupted.

Red glanced in Zeke's direction, and he could have sworn he saw disappointment, or maybe it was betrayal, in her eyes. That was ridiculous. They had not known each other long enough for him to have disappointed her, and they weren't close enough for betrayal. Still, it hurt like very few things ever had.

"Hey, leave me out of this," Zeke said.

"I'm not trying to get you into trouble. I thought it would be nice if my daughter could do the nice thing," Ms. Gardner continued to push. "You're both living alone. It might do you both some good to have a little company."

With a sort of growling grunt, Red turned to Zeke with an un-encouraging fire in her eyes and shot out, "Would you like to come have dinner at my apartment with me?"

"I'm fine, really," Zeke replied unsure of what the best response would be.

"No, seriously, apparently it's the only way we are going to shut my mom up!" She was practically yelling now as she tried to control her raging emotions.

"Sallee Roxanne!" Ms. Gardner snapped.

Red threw her napkin onto the table and stormed out of the room. Kris cleared his throat, and Zeke noticed that everyone in the room had stopped eating during the altercation.

"These biscuits are amazing, Mom," Kris said shoving a big bite of biscuit in his mouth. Michael nodded and followed suit by shoveling his own food into his mouth. Ms. Gardner made no acknowledgement of the compliment but went back to eating. Zeke tried to finish his own meal, but he couldn't shake the image of rage painted across Red's face like a canvas.

"I'll get those for you," Zeke offered after diner as he took a plate from Ms. Gardner. She smiled but didn't make any other response.

"I can give you a hand," Michael offered.

"Nah, that's ok. You've got an early appointment tomorrow. It wouldn't do the patient or your practice any good if you fell asleep while numbing their mouth."

"I've got it," Kris chimed in.

"You're going to do dishes?" Zeke scoffed knowing how Kris felt about washing dishes. "I may not be able to cook, but I wash a mean dish." Zeke was not trying to be selfless, far from it. He could hear a heartbeat, Red's heart beat, in the kitchen, and he had heard running water. Red was already getting started, and Zeke wanted to be in there with her.

Kris looked to the open doorway where his mom had already left out, and then he said, "Alright, man, I won't stop you."

"Kris," Michael scolded.

"Hey, the man really wants to wash dishes."

Zeke didn't stick around to hear how that conversation would play out. He slipped quietly into the kitchen. He sat dirty dishes down on the counter next to Red. "How is it that I always find myself apologizing to you while we wash dishes?"

"You didn't do anything wrong. I'm the one who should be apologizing... You're welcome to eat with me after work."

"I don't want to put you out. It's not like I'm starving. Like I said those frozen dinners are pretty good if you know which ones to get."

"I mean it. It really is a good idea. We could even split the grocery bill. I just don't like being bossed around like that. I'm an adult now."

"I can imagine. Both your brothers seem a bit... overbearing when it comes to you. I could see where one more person bossing you would be too much to handle. When you lash out, your mom is the easier target."

Red looked at him like she had never thought of it that way. There was something else, too, in her expression that he couldn't read. He wondered if he had said the wrong thing.

"I guess," she finally mumbled. "So, are you interested?"

Was he interested? He was more than interested. His heart was pounding with an excitement of adrenaline, but he had responsibilities. "Yes," he heard himself say. Where had that come from? He hadn't meant to say that.

"Good." She gave him directions to her apartment, and they made plans for him to meet her there as soon as he could get there from work. "I was planning on chicken and stir fry Monday. Will that be okay with you?"

"It sounds delicious."

"Okay, good. I should be getting back; I'll see you Monday."

"Yeah, I should hit the road too."

The whole drive home, Roxie had only one thing on her mind. Had she seriously just invited the very hot, very charming Zeke Miller to her apartment for diner? No, she had just offered him a standing invitation for every week night. For a brief, disappointing moment she thought he might still refuse. It couldn't possibly be for the riveting company. Their only two meals together thus far had not fared well. Maybe the frozen dinners weren't as passable as he tried to pretend. It didn't matter. Whatever his reasoning, Zeke was coming over Monday night.

Chapter Four

Roxie spent the weekend cleaning. She had to be sure that everything inside her apartment was presentable. She didn't keep a mess, but she wasn't necessarily used to having a lot of company over either.

"How did it go?" Lucy squealed Monday as Roxie walked in the office.

Roxie smiled and continued walking, without a word, to her own office. Lucy followed and waited impatiently for her answer. "Well," Roxie started, "Mom practically shoved Zeke at me. She's worried that he isn't eating well, and she wants us to eat together throughout the week. Long story short I lost my cool when she tried to force me to do things her way. After I calmed down, Zeke and I made arrangements to start eating together tonight. He's going to come over to the apartment when he gets off work."

"Wow."

"That's all you have to say?"

"Wow," Lucy repeated and turned to go back to her outer office without anything else.

Lucy worked without mentioning diner with Zeke again until lunch.

"Hey, Luc, what are you doing for lunch?" Roxie asked.

"A pizza and girl talk?" Lucy answered question in her voice.

"Sounds great. I'll order the pizza."

Twenty minutes later Lucy and Roxie were shut in Roxie's office hunched over a box of pizza. "So?" Lucy pressed.

"So what?"

"Tell me," Lucy insisted.

"I told you already."

"What are you cooking?"

"Chicken and stir fry."

"Not bad... So, there is really nothing more to tell?"

"No, there really isn't. I can't get him off my mind, but there isn't anything to tell... yet, maybe tomorrow."

"Chinese tomorrow?"

Roxie nodded with a conspiratorial smile.

Work flew by after lunch. It was rather slow for a Monday, but that suited Roxie fine since she was distracted today anyway. If this became a more permanent arrangement for Zeke to eat with her, would it always be such a distraction? She couldn't imagine Zeke ever not being a distraction. Logically she knew that she didn't need those kinds of distractions. She had to learn to focus whether he was in her life or not, especially if he wasn't even physically with her at the moment. In a way, though, she liked being distracted by Zeke, and she genuinely did not want to give up that distraction.

Roxie rushed home and got started on the chicken and stir fry, a little too quickly she was beginning to worry. The food was done. If it waited too long the stir fry would be overdone. She should have waited a little longer knowing that Zeke had two hours to travel, but before she could finish this trail of thought, there was a knock at the door.

"Nice timing," Roxie said with a smile as she opened the door for Zeke. "I just finished cooking, and we're ready to eat."

"Wow, so much for lending a hand," he replied.

"Don't worry about it. It was no problem; I was going to be cooking anyway. Come on in. It isn't a big place, but the table is ready." Roxie ushered Zeke inside and gestured to the easily visible table.

Now, that she took a more critical look around, Roxie realized how small her apartment really was. A larger table could never fit in the tiny space, yet the miniscule table barely held room enough for two people. There was a loveseat, a recliner, and a TV squeezed into the living area. The diminutive kitchen could hold only one at a time. A narrow hallway led off to the one bedroom and bath not visible from here.

"I hope you don't get claustrophobic in this miniature apartment," Roxie tried to laugh it off making her way around the table.

"I've lived in smaller areas before... Something smells good."

"Oh, yeah, let me grab-"

"I'll get it," Zeke cut her off. He laid a hand on the small of her back. Chills slithered up and down her back radiating from that one simple touch. His warm hand was scalding her back at the point of contact. He slid behind her into the small kitchen to get the food.

Roxie swallowed hard and took her seat. "Thank you."

Zeke gave a slight nod. "You did all the work."

Roxie served her own plate then waited for Zeke to serve his. "How was your day?"

"Good, yours?"

"Good, it went quickly."

"Is that a good thing or a bad thing?" Zeke wondered.

"It's a good thing. I got everything done that I meant to; it just seemed to take no time at all."

Zeke still couldn't believe he was sitting across from Red in her apartment. He had not noticed before how full her lips were. He couldn't stop staring at her lips. She didn't seem to be aware of his stare, or maybe she just didn't care. Her bottom lip jutted out slightly further than the top lip. Although both lips appeared delectably kissable, the bottom just looked like it was reaching out to be caressed, and Zeke longed to caress it with his own, to taste her. He wondered what she would taste like. Her beautiful, alluring lips quit moving, and he realized that she was awaiting a response. "What?"

"What are you going to do with your time off next month?" Red repeated.

"What time off?"

"Did Michael not tell you?"

"I guess not."

"My family goes camping each year. My dad used to love camping, so our annual trip is sort of a big deal, like a memorial so to speak. Michael always closes the office down for the week we're gone."

"It sounds like fun."

"It is. You should come." Red looked suddenly astonished as if she had not meant to say that.

"I wouldn't want to intrude on a family thing."

"It's not that exclusive. We've all had friends go along over the years. Besides, Mom seems to like you more than most of Kris's friends already."

"Are you and your mom... okay?" Zeke inquired.

"Oh, yeah, we're fine. We just needed time to cool down; that's all. Be glad you missed my rebellious teenage years. The other night was nothing in comparison. I mean, I'm not saying that Mom and I fight a lot, but every so often, I guess everyone does, right?"

"I guess so... This is really good," Zeke complimented as he took another bite of broccoli.

"I'm glad you like it."

"I do, and I'm not usually much of a vegetable eater."

"More of a meat and potatoes kind of man, huh?"

"More so just the meat."

Red laughed, and Zeke realized just how much he had missed that laugh. It was a joyous sound even in a world where there wasn't much joy to be found.

"What?" Red asked defensively.

He must not have had as much control over his expression as he thought. Zeke couldn't think of a plausible excuse quickly enough, so he settled for the truth. "I like your laugh. It's a happy sound."

"Laughing usually is happy."

"Not always. Even when people are genuinely laughing, many of those people still don't sound truly happy. There's just no joy behind it, but you sort of fill the room with joy when you laugh. It's pleasant."

"Oh, thank you."

"Sure... I, um... I hate to eat and run, but I have some things I need to take care of tonight." Zeke was almost positive that he had figured out how to make diner work out with all his other responsibilities. Red's apartment was not too far from his home, and all the gang activity so far had been confined to the area between her apartment and his home. He could park his car not too far from here, abandon his clothes, and take care of what needed to be taken care of. Then he could pick up his car and clothes and return home.

"Right, no problem. You've been out all day; I bet you're ready to get home... Are you coming tomorrow?"

"Are you sure I'm not intruding?" Zeke asked skeptically.

"I'm sure. Tonight was nice. It's nice to not eat alone."

"Well, if you're sure."

"I'm sure, and I'll see you tomorrow. Now go home and get some rest," Red instructed with confidence. Zeke had never been one to follow directions well, yet he had no hesitation to follow Red's, except for the fact that he would have to make a stop on his way home.

The timing turned out to be perfect. By the time Zeke had parked his car and shed his clothes, he had gotten to the warehouse/office building used in the newest gang activity just as things were picking up. Tonight's agenda was focused on one specific person, the gang's top hit man. He wasn't the top boss, but he was no less evil. He made his living by murdering anyone the boss named without so much as questioning the boss's motives. They weren't targeting only members of other gang members anymore. They were branching out and going after anyone who would not bend to their will. Taking out this slimy murdering criminal would be doing all of society a favor.

Zeke sat outside and watched the hit man walk inside for his instructions. Zeke continued to wait patiently, lurking in the shadows. When the hit man came back outside to the empty alleyway, Zeke made a shuffling sound with his paw still in the shadow. He was dressed better than Zeke had expected. Honestly, Zeke had expected a jeans and T-shirt at best. Perhaps he would have been ragged, scruffy, even dirty. A man as evil as all that should somehow look the part, at least have an evil gleam to his eyes, but that wasn't the case. It was almost never the case. The brute was handsome and well dressed. His dark hair was perfectly styled and gleamed with the dim light in the alley. He was wearing dark pants and a mint green, silken button up shirt. He looked like any other man walking through the business district.

The thug eased over to the shadows to investigate. As soon as he was engulfed in shadows, Zeke lunged.

The man let out a gurgled scream as Zeke clamped down on the man's throat. He put up an impressive fight. He could not best Zeke, but he was holding, however temporarily, onto his life. He sent an upper cut to Zeke's gut then dug his thumbs into Zeke's jaw in an attempt to pry the sharp, cutting teeth from his neck. Zeke raked his claws across the man's chest, leaving deep gashes in their wake and a slashed-up shirt.

Without warning a boom interrupted the battle from behind. A siring, burning pain sliced through the side of Zeke's neck. Immediately Zeke recognized that he had been shot. The bullet had grazed his neck and exploded through the hit man's trachea. He fell gasping to the ground. He would not live much longer without help, and Zeke was going to see to it that help did not come.

Zeke turned and pounced on the shooter who must have heard the hit man's scream and come to assist. This man was not nearly as strong as the hit man had been, but he was heavily armed. The shooter fired again, but the bullet went wide easily missing Zeke. Biting the shooter's arm, he jerked, and the gun went flying. Zeke went straight for the shooter's jugular as the shooter went for a knife strapped to his leg. Zeke made quick work of the shooter, but it was not quick enough to avoid being stabbed in the hind, left leg.

Zeke chomped tight around the knife and dislodged it from his leg. He then dropped the bloody knife next to the shooter's lifeless body and limped pitifully back to his car.

Chapter Five

Lucy didn't say anything more than "Good morning" as Roxie walked through to her own office, but she looked at Roxie with a mischievous grin. She did not mention last night's diner all morning long, so neither did Roxie. At exactly twelve noon, Lucy walked boldly into Roxie's office carrying a sack of Chinese delivery.

"Time to talk, girl," Lucy thrilled.

"I thought you'd never ask," Roxie almost squealed as she pushed her work away. "He got there literally as I finished cooking. It couldn't have been timed better if I had orchestrated it myself... I wish you could have seen him. You would have enjoyed the view. I've never seen anyone make khakis and a polo look as good as he does."

"I'm sure. How was the food?"

"Good, Zeke enjoyed it, I think."

"You think?" Lucy pursued.

"Well, he admitted to being more of a meat eater. He doesn't care too much for vegetables."

"Oh Rox." Lucy's voice was saturated with disappointment and sympathy.

"It's okay. He said he liked the stir fry. In fact, he acted genuinely surprised that he liked the vegetables so much."

"Well, that's okay. How was everything else?"

"He likes my laugh... He said it sounds happy and joyous. Is that weird?"

"Nah, not weird. It's good; it's an interest."

"Maybe. He didn't stay long. He had things he needed to do, or that's what he said."

"I'm sure it was the truth."

"I sort of invited him to go camping with my family next month."

"The big annual camping trip? What do you mean sort of?"

"I told him he should come, but I don't think he was convinced. I also invited him to come back for dinner tonight."

"And?"

"And, he's coming over."

"What are you cooking? Something with more meat I hope?"

"I'm thinking about beef stew."

"Sounds good, plenty of meat for him a few vegetables for you."

"Right."

"There's more; I can see it in your face. Tell," Lucy insisted.

"I feel like a little girl giggling over her first kiss."

"He kissed you?" Lucy practically squealed.

"No, nothing like that. It's much sillier than that... He touched me."

"An innocent touch?"

"Of course. It was just a casual brush; he laid his hand on my back to get around me into the kitchen to grab the food. It was a normal, everyday touch, but there was nothing normal about it. It was like nothing I've ever felt before. It was so much hotter than any every day, innocent touch has a right to be."

"Are you sure it was the touch that was out of the ordinary, or is it your emotions that are out of the ordinary?"

"Probably my emotions, but it's just that I've never reacted that way to anyone before. His touch was scalding. I had chills that ran up and down my spine and radiated out my arms and legs. All that is normal enough, I suppose, but it wasn't just the chills. There was this tingling I've never felt before. There was a tingling, like a slight pulsing, right beneath his touch."

"A tingling? That's not exactly unusual. It's all a state of mind."

"I guess, but it is not usually something that I personally feel. Never before."

"So, you're in uncharted territory. That doesn't mean that something is wrong."

"I didn't say anything was wrong," Roxie pointed out.

"You didn't have to you've got that curious but suspicious look on your face."

"I know it sounds normal, but it felt anything but normal. It wasn't bad. It felt... wonderful, but there was definitely something abnormal about it."

"But, abnormal in a good way?"

"A very good way."

"Maybe he's the one, Rox." Roxie gave Lucy a skeptical look, and Lucy continued. "I don't know. It could be. All of the sudden you're feeling tingles that you've never felt before. Everything feels... different. Maybe that's the difference."

"No, no, that cannot be it. It probably has more to do with the fact that I'm attracted to one of my brother's friends. The lure of the forbidden and all that. You don't just get tingles that tell you someone is the one especially after only the fourth time you lay eyes on them."

"You're too practical, Roxie. Listen to your heart. This may be the only impetuous thing you ever do in your life."

"He is Kris's friend," Roxie felt compelled to protest. It just couldn't be. Kris would never approve, and she would never jeopardize one of her brother's friendships.

"What you mean is that you're scared."

"Yes, I'm scared of ruining a perfectly good friendship, maybe two."

"Fine, you're stubborn. Do it your way."

After the "girl talk," Roxie threw herself into her work. She had been distracted enough lately. If spending time with Zeke was to become a regular occurrence, she had to learn to balance the two. She couldn't let her work suffer. She had worked hard to get where she was today, and she could not throw it all away on a wild, runaway feeling that was more likely all in her imagination.

The timing was not as perfect on Tuesday. The beef stew had been done and simmering for almost ten minutes when Zeke arrived.

"Come in," Roxie smiled.

"Hi, Zeke said with a warm returning smile. His white teeth gleamed in the setting sun. Roxie marveled at how sharp his teeth appeared, sharper than any other human set of teeth she could recall noticing. Surely her imagination was still running rampant. Honestly, sharper than any other human? Where had that arrant thought come from?

"How was work?" Roxie inquired.

"Busy, I believe every person in that small town came in today complaining of toothaches. Has that town ever heard of dental hygiene? Not a single one of them left without making a follow up appointment to get a filling."

"Uh-oh," Roxie chuckled.

"How was your day?"

"Fantastic, I really focused today."

"That's... good."

"That's very good. It's hard to lead others when you cannot focus yourself."

"Good point."

"I hope you're hungry."

"I'm starving. Beef stew?"

"You have a good nose." He had a somewhat flat nose but interesting in its own rights. His nostrils flared as he breathed in and out slow and evenly.

"I do, and it smells heavenly."

"I don't know about heavenly, but it is full of meat."

"I hope that wasn't for my benefit. I would hate to think that you are going out of your way for my sake."

"It is full of vegetables for me as well."

Zeke smiled and Roxie's breath hitched in her chest. For a full three seconds, she forgot completely how to continue drawing in air. When she finally drew in her next breath, she gasped in panic.

"Red, are you okay?"

In one instant, all Roxie could think was that he had called her Red, and in the next instant, she realized that he was reaching for her. One hand cradled her head while the other cupped her shoulder. "Red?"

"I'm fine, fine. Sorry, I was just having a moment." Roxie meant to pull away from his touch. She knew she should. To be honest, she tried, but her mind and body would not work together. For once in her life, Roxie's mind and body were not of one accord, and she did not care for it one little bit. It was an unsettling feeling. She felt disconnected, unsure what to do or how to do it.

"Are you sure you're okay?" Zeke asked.

"Yes, I'm fine."

"Okay." He slowly let go of Roxie's head and shoulder. He moved his hands painstakingly slowly. The friction was driving Roxie up a wall. The whole thing felt more like an intensely intimate caress than a withdrawal.

"So, beef stew?" Zeke asked awkwardly. Was it even possible that he was half as uncomfortable in the moment as she was? Maybe her thoughts had shown all over her face. Too bad, her lack of comfort had been a result of pleasure; her reaction had undoubtedly been the root of his unease.

"Yeah, it's on the table if you're ready."

"I'm always ready to eat. Maybe not as much as your brothers though."

That got Roxie laughing. She couldn't help herself, and just like that she was comfortable again. She took a seat across the table from Zeke.

"It smells amazing," Zeke complimented.

"Thanks."

"Mmm," Zeke moaned with his first bite.

Roxie smiled. "Better than the stir fry?"

"The stir fry was good."

"But?" she prompted.

"But... This. This is better. You added meat for my benefit."

It wasn't a question, so Roxie did not try to deny it. Nor did she admit to anything. Instead she took a bite of carrot. "There are vegetables in there, and they are good for you."

"You sound like my mother. What is it with you Gardner's and taking care of people?"

"What do you mean?"

"First, Michael takes me home to eat with your family, because he was worried I wasn't eating well. Then, your mom forces me on you, because she, too, is worried I'm not eating well."

"That was two birds with one stone. She also worries about me being all alone two hours away," Roxie interjected.

"Next," Zeke continued as if he had never been interrupted. "Michael was worried about me getting lonely. Now, you are worried about me eating all my vegetables."

"I don't think I said you had to eat all your vegetables. I only mentioned that they were good for you. Why is Michael worried about you getting lonely?"

"I don't know. All day long today he was talking about the camping trip you mentioned last night. He asked me to go, and won't take no for an answer, saying that he doesn't want me staying here all alone while y'all are off having fun."

Roxie nodded. There wasn't much to say. She agreed with Michael. She had invited Zeke herself just last night.

"What is that nod supposed to mean?" Zeke demanded accusingly.

"I agree with Michael."

"It's awful suspicious that you mentioned the camping trip last night. I declined your invitation, and today that was all your brother wanted to talk about."

"You're right. That does sound suspicious. Lucky for me I haven't talked to Michael, so I cannot be accused of anything."

Zeke did not look convinced. "How do I know you haven't talked to Michael?"

"Hmm, I guess you don't. You can believe me or not."

Zeke smiled. Man, this guy could charm the devil with that smile. "I think I'll believe you this time, but you have to admit the whole situation is convenient."

"Did you decline Michael's offer?"

"It was a little harder to decline Michael's offer."

"How so?" Roxie couldn't keep the irritation from her voice. What was it that made Michael so much more persuasive than her?

"You know, a boss versus a friend? One can fire you; the other one can't."

"So, you aren't worried about letting a friend down then?"

"I didn't realize that we were already so close that my turning down the opportunity to go camping with your family would offend you. My apologies."

"Ha, ha."

"I'm going," Zeke deadpanned.

"Zeke, please, calm down. You don't have to get so excited."

He smiled again. Roxie was quickly becoming addicted to his smile. She would do almost anything to witness and gawk at that smile again and again.

"We really do have a lot of fun. Do you like the outdoors?"

"I do."

"That was vague."

"That was direct. What exactly are you wondering about?"

"I don't know. What sort of things do you enjoy outdoors?"

"I love the outdoors. I enjoy almost anything if I can do it outdoors."

"So, you camp a lot?"

"Not so much."

"Have you ever camped?"

"Not since I was a kid. I guess it was sort of a novelty for my family."

"You'll have fun."

"I'm sure I will." The corners of Zeke's mouth sneaked upward, not in the smile that Roxie had become so fond of but a more seductive grin that Roxie found herself just as fond of. She watched as he took another bite of meat and chewed, his strong jaw working as he did.

"You not hungry?" Zeke asked.

"Hmm?"

"You're not eating."

"Oh," Roxie mumbled and with great effort forced her attention back to her plate.

"What sort of things do you enjoy about camping?" Zeke wondered.

"I love hiking. I'm not much of a fisher. I leave that to the boys. I don't like any contact with the fish whatsoever until it more closely resembles something from the grocery store."

Zeke chuckled, a soothing sound accompanied by his glorious smile, and Roxie continued. "I do like just relaxing at the lake though. Roasting marshmallows is always fun."

"I've never done that," Zeke admitted.

"You've never had s'mores?" Roxie asked in disbelief. Zeke shook his head no. "Oh, you will love them! No. No, you won't. I almost forgot that you don't like chocolate. I've never tried s'mores without the chocolate, but still roasted marshmallows are still good on their own."

"I have an allergic reaction to chocolate. Too much can make me sick."

"Oh my goodness! You should have said something at Mom's. I told you she would not have been offended. She might, however, be offended if she thinks you risked an allergic reaction to avoid offending her."

"Good reason to keep this between us." Zeke's dark eyes seemed to be pleading with Roxie. Intoxicated with his stare, Roxie couldn't do anything to stop her head from bobbing up and down like some relentless bobble head. "Thank you."

"We make s'mores every year. What are you going to tell my mom then? You can't possibly eat them."

"I can handle a little chocolate without getting sick. I simply don't care for it."

"No, absolutely not. You are not purposely eating something you are allergic to on my watch."

"Good thing I'm not your responsibility then."

"Zeke, I'm serious… You can't." Now Roxie was the one pleading.

"I'm sure I'll come up with a polite way to excuse myself between now and then." He stood up and started toting dishes to the kitchen sink.

"I'll get those," Roxie said.

"It isn't fair that you do all the cooking and all the cleaning as well. You cleaned up last night. Sit down, and let me clean up tonight."

Roxie tried to push her way into the cramped kitchen area, but Zeke backed her out. "Go, you don't have a choice in the matter."

Giving in, Roxie settled in on the couch underneath the softest blanket she owned. There wasn't much on TV, but she found something to fill the time while she cuddled underneath the blanket and dozed in and out.

Roxie woke with a start as a warm tingling sensation overtook her, and she realized with dizzying awareness that Zeke's hand was laying on her shoulder. "I'm going to go. Everything is cleaned up. Get some rest," he said softly and took his hand away.

"Tomorrow?"

"I'll be here."

Roxie barely had time to nod groggily before Zeke was gone. He wasn't kidding. The kitchen and the table were spotless. With a satisfied and grateful smile, Roxie shuffled off to bed.

The next day Zeke could smell the scent of chili wafting through the air before he even reached up to knock on Red's apartment door. His mouth watered as he rapt at the door.

"Coming," he heard Red's voice call from inside. She opened the door with a smile and his heart fluttered in his chest. "You know, I really should get you a key. It would make things easier than having to go through this ritual every day. Of course I could just leave the door unlocked, but I don't exactly feel comfortable doing that."

"No!" Zeke tried to reel in the panic he felt at that suggestion and push his words out calmly. "No, don't do that. You're too close to all the trouble that is stirring."

"What trouble?" Roxie asked as she sat down at the table expecting Zeke to follow, which he did.

"What do you mean, what trouble? You were attacked."

"That was one guy."

"He may have been alone that night, but he is far from the only one causing trouble around here. I wasn't joking or exaggerating when I said that there was gang activity going on out here."

"I thought that was just rumors."

"There's truth to it."

"How do you know?"

"I know."

"How?"

"Does it matter how I know?"

"Well, I was thinking about the camping trip today, and it occurred to me that I really don't know much about you."

"Are you accusing me of being involved with a gang?"

"No, of course not. I was just curious how you knew."

"I live around here. I've lived here all my life, and I've seen a lot of changes. I notice things that other people, who haven't lived here as long, might not notice."

"Things like what?"

"Things like gang activity. Just because the police haven't found out yet, doesn't mean they aren't there."

"I guess... The chili maybe a little hot," Red warned several bites into dinner.

"It's delicious. I like hot."

Red gave him a shy smile strong enough to melt him into a puddle of goo. "Zeke... tell me about yourself?"

Red flags were waving high. "What do you want to know?"

"Anything. Like I said, I realized today how little I know about you. Share anything you want."

"I don't know what to tell you. You know that I was in the military with Kris. You know I live a few miles from here and that I work for your brother. What else do you want to know?"

"What do you do for fun?"

"Uh," What did he do for fun? Zeke couldn't remember doing much of anything just for the fun of it since his family died. It wasn't to say that he hadn't had any fun, but it had all come indirectly. He hadn't done anything with the sole purpose to simply relax and have fun. "I guess I don't do much anymore. What do you do for fun?"

Red sucked her bottom lip into her mouth and pressed it tight between her teeth. "Oh, well... I don't have a lot of extra time. It takes time and hard work to get ahead in the business world, especially for a girl."

"You've done well for yourself. It's nearly impossible for a woman to get where you are."

"Thanks, but what about you?"

"Business wasn't really my thing. It was just another job."

"What is your thing?" Red asked with honest curiosity in her voice.

Zeke answered the only way he knew how and still be honest. "I liked being in the military."

"Why did you quit?"

"I had responsibilities."

"That simple? What kind of responsibilities?"

"Taking care of the house and land mainly."

Red looked down at her bowl guiltily. "What?" Zeke wondered.

"I'm sorry. Was that when your family died? While you were gone, I mean?"

"No, they died before I left. I had already made the decision to join the armed forces. They didn't like it, but they knew my plans. After they... died, I went through with it anyway. I guess I was running away. I stayed in the military for years, but someone had to take care of things here. I was the only one left to do it."

"So, now you're not happy? Why don't you sell the place?"

"It's my family's home. I could never sell it."

"But, you're not happy here," Red pushed.

"I just haven't found my place in the world."

"What about in the military?"

"I liked it in the military, but that wasn't where I belonged. It was a distraction."

"From what?"

"Life."

"What will you do now?"

"Well, for the time being I'll work for Michael and take care of things back here."

"You make it sound like you are taking care of the whole area," Red smiled.

"Tell me more about you," Zeke dodged. "You worked hard to get where you are, but are you happy?"

"Yes, I'm very happy. I mean for now. I'm not going to be satisfied with the status quo forever."

Zeke worked hard to keep his lips from quirking up into a smile. "What does that mean?"

"I love my position. I want to stay there, but maybe not here. This apartment is tiny, and... Don't tell my mom, but it does get lonely from time to time. I'd like to get married, get a bigger place, and start a family someday, but..."

The thought of Red married to some stranger and having his kids had Zeke seeing red. He grit his teeth together and pushed himself to speak despite the fact that his voice sounded rougher than normal. "But?"

"But, working the hours that I do, it's not easy to get out there and meet people. I have to get to a point in my career where I can focus on other things. That's what Mom doesn't understand. I don't want to sacrifice my career, and that's what would happen right now. What about you? Do you date much?"

"Ah, no, not really."

"Why not? You're a good looking man; I'm sure you wouldn't have trouble meeting women." Red's face suddenly flushed as red as her hair as if she had just caught what had slipped out of her mouth unnoticed.

Zeke smiled at the compliment. Red wasn't the first woman to tell him he looked nice, but it was most certainly sweeter coming from her mouth. "I realized some time ago that dating just to be dating is a waste of both my time and the young lady I'm out with. Unless I see it as something that could last, I don't bother." He left out the part that he would know more precisely than normal people when he found the one.

"That's... not very practical at all, actually. If you refuse to date until it's serious, how will it ever become serious, and how will you know when you find someone who things could be serious with?"

So much for keeping some things to himself. "I'll know."

"How?"

"Does it matter? I'll just know."

Red shook her head, but let it go. "Okay, so you don't date. You take care of the family house, and you work with Michael. There must be more to your life."

She had no idea, but what he did otherwise would send her running for help. "Not really," he lied easily.

"What about your weekends?" She was not going to let go easily.

"I work around the house. What about your weekends?"

Red looked down at her bowl sheepishly. "I bring a lot of work home with me. I don't like staying late at the office, but nine to five hours are a myth in my line of work."

"I'd much rather you bring your work home with you than stay late again. I still feel bad about that."

"Don't. I told you it wasn't your fault I was behind that day."

Zeke caught Red's gaze and could not pull his eyes from hers. "Do me a favor? Don't work late anymore. There is some bad stuff going on around here, and I'm starting to grow kind of fond of you?"

Red smiled and her eye lids fluttered breaking the strangely mesmerizing hold her gaze had on him. "I promise not to work late unless it is unavoidable."

"That's not good enough," Zeke said not willing to bend. "If you insist on working late at least call me. I'll walk you to your car. It's not safe for you to be walking out there alone, much less after dark."

"You sound like my brothers," Red accused.

It wasn't meant as a compliment. Zeke knew how she meant it; she meant that he was being overprotective. Kris and Michael both cared for her very much. Her statement could be easily taken as a compliment despite how she meant it, yet being compared to her brother still didn't feel like a compliment. It felt... hollow, not nearly strong enough, but that was ridiculous. They didn't know each other well enough for them to have a relationship stronger than that of a brother. They didn't know each other well enough for a relationship as strong as a brother even, but then, wasn't that the point of this conversation? Wasn't Red trying to get to know him? Funny, a part of him wanted that, but he couldn't have that relationship. He had not wanted to be that close to anyone in a long time. He was probably as close to Kris as he was to anyone, and Kris didn't know much about him.

Zeke looked up from his bowl only to find himself under Red's scrutiny. "Why are you being so elusive?" Red demanded.

"Elusive?"

"Yes, elusive, mysterious, vague."

"I know what it means."

"Well?"

"I don't think I'm being elusive," he lied smoothly. "I've told you as much as you've told me."

"That's hardly fair. You know Kris and work with Michael. You could ask whatever you want behind my back."

"I wouldn't do that."

"Sure, do you want more?"

"What?"

"Chili?" Red offered reaching across the table for his empty bowl.

"Oh, yeah, thanks."

"You must be hungry tonight." He was hungry. He always got hungrier the closer it was to a full moon. It was a myth that the lunar cycle affected the change; however, it did cause other interesting side effects. Side effects such as increased appetite, but there was no reason to tell Red any of that.

"I am sort of hungry, and this is really good."

"There you go with the compliments again. Has anyone ever told you what a smooth talker you are?"

"I might have heard something to that effect once or twice. I've heard it just as often, though, that my smooth tongue is more offensive than anything."

"Well, I am thoroughly enjoying the compliments."

Red's smile warmed Zeke's heart in a way that he hadn't felt in a long time. He smiled back confidently, triumphantly and said, "Good." It was dangerous to get too close to Red. Zeke knew that, but he also knew that it was going to be hard to give her up now. "If you aren't busy this weekend, would you like to come over and see the house?" Zeke heard the words come out of his mouth, but it took a minute before it really registered what he was saying.

"Hmm?" Red nearly choked on her chili.

"You wanted the chance to get to know each other better. Come over to the house; I'll give you the grand tour."

"Oh, um, sure." She didn't sound entirely sure at all. Once again her face was the same shade as her tantalizing red hair.

"Don't let me twist your arm."

"No, I'm sorry. It sounds like fun."

"Don't worry about it. You're right; we really don't know each other all that well. That makes my invitation wildly inappropriate and probably makes you uncomfortable. I shouldn't have even asked." Zeke felt like the biggest idiot on earth and a jerk to boot.

"Are you withdrawing the offer now that I've accepted?"

Was that actual pain in her voice? It couldn't be. She was not interested to begin with. She must have been offended. First he extended an inappropriate invitation, and then reneges. Offended sounded like the most probable reaction. Zeke was making a terrible mess of things, and he wasn't sure how to fix it.

"No, that's not it. I just don't want you to feel pressured, like you have to come."

"I know. I want to come. I've always wondered about the lone house sitting in the middle of the business district."

Zeke smiled. She had wondered about his home... for years. What might have happened if they had met earlier... maybe before he met her brother? The age difference would have been an issue. He would have been forced to sever ties by now, and all the same road blocks he had now would still have been a problem then. They would never have worked out. They were never meant to be.

"Maybe I can answer all your questions this Saturday. I could cook for you for a change."

"No thanks, not if what I've heard about your cooking is true."

"I could take you out for a change," Zeke suggested. On second thought, that sounded too much like a date, and neither one of them needed that right now.

"Sounds like a plan," Red agreed as she toted dishes to the sink.

"I'll get the dishes."

"You got the dishes last night."

"And, you cooked. So? Let me do something to help."

"I'm fine, really."

It was obvious that Red was not going to willingly move out of his way, so he pushed his way into the tiny space, gently of course;

he didn't want to hurt her. Opening the dishwasher, he crowded her into a very minuscule spot opposite from him. She didn't have space to turn or move about without hitting her shins on the dishwasher door. Zeke rinsed the dishes and handed them off to Red to load in the dishwasher. A tag team compromise seemed to be as close as either of them were going to get to their own way. The close quarters caused by the compromise was not unpleasant either.

She was close enough that heat from her skin was flowing over Zeke and hitting him like straight line winds. He could tell that she was fevered, but she didn't appear sick in any other way. The fevered warmth spilling from her was satisfying in an unsettling way. Zeke had never been a cold natured person; it wasn't myth that werewolves tend to run hot, but now, the side farthest from Red was uncharacteristically cold. He realized now how cold he had been all his long life as he tried to survive alone. Wolves were pack animals; they were never meant to be alone in this world. The person he needed was Red and all her heat to keep him warm.

He could hear her heart beating wildly, blood rushing through her veins like rapids. Her breaths were coming more hastily than normal as well. In Zeke's experience, if a person wasn't sick, there were two main reasons for such reactions, excitement or fear. Zeke meant to glance over at Red's face for only a second, an innocent peek, but when he saw her flush, he couldn't help but revel in her exquisiteness. He had never quite found a moment that called him to use that word to describe anything, but that was what Red was, exquisite. Her grey-green eyes were more green than grey. Green was a typical eye color for red heads he reminded himself again, but the grey undertone made her eyes anything but ordinary. It gave them an air of mystery that Zeke had never seen in anyone before, and right now those mysterious, grey-green eyes were boring straight into him with an intent stare. How could eyes so vibrantly green harbor a hint of grey at the same time? Despite her accelerated heartbeat and flushed skin she did not appear sick; she appeared... hungry.

Zeke swallowed hard trying to fight back his own hunger that was now intensified by the hunger he imagined seeing in Red's eyes. Breaking eye contact he forced his gaze down to where light brown freckles danced across her high cheek bones on porcelain smooth skin. Funny how things he never noticed on people before, on Red could call so loudly to him now. He turned back to the sink and the bowl he was supposed to be rinsing. He closed his eyes for only a second and took a deep breath.

Zeke could smell the scent of soap and shampoo, as well as a more flowery scent that was all Red. He could almost picture red flowers to match her scent, flowers the exact shade of red as her hair. The blooms were full, numerous, and lovely to behold. Their fragrance could be detected from up to a mile away, and its enticing aroma would be strong enough to bring both men and beast to their knees. The red flower that held her scent would be beautiful, but not nearly as beautiful as Red herself.

She smelt good enough to eat, and Zeke so desperately wanted to sample what Red would taste like. Just one quick kiss was all it would take to capture her taste on his tongue, and that was why he had to get out of there, fast.

He handed off the last dish to Red, quickly dried his hands on the dish towel, and made a mad dash towards the door. At the last second Zeke looked over his shoulder and asked, "Tomorrow?"

"Yeah, I'll see you then," Red answered with false cheerfulness. Her face was confused, concerned. Any hunger he thought he had seen before had effectively been doused.

<h1 style="text-align:center">Chapter Six</h1>

"Girl, you know you've got it bad when simple chores like loading the dishwasher with a man can get you all hot and bothered," Lucy sympathized.

"I know. I know," Roxie responded almost desperately. She was hopelessly lost, and there was nothing she could do about it. It couldn't go anywhere.

"So what are you going to do about it?" Lucy wanted to know.

"Nothing."

"Nothing? You're going over to his house for a grand tour Saturday, and he is taking you out. That sounds an awful lot like a date to me. How long do you think you are going to be able to deny this? Better question is how long do you think you'll be able to hide this from Kris. He's going to see what is obvious to everyone but you."

"He isn't going to see anything, because there is nothing going on."

"Keep telling yourself that if it makes you feel more secure."

That night Roxie cooked meatloaf, mashed potatoes, and English peas. Zeke should have been there any second, so Roxie unlocked the door and started putting food on the table. She had barely gotten started when there was a knock on the door. "Come in," she called.

The door knob turned slowly and the door opened tentatively. Zeke poked his head in before entering and shutting the door behind him. "I thought we agreed that you would keep the door locked."

Roxie glanced over her shoulder at him. Man, he looked disappointed. "Calm down. I just unlocked it, like less than two minutes ago, because I knew you would be here any second. And... here you are, so no harm."

"No harm this time, but it might not always be that way."

"Sure," Roxie tried to blow it off as no big deal. She hoped that if she treated it with a nonchalant attitude maybe he would too, but that wasn't going to happen.

"Red." He had called her Red again, but Roxie quickly put that on the backburner when he crossed the room arms extended and took hold of her by her upper arms. She had shed the suit jacket as soon as she walked in the door, and her sleeveless shirt left her arms bare and vulnerable to his embrace. His hands were like a scorching vise. She couldn't have escaped if she wanted to, which she didn't. That scorching heat was searing through her entire body faster than anything she had ever felt before. Her heart kicked into high gear with a jolt, and a now familiar tingle took over her. Although familiar now, it wasn't a common tingle; it was Zeke's tingle, the sensation that only he could cause. "Listen to me. I wasn't kidding when I said that there was gang activity threatening the area. Lock the door... please."

"I'm sorry. I honestly didn't think about it being a problem for just a minute. I'll… I'll keep it locked from now on."

"Promise?" Zeke was rubbing his thumbs back and forth now across the front of her arms. Just like that, Roxie forgot what they were talking about and what Zeke wanted from her. She forgot anything past his touch on her arms. Something in the back of her mind continued to scream that it was nothing more than an innocent touch, but it felt anything but innocent.

"Promise," she parroted even though she had no idea to what she was promising.

"Good," Zeke said letting his hands drop back to his sides. "Something smells great!"

Instantaneously Roxie felt the chill of the air as it hit her skin like millions of pin pricks all over. She instinctively wanted to turn up the thermostat, that is, if she couldn't get Zeke to wrap his arms around her instead. One would draw attention, and the other was not going to happen. Roxie dug her feet in, so to speak, and readied herself to work her way through the cold.

Roxie sat down at the table to eat with Zeke, but all she could think about was the night she was attacked. All the talk of locking doors and gang activity had made those terrifying memories resurface; except, she didn't feel at all frightened anymore. She was much more interested in the wolf that no one else seemed to believe existed.

"I talked to Michael last night," Roxie mentioned with what she hoped was an air of indifference as she took her seat at the table.

"Oh?"

"He still doesn't believe me. I'm pretty sure he thinks I'm nuts."

"Did he say that?" Zeke wondered.

"Not exactly." He hadn't had to say it. He danced all around it. He all but suggested she go see a shrink. "He implied it."

"I'm sure Michael doesn't think you're crazy. What is this all about anyway?"

"The wolf."

"Oh, I see. It's public record now that the guy was attacked by an animal. He believes you were attacked. Why is it so hard to believe that you saw what you said you saw?"

"I don't know, but I don't think Kris believes me either."

"I think Kris is more scared than anything. It's harder for the tough guys to admit when they are scared. Kris has devoted his whole life to protecting, and now he doesn't know what to do to protect you."

Roxie wasn't sure whether or not she should be insulted. She knew that Kris had always been overprotective. She admitted it openly, but that didn't mean that she was helpless. "I don't need his protection. I'm an adult now."

"It's not just you. Sure, it started with you when you were young kids, but that was only the beginning. When your dad died, it was your mom, and when he joined the military, it was the whole country, the entire world for that matter. Why do you think he doesn't work? He feels like he's too busy taking care of everyone else."

"He said that?" Now she felt bad; Roxie had assumed that he was just being lazy.

"He doesn't have to say it."

"And, you think he's scared?"

"I know he is... I don't know if Kris ever talks about the things we saw overseas." Roxie shook her head vehemently. "Ok, well, we saw a lot. You learn what scared looks like in yourself and in your friends."

"So, you think he believes me?"

"I don't know. I don't know that he is sure what to believe at this point."

Roxie gave an instinctive sigh before catching herself. She had almost believed Zeke, believed that Kris might take her word for it, but that wasn't the case. "The police don't believe it was a wolf. They put down that he was attacked by an animal, probably a stray dog, but they don't believe it was a wolf. Kris is taking their word over mine... Mom has been avoiding the subject. I don't think she wants me to know that she is taking Michael and Kris's side."

"Maybe not, but why does it have to be about sides?"

"It's not about sides. I know what I saw, and it would be nice if my own family would believe me."

"I'm sure they want to believe you, but it is odd for a wolf to be in the middle of a city, especially the business district. It doesn't help that the wolf did not act like a normal wolf."

"You're right. It didn't behave like a regular wolf, but it didn't look like a regular one either."

"Exactly."

"So, you're on their side too?" It didn't make any sense for Roxie to feel betrayed. She barely knew Zeke, and her own family did not believe her. Nevertheless, that was exactly how she felt, betrayed.

"We're back to taking sides again?" Zeke asked with an accusatory tone.

"No, yes, I don't know."

Zeke frowned. Roxie did not like his frown anymore than she liked the feeling of betrayal. "What do you think, honestly?" she asked.

"Honestly?" Roxie nodded, and Zeke paused a moment. She could practically see the wheels turning in his mind. "I believe that if you say you saw a wolf, than you saw a wolf. Wolves are pack animals, so I believe that a lone wolf this far in the city, would naturally act unusual."

"You believe me?"

"Yes."

"You're the only one."

"Does it matter?"

"I guess not... You want to hear about the wolf?"

"Um... sure, I mean if you want to talk about it, I'll listen."

"It was beautiful."

"What?"

"It was beautiful with long, dark fur. I guess you could call it chestnut, not quite black, but it was dark. It was as dark as the night around us. It was large, tall, wide, long, and it was so muscular. His fangs were sharp and bone white."

"Teeth usually are white," Zeke pointed out with a smirk.

"True, but his teeth were perfect."

"So, a large, dark-furred wolf with perfectly white teeth?"

"That's not even the most amazing part. Those eyes..."

Zeke looked leery when he asked, "What about the eyes?"

"They were dark, mesmerizing. They were almost human looking. I keep getting the feeling that I've seen those eyes somewhere before."

"The wolf's eyes?"

"Yeah, his eyes were amazing, the kind of eyes you could get lost in if he were human. They were..." Roxie looked up and her own eyes bugged out. "They were just like yours..." Zeke didn't say a word; he just stared at her with intense, beautiful eyes. "Maybe that's why I thought I had seen those eyes before. The wolf's eyes were so much like yours, and I had just met you earlier that day."

"Mmm, maybe," he responded, but he didn't look like he believed her.

"You think I'm crazy now, don't you?"

"No, not at all."

All Roxie could do was smile; not only did Zeke believe there had been a wolf, but he didn't think she was crazy even after her description of the wolf.

Zeke cleared his throat and said, "This meatloaf is wonderful."

"You've barely touched what little peas you put on your plate," Roxie scolded with a laugh.

"Haven't we had this conversation before?"

"Still, you should try to eat more vegetables; they're good for you."

"You want to hand feed them to me? I might eat them that way," Zeke offered.

"My brothers would beat you, if they ever heard you joking like that."

"Probably," he smiled. "Good thing they aren't here."

"I guess so... Thanks."

"For what?"

"Believing in me when no one else did."

"I'm just taking all the facts into consideration," Zeke said modestly, but it was so much more than that. Taking the facts into consideration is what everyone else claimed to be doing too. Zeke was the only one who saw the same set of facts and believed.

"Thanks all the same... Are you coming tomorrow night?"

"Are you sure I won't be an inconvenience?"

"Sure, I'll be cooking anyway. It's just as easy to cook for two as it is one."

"I'll be here."

"Taco salad?" Roxie threw out.

"Sounds good." Zeke stood up and started staking dishes. "Don't rush; I'm just going to get this stuff started. You finish eating."

"You don't have to do that."

"I know. It's not about what I have to do. I told you I want to help out, pull my own weight. I can be very stubborn, so you might as well give in."

"I've been known to be stubborn myself," Roxie warned.

"Well, you feel free to join me after you finish eating, but finish eating first."

Roxie wolfed down what was left of her meatloaf and joined Zeke in the kitchen. He was forced to scoot over making room and leaving her at the sink. It didn't take long to get the work done, and Zeke wasted no time disappearing.

Work the next day was exceptionally slow for a Friday, but Roxie managed to muddle through somehow. All the while what she really wanted to do is get home, cook, and wait for Zeke. She really was beginning to look forward to her dinners with Zeke way too much. They were the highlight of her day.

Taco salad was a quick and easy fix. Chopping lettuce and tomatoes took the longest of anything. Still, Roxie was not quite finished when Zeke arrived.

"You're early," Roxie squeaked as she opened the door for Zeke.

"Yeah, Michael finished up early. I think he was ready to take off. Some hot date or something."

"Oh."

"Was I not supposed to say anything?" Zeke asked guiltily.

"I don't think it really matters, but Michael doesn't really talk with me about the girls he dates. It is probably a weird subject to discuss with your baby sister."

"Maybe... Look, don't say anything to Michael. I didn't mean to do anything to upset him."

"Don't worry about it. I won't say anything. I'm really not all that interested in who he dates. He'll say something if he ever finds someone who he's serious about."

"Thanks. Is there anything that I can do to give you a hand?"

"Nah, I think I've got it... I was kind of surprised you came tonight."

"Why? Did you have plans?"

"No, no, not me. I'm a workaholic. Remember? But, why don't you have plans?"

"Me? Kris is the party animal, not me."

"What about you?"

"What do you mean?"

"You're not a party animal, but surely you have some kind of social life. Don't you date?"

"Not in years actually. What about you, don't you date?"

"Not really. I dated a little in high school, but I've been too busy building a career since then. Besides, I have no interest in the guys who usually hit on me."

"A lot of them then?"

"A lot?"

"Guys who hit on you?"

"Oh, there are a few from time to time, I guess."

"You guess? You don't know how many guys hit on you?"

"I don't pay them much attention."

"Why not?"

"Not interested?"

"Do your brothers know?"

"Know what?"

"That you're... not interested in guys," Zeke said in a tone that suggested that her interests might swing in the opposite direction.

"Ha, ha."

"So, you are interested in guys then? What kind of guys do you date, or would you date?"

"Um, I don't know. I haven't ever sat down and made up a criteria list for the perfect guy if that's what you're asking."

"No such thing. Is that what you're holding out for?"

"No, I don't know what I'm looking for. Ok, turn this conversation off of me. What about you? What kind of woman are you looking for?"

"Not looking all that hard," Zeke commented nonchalantly.

"Why not?"

"It is a tiring never ending search."

"So you just choose not to date?"

"I think we've had this conversation before," Zeke said with a wink. "You never answered the question."

"What question would that be?"

"What are you looking for in a guy?"

"I think I steered that conversation away from me," Roxie pointed out somewhat desperately.

"Mmm… so, how wild do you like them?" Zeke asked with severe seriousness.

"Wild? What?"

"You don't want to talk about it, almost as if you are ashamed."

"That is not it… It's a sort of embarrassing subject to talk about with someone you haven't known very long."

"And, yet you wanted me to talk about it. I tell you what I'll tell you if you tell me." When Roxie hesitated, Zeke added, "Come on. How awful could it be? I won't ridicule you or even try to morph into whatever type man you describe."

"Well, okay, but you go first."

"That's easy. I'm not looking for anything in a guy; I like girls. Your turn."

"Zeke!"

"I never said I played fair."

"I'm not following that."

"I don't have any specifics like blonde hair, blue eyes or even a type A personality. I just want someone who I can connect with."

"That's very vague. Don't you have any idea what kind of person you might connect with?" Roxie asked for clarification.

"No, do you?"

"Of course,... Someone like my brothers but sort of between the two. He's got to be pretty tough to survive my brothers, not to mention I've been protected all my life by two big tough guys. I don't think I would know how to act if there wasn't a guy there to protect me. I want someone with Michael's work ethic. I also want someone who is fun like Kris... Somewhere in the middle. I want a good man. Someone who takes notice of moods and acts accordingly, but not someone who is overly sensitive, like almost prissy or something."

"Hmm, so you looking for someone who is sensitive but not sensitive, who is a hard worker but a goof. That's not contradictive in the least. Why do people do that? In essence, you're no more sure what you're looking for than I am. Why not just say you're looking for someone who you connect with?"

"How does that work? You may connect with all sorts of people."

"Sure, but give me a little credit. You're going to connect with people on a different level. I connect with Kris, but that doesn't mean that I'm attracted to him or think we should run off to get married. At the same time I connect with Michael, but not the same way as I do with Kris. Kris and I are goofballs when we get together. Michael wouldn't much appreciate that behavior at work. Or, take us for example, I would never sit down with either of your brothers and have this sort of conversation."

"I would hope not; they would likely break your nose thinking you were hitting on them."

"Are you hitting on me?" Zeke questioned with a cocky smirk.

"Not the same."

"Why is it so important that you know what type of person you are looking for anyway?"

"I don't guess it is... unless..."

"Unless?"

"I can't believe guys don't have the same problem, but no one ever gives Kris a hard time. The older a girl gets the more she is expected to settle down. If she doesn't, everyone and their brother start trying to set her up. It's nice when they're trying to set you up all the time to have a relative type to give them so that each time is not some obscure set up."

"Why let them set you up at all?"

"No isn't always an option," Roxie pointed out.

"No is always an option."

"For guys maybe."

"For anyone."

"Okay, change of subject please." Roxie wanted to change her thought process as much as she wanted to change the subject, but now that Zeke's dating habits had been brought to the forefront of her mind, that was all she could think about. He could probably have any girl he wanted. He probably dated only the most gorgeous women... come to think of it..."I'm impressed. Most guys would go straight to looks when they started talking about their type, but you are more interested in the connection." Roxie hadn't meant to say that aloud, but before she thought better of it, it had already slipped out.

"Mmm."

Roxie was not sure if he was mmm'ing at her statement or the huge bite of taco salad he had just put into his mouth. Roxie studied Zeke's plate for a minute then asked, "Did you get any lettuce at all, or corn chips for that matter?"

"A little," Zeke mumbled guiltily.

"You know heart disease does not discriminate. Many people who appear to be in tip top shape have had heart attacks."

"My heart is fine."

"If you say so."

"Do you have a physical preference in guys? If I were setting you up for example, what would you tell me?" Zeke wondered.

"I'd tell you exactly what I have already told you. I might also add that it would probably be detrimental to your health to set me up."

"Your brothers?"

"Yep, a girlfriend setting me up is one thing, but..."

"I guy setting you up is just forward. I can see their point."

"I don't. That's never stopped them before though."

"Have you ever thought that you had maybe found a connection?"

Now Zeke's questions were getting extremely personal, but Roxie did not much mind since she had every intent of returning the favor, as long as he kept his word. "Looking back, I don't think I was ever really that close, but every teenage girl thinks she's in love at some point. I was no different."

"What happened?"

"Kris happened."

"Bummer."

"Yeah, Kris saw him kiss me goodnight. Kris came barreling onto the porch. He sent me inside, and the rest was history... It was only our first date."

"Wow, did you ever make it past the first date?"

"Yeah, but it was always when there was no spark. I guess that was the way that Kris and Michael liked it."

"I imagine so."

"What about you? Have you ever been close to a real connection?"

"I thought so once. I was young and foolish. We were from different worlds. In the end there was never any connection but the physical one."

"Tell me about her?"

"All I can remember about her now is how she looked. It was all so long ago. She was beautiful. Red head, dark skin, I think she was part Native American, part Irish. Funny that the red hair would come out especially with that dark skin. It made her seem more a mystery. She had dark brown eyes that you could look into a thousand times and see something new every time. She was tall, very close to my own height and curvy." Zeke's eyes had taken on a kind of dreamy state while he talked about the girl from his past.

"She sounds beautiful," Roxie said sympathetically.

"She was, and I swore to myself that I would never be that stupid again. There is so much more to life than beauty, and there is so much more to real connections than mere physical."

"Yeah, right. Haven't you ever noticed that the beautiful tend to end up with the beautiful? It's no wonder the closest you ever came was with someone beautiful," Roxie mumbled. She was only half talking to Zeke, mainly grumbling to herself. Her self-esteem was not so low to think herself ugly, but she was no beauty queen either. A good description for her would be average.

"Uh... thanks?" Zeke's usual confident air was suddenly shaken. He was looking at Roxie warily unsure of himself. "How was your day?" It was a sad attempt to change the subject at best.

"Uneventful, which isn't a bad thing. How was your day?"

"Same, uneventful. I'm looking forward to next week though," Zeke said with an amused, mischievous grin.

"What's happening next week?"

"Michael has an appointment with a kid who bit him last time he was in for a filing. It should be interesting."

"Sounds like."

Together they ate in silence for a few minutes. Roxie could not seem to force her gaze off Zeke. His jaw worked rhythmically, the muscles tensing and showing off pure strength. She watched his lips moving and couldn't stop herself from wondering what those lips would feel like moving against her own. Would they be as soft as they appeared? Strong? Demanding? Soothing? They would definitely be distracting; they were already distracting without any contact. If she hadn't been watching his lips so closely, she wouldn't have noticed he was speaking again.

"What would be your idea of a perfect date?"

"A perfect date? A meal at a nice restaurant, somewhere I'm not cooking or cleaning afterwards, with someone I trust. Good conversation and a comforting feel."

"So that's it? Just a nice meal?"

"I don't know. I've never been charged with planning the perfect date. What would you do if you were going to take a girl on the perfect date?"

"Maybe start with a dinner at a nice restaurant; you women seem to like that." Roxie scoffed, but Zeke continued. "A walk under the moonlight would be nice, a full moon."

"That's it?" Roxie asked when he did not continue.

"What more do you need? A full moon can be very intoxicating. Have you ever walked beneath one?"

"Uh, I'm not sure. I've never taken much notice."

"You should. Full moons are amazing. The next date you're on try going for a walk under a full moon and see if you don't fall in love faster."

"You're serious?"

"Just try it before you knock it."

"I'll try to keep it in mind. I don't suppose you know when the next full moon is?"

"Not 'til next month. It actually falls during the camping trip," Zeke informed.

"Well, there will hardly be any romancing going on there, but I'll try to pay attention to the full moon nevertheless."

"Good idea, you know people say that a full moon can make people act crazy."

"Do you believe that?"

"I don't not believe it," Zeke answered vaguely. "I've heard teachers, ER nurses, and countless others profess to the fact, but I don't know any scientific rational why it should be true."

"That doesn't mean there isn't one."

"True, so do you believe it?"

"No," Roxie answered simply.

"No?"

"I don't believe that the moon has anything to do with people's behavior. I believe that people control their own behavior... I can, however, imagine that the light from a full moon could provide a romantic ambiance."

"Mmm, the full moon is very enchanting."

Roxie stared at Zeke, the intense look on his face like he believed whole-heartedly in what he was saying. Not only that, he looked intent, content, romanticized himself. He was staring right back, straight into her eyes. His dark eyes were so... mesmerizing, and was she imagining that look in his eyes? Was he looking at her as if she was as fascinating as that full moon he seemed so taken with?

Roxie's breathing started coming in short, rapid breaths and shallow. She couldn't catch her breath. Was she hyperventilating? No. There was no panic. She didn't feel that there was a threat of not getting enough air, not really. If anything, it was a good feeling. Excitement. It was the kind of difficulty breathing that comes when you get excited about something. What was going on? Roxie knew that it was irrational, impossible, but there was something uniquely exciting about Zeke's eyes and the way she felt with his eyes watching her.

That was ridiculous! She was still staring at him. What was wrong with her? Roxie cleared her throat and looked away awkwardly. "Um, would you like some more?"

"What? Oh, no, I'm stuffed, couldn't eat another bite," Zeke replied.

Roxie started collecting dishes, but Zeke put a staying hand on her arm. "Let me," he said softly. Roxie's attention was captured by Zeke's hand on her arm. It was warm and calloused and strong. "Sorry," he said and jerked his hand away as if she had burnt him.

"I've got it tonight. I'm sure you have better things to do on a Friday night. Go on; these won't take me very long. I'm just going to take it easy tonight, try to unwind."

"Are you sure?" Zeke asked uncertainly.

"Yes, go on. I'll see you tomorrow."

"Tomorrow." With that Zeke was gone, and Roxie was left alone.

Chapter Seven

Zeke was so stupid! He shouldn't have touched her. He had no business touching her. He had no right to touch her. The look on her face when he touched only her arm was shock to say the least. Was she... mortified? She couldn't possibly have felt the same thing he had felt at that exact moment. It was an intense tingle that he could feel all the way down to his toes.

Zeke parked the car and began stripping out of his confining clothes. He had a full night ahead. He had been watching the gang. He knew their schedule almost as well as they did. He knew their guards, and he knew their guards' weaknesses. After allowing his wolf form to take over, Zeke loped silently, stealthily through the shadows, but his thoughts remained with Red back at the apartment he had left.

She was an amazing woman. He had not met anyone like her in... generations. She was more than beautiful. She was intelligent, funny, practical, good company. He loved just being in her presence she gave him a sense of calm. Even on a night like tonight, when he was off to handle some unpleasant business, she had the power to calm him... except when she didn't. He sure didn't feel calm when he was touching her. He felt anything but calm; he hadn't felt like that in many long years.

Zeke crouched close to the ground hidden away in the shadows and settled in to wait. As he waited, he thought. Zeke was sure, if given the chance, he could be everything she was looking for in a man, but that was a chance that Zeke was not afforded. Her idea of the perfect date was so simple, so easy. Zeke could show her everything that she was missing. She could be so breathtaking underneath a full moon.

Activity began. Men of all ages and sizes began pouring inside carrying all types of booze. It wouldn't be long now before the women began to arrive, and shortly after that everyone with the exception of the guards would be intoxicated.

The women came in eagerly and scantily dressed. They were sleazy at best and no better than the men they came to seduce. The women were easy, but not easy to love in the slightest. Red, now she was a woman who would be easy to love, and she was so much more beautiful in her more conservative clothes than these scantily dressed women on their best day.

Things always got louder inside before they began to get quiet. Tonight Zeke was not waiting for the quiet. Their best and strongest man had guard duty tonight. He would be the lone man on the main street. There would be no witness to be found. Everything this close to the business district was abandoned this late on a Friday night, except, of course, for the trouble makers themselves. Tonight Zeke would strike when the party reached its loudest. He would strike quickly and silently. He would be deadly in his strike, and no one would be the wiser until it was too late.

The guard was tall and thin but not small. He had long sinewy muscles. Zeke had not seen the man use his gun but had no doubt that the guard knew just what to do with it.

Zeke leaped out of the shadows and onto the guard before the guard even knew he had been stalked. Zeke went straight for the throat for two reasons. One, it would keep the guard quiet, keep him from sounding an alarm. Two, it was the fastest kill. The guard put up very little fight. By the time he figured out what was happening, it was too late to do anything about it. He had been as good as dead from the moment Zeke set his sights on the guard.

It was far from Zeke's first kill, as distasteful as it might be. He had killed in both wolf and human form. Back before the world had become "civilized," things had been simple, a life for a life. You fought. There was a winner and there was a looser. He had fought off many threats to his family while in wolf form. Once upon a time, nearly two centuries ago, wolves had fought one another for territory. Although his family had never been one to invade or take others' territory, many had tried to take what was theirs. Many wolves like himself had died by his muzzle.

In human form, he had killed for very similar reasons. In human form, however, his battle had been on a more grand scale. He did not fight for his family's small plot of ground, yet he fought for an entire country. He had served as an assassin in the military. It didn't matter which form he chose. He could kill expertly in either form, but he preferred to kill in wolf form. Somehow it seemed less inhumane.

Zeke made his way slowly back to his car. He dreaded the part when he shifted back to human form with the taste of blood still in his mouth. The taste was not a pleasant one in either form, but at least in this form it was tolerable. In human form it was nauseating. If it weren't for his car, Zeke would have walked back home and stayed in wolf form until morning, but his parked car would cause too much suspicion.

By the time Zeke got back to his car and phased back to human form. The taste was not as bad as he had survived before, but it was still bad enough. Before he could even redress, Zeke found himself doubled over and vomiting. His stomach emptied in record time, and he regretted the taco salad he had eaten with Red.

Zeke stood up and grabbed inside the car for his shirt. He quickly wiped his mouth with his shirt and left it on the side of the road as he pulled his pants on, climbed in the car and drove away cursing himself for being so stupid. He had a clear plan of how he wanted tonight to go, and he knew the result would be violent vomiting. Taco salad had been a stupid move, but he couldn't bring himself to regret the time he spend with Red tonight.

What was with this gang anyway? How many of their men had been killed by what they believe to be a wild animal? He guessed wild animal was as apt a description as any; he had been pretty wild once upon a time. No one could control him, but he had a job to do now. Why had these stupid idiots not been scared away from the area yet? How many more would he have to kill? What was it going to take to get this band of criminals out of his territory?

Zeke pushed the dismal thoughts from his mind. He didn't even know the results of tonight's mission yet. Unfortunately, or maybe it was fortunately, the only other place Zeke's thoughts were headed that night were straight back to Red. He thought of the way the light shined off her lip gloss when she smiled. He imagined how her lips would look shining in the moonlight, or better yet, how her lips would feel gliding across his own.

Zeke shook his head and focused on the road as he turned into his drive. Thoughts like those were going to get him into trouble.

Red was the sister of a friend, and if he was lucky, she was a friend. Tomorrow he had better be on his best, friendliest behavior if he ever wanted to be on friendly terms with Red again.

That night Zeke could not sleep. He was jumpy and had too much energy. He had never reacted like this to a kill before, so it must have been due to something else. Zeke tried to tell himself that it had nothing to do with Red's visit, because she was just a friend. There was nothing to get so worked up over. Zeke has had friends over to the house before; of course he had.

By the time the sun came up the house was spotless, yet Zeke was still finding more and more to do. Since the house was as good as possible, he moved on to the yard. They had not set a precise time for Red to come over, but Zeke imagined that he had at the very least a couple hours to kill. He mowed the grass, pulled weeds, and trimmed bushes before retreating back to the house for a shower.

He hadn't slept, and he hadn't stopped working since last night. Zeke knew from a logical standpoint that he should be exhausted even though he had more stamina than most humans, but instead he was wired. He was just stepping out of the shower when he heard Red walking up the sidewalk toward the front porch. It didn't make sense that he should recognize her footfalls distinct from any others, yet he did. He slipped into his pants as quickly as possible and tore out of the bathroom.

"I'm coming," Zeke called as he ran down the stairs. He opened the door and took in Red standing out in front of the sunlight. The sun shone all around her like a halo. There was no denying how angelic she looked in the early afternoon light. Then again there was no denying that she looked devilishly attractive either. She was literally the best of both worlds, and right now she was staring at him like he was the most delicious piece of cake ever.

"Oh, I'm sorry. I came at a bad time. We never set a time. I wasn't sure... I-I can come back later," Red suggested uncomfortably. She was stammering, but why?

"No, no, come on inside. The timing is perfect."

"But you..." She gestured to his bare chest.

Zeke glanced down and realized that water still dripped down his chest. "Oh, that?" he asked as he swiped at some of the water, but all he succeeded in doing was to spread the water. "I just stepped out of the shower. Give me just a minute. I'll be right back; make yourself at home."

He just stepped out of the shower? Wow! Maybe her timing was perfect. He looked absolutely... delectable. Yes, that was it exactly. Roxie hoped that he was not going to go dry off and finish dressing on her account, especially since she preferred him just the way he was. Oh well, more's the pity. She watched as Zeke rushed up the stairs. The way his body moved was, to use a cliché, poetry in motion. It was almost as nice as seeing him bare chested and water running over his perfectly sculpted muscles... almost.

What had gotten into her? Roxie did not react to men like that, like some hormone crazed animal. She gave herself a mental shake and moved past the foyer. The house had a rustic but homey feel. There was hard wood flooring and wood furniture in the foyer.

As Roxie moved out of the foyer, she was greeted by a cozy living room. The large fireplace was covered in ash and proof of regular use. Over large brown leather furniture was scattered around the room, and on one wall hung a big screen TV. A coffee table sat in front of a cushy leather couch, also a light brown color. The table was clear of all clutter or nick knacks. A few family photos hung from the walls around the room, but other than those few family photos the room appeared void. It could have passed for a show room; it did not appear lived in at all.

Roxie wandered around the room for a couple minutes before Zeke walked back in. "So, this is the living room," he said uncomfortably. Roxie turned to see Zeke standing in the doorway. He still had on his loose fitting pair of jeans, but he had thrown on a T-shirt and run a towel through his hair.

"It's nice."

"Yeah, I guess. My mom liked this room. She said it was a place we could all come together. I've kept it updated for her sake, but I don't use it much myself. It seems pointless; it's just me. Who am I going to get together with?"

"Oh."

"The only rooms I really use are the kitchen and my bedroom."

"In this big house, you only occupy two rooms?"

"I guess so, but I don't need a lot when it's just me... So, do you want to see the rest of the house?"

"Definitely." Roxie tried to smile encouragingly since Zeke was so clearly uncomfortable.

Zeke tried not to choke as he spoke, but it was simply unbelievable. Red belonged. She was a natural fit in the house, in the living room. Zeke had felt out of place for years here in this big house all alone without any family, but Red looked like she belonged there in his family home.

It was crazy, and Zeke gave his head a small shake as he turned his back on Red and said, "This way."

He moved toward the kitchen. It was spotlessly clean thanks to his late night bundle of nerves. Usually the sink was full of dirty dishes and he had papers or whatever laid out across the kitchen table.

"Oh, it's… big," Red said in wonderment. Zeke looked around him. He had not thought about it before.

"Yeah, everyone in my family cooked. We are… were kind of big. It takes a lot of space to accommodate us all."

"Wow… You and Kris really are opposites. He almost never picks up after himself, and I'm not sure he even knows how to wash a dish," Red smiled.

"He knows how," Zeke smirked remembering their time together in the military. "I'm not normally this neat. I had a little time on my hands last night, so I did a little cleaning."

"I hope it wasn't on my account."

"No, like I said I had extra time. I needed something to fill it."

"You didn't leave my apartment early last night. How did you have extra time?" Red asked.

"It wasn't as much extra time as it was extra energy. Since I couldn't sleep, I filled the time."

"Oh, how much sleep did you end up getting?"

"I haven't slept yet."

"Oh, Zeke! We can do this another time, seriously. If you need to get some sleep…"

"I'm fine. I'm honestly not tired yet. I'll sleep like a baby tonight, I'm sure."

"Yeah, well, if you're sure you're. Ok," Red agreed hesitantly.

"Come on," Zeke said turning to continue the tour and effectively putting an end to the conversation. "This is the dining room."

The dining room was done in earth tones like the rest of the house. There was a long, huge dining table that looked vintage. "How long has that table been in the family?" Roxie asked.

Zeke looked at her thoughtfully before answering. "Centuries, I believe. It was built the same year as the house."

"Wow, it was hand built by your family?"

"Yeah, there weren't a lot of furniture stores around back then."

"Oh yeah, I guess not." Roxie felt her face flush with heat. Of course there weren't any furniture stores back then. Way to embarrass yourself, Roxie.

Zeke nodded his head toward the exit. "This next room has had many purposes throughout the years. It started out as a parlor or sitting room. It's been a spare room, a library, a den, and so forth over the years. Its latest purpose is library slash den. There is a bathroom off of this room. It's not the most convenient location for a bathroom, but it was added on later. At least there is indoor plumbing; that's something to be thankful for."

Roxie walked into a much more modern room. The big screen TV was set up with gaming consoles and all sorts of extra gadgets.

There were overstuffed recliners that looked well used. No family photos adorned the walls, but the room had a feel of togetherness.

"I use this room from time to time when I have friends over," Zeke informed. "It's more or less my entertainment room. Seriously, though, the only time I really use this room is when I have friends over. I don't exactly feel comfortable having a bunch of people in my bedroom, but in here it's more like public space. Does that sound crazy?"

"Not at all."

Zeke smiled and said, "Come on. There's one more room on this level. The master bedroom, my parent's room." He lead the way to the master bedroom where there was a king size bed and matching dresser and chiffarobe. There was even clothes draped across the foot of the bed as if someone had laid them out to put on. "I haven't had the motivation yet to change anything in here."

"It's still the same way your parents left it?"

Zeke nodded.

"Even the clothes laid out on the bed?" The clothes looked old fashioned, much too old fashioned for his parents' time. Roxie wondered idly what they had been planned for, but didn't dare ask.

Zeke nodded again.

Roxie was not sure what to say. How could you respond to something like that? She wasn't sure how long it had been since his parents died, but surely long enough that he should have accepted by now. She smiled tentatively and slid her hand into his.

"There's a bathroom through that door," Zeke said pointing to a door across the room using the hand that Roxie was currently clinging to. "It's not much, only a hole in the wall."

Zeke seemed reluctant to walk through the doorway, so Roxie asked, "What's upstairs?"

Zeke gave her hand an acknowledging, grateful squeeze. Then he started making his way back to the stairs without letting go of Roxie's hand. "Look up. See the way the ceiling was done? See the plane strokes? They go across the boards. You can see where they were put up first then someone used the plane on them." Roxie might have been mistaken, but she could have sworn that Zeke looked bored with the information, like it was a well rehearsed speech.

There were four bed rooms upstairs. Three had belonged to his siblings. "I did not change much, but I use this as a guest room now. I don't have a lot of use for guest rooms, but they are here if I ever need them... And, this is my room." Zeke threw open the last door and gave Roxie a small nudge through the doorway."

Zeke's room had a king size bed as were all the beds in the house. He had mismatched furniture, but it all looked handmade like everything else in the house. "Is this furniture handmade too?" Roxie wondered.

"Yeah, it's um... ah, I made it. That's why none of it really matches. I couldn't settle on a style, so I just made a little of everything."

Roxie's breath caught as she looked at the beautiful bed and fully took in what Zeke was saying.

Red let Zeke's hand fall from hers as she absently moved toward his bed. She softly trailed her hand up and down the bed post. "You really made this?" she asked.

"Yeah."

She turned to look behind at his haphazard dresser and asked again, "All of it?"

Zeke watched as she wondered aimlessly staring at the dresser. "Uh, yeah."

"Wow, Kris never told me that you did woodworking."

"Well, you can see why I don't very often."

"Why?" Red twirled around to face him with wild surprise in her eyes. "This stuff is so beautiful. Why would you not want to do it very often?"

"Well... it's just all the other furniture in the house matches, at least from room to room. None of this stuff matches."

"But, it's all so wonderful. Why should it matter if it all matches? It gives the room character."

"You think?"

"Yeah I do."

"It's been a long time since I've made anything with my bare hands. Sometimes it is just easier to go buy what you need."

"Sometimes?" Red challenged.

"Ok, it's always easier, but it doesn't always mean as much."

"It's a shame that you don't woodwork anymore. All the other people I've ever known to woodwork made smaller stuff, much smaller stuff. I've never known anyone before who could make large scale furniture like this. It's extraordinary."

"It's not as hard as you would think. It takes making yourself do it. Of course, the fancier you want things, the more intricate work you'll have to put into it. That's why I went simple."

"I like it. I think simple fits you better than all that fancy stuff."

"Yeah, that's me, the simpleton," Zeke smirked at Red. He caught her off guard. She blushed a beautiful shade of red but couldn't hide her smile.

"That's not what I meant. It's just that most of the time the more intricate the details on something, the more feminine it starts to look."

"Ah, I see. Come on."

"Wait a minute," Red said as they started back down the hall toward the stairs. "Is there no bathroom up here at all?"

"Afraid not. Indoor plumbing is a good deal newer than the house, so it was a little hard to go back and add a bathroom upstairs."

"Oh, that makes sense."

"You hungry?"

"Starved."

"Let's go eat." Zeke wanted Red's hand back in his, but he couldn't work up the courage to make that move. It was a bold move, and even though Red had reached out for his hand, he knew he shouldn't return the gesture. He was getting too close to crossing a line that could only lead to heart ache.

He showed Red back outside and held the passenger door to his car open for her.

"Where are we going?" Red asked as she eased into the car.

"Ah, surprise," Zeke answered quickly then hurried around to the driver's side and got in.

"A surprise?"

"Yeah, I think you'll like it, and I bet you never even knew it was there."

"Alright." Red smiled playfully, and Zeke allowed himself to be distracted by her smile. The car started drifting to the left, and he jerked it back just in time for a car to go whizzing past. He cleared his throat nervously and turned his attention back to the road where it belonged.

The rest of the ride was silent, yet it was not an uncomfortable silence. It was not a very long ride either. Less than ten minutes after their start, they were passing by Red's office and parking less than three blocks away.

"Where are we going?" Roxie asked again after Zeke parked. They were within walking distance of her office. Where could they possibly be eating here in the middle of the business district?

"I told you it was a secret," Zeke shot back with a wink. He got out of the car, so Roxie followed his example.

With a mischievous grin she said, "I thought you said that this area was dangerous."

"It is. Good thing you have me to protect you." Roxie couldn't see Zeke's face as she followed him briskly across the sidewalk, but she could swear she heard his over confidant smirk. Her heart fluttered, and she could not keep herself from smiling. She was flustered by him in a very nice, very exciting way. It made no sense. His macho double standard should not affect her in any way. It did though. She instantly loved the idea of big, strong Zeke protecting her. Her brothers had protected her all her life, yet Zeke's protectiveness felt somehow different, more exceptional.

"Seriously, where are we going? There is nothing out here."

"I told you that you wouldn't even know it was here." Zeke pulled on a door to a small hole in the wall kind of space and held the door open for her. "Come on."

Roxie walked inside where she was met by a short middle aged woman with dark hair. "Two?" the lady asked. Roxie nodded, and the lady immediately started to lead her into the back area where there was indeed a very small restaurant set up.

Zeke placed his hand on the small of Roxie's back as they followed the woman back. His warmth was a sudden pleasure, and the tingles started at once racing one another all along Roxie's body. Suddenly Roxie did not care where the woman led; all she cared about was where Zeke was guiding her. She knew without doubt that she'd go anywhere he instructed her without argument. When had that happened?

All too soon, they stopped at a booth in a secluded corner. Roxie breathed out a silent sigh of longing as she lost the warmth of Zeke's touch against her back.

"What can I get you to drink?" the woman asked. She and Zeke both ordered water, and the woman rushed off to get the waters.

"So, what do you think?" Zeke asked.

Roxie looked around her truly taking in her surroundings for the first time since they had walked through the door. The lighting was dim with candles on each table. When had the woman lit that candle? How had Roxie not noticed her lighting a candle before they sat down? The walls were decorated with wine and grape paraphernalia, and the place had a distinctly Italian smell, strong with garlic and oregano. "It's nice. Smells good in here."

"If you like that, you'll love the food."

The waitress returned with waters, salad, and breadsticks; then she bustled off again giving them a few minutes to look over their menus. It didn't take Roxie long to decide. Spaghetti was her all time favorite food. She looked up from the menu to find Zeke studying her. "Do you know what you're getting?" she asked.

"Yes, you?"

"I think so," Roxie answered just as the waitress walked up to take their orders.

"I'll have the spaghetti and meatballs," Roxie ordered.

The waitress looked to Zeke, and he replied, "I'll have the same."

"Surprise, surprise," the waitress commented with a grin as she walked away.

Zeke looked across the table at Roxie's confused look and explained, "I've been here a few times."

"We've got to teach you to cook."

"It's a lost cause," Zeke chuckled. "The couple who started this place moved here from Italy about eighty years ago, and when the county started buying up land, they didn't have the money or power to fight them."

"But it is still here?" Roxie interrupted.

"I'm getting there. So, they cut a deal with the county. They would sell their property, which they still owed money on, for a very fair price. It was much less than what others were getting for their land, but in return the couple was given this little slice of building to continue their restaurant. The government agreed, because it was a win-win for everyone involved. The government would never miss this small piece of property, obviously since most people don't even notice it's here, and they actually saved money on the deal. The couple didn't do so badly themselves; they sold their land to the government for more than what they still owed on the land. They were able to pay off their debt and still have enough money to get this place set up for business. Our waitress? She is their granddaughter, and for the most part she runs this place now. The couple both retired years ago and left this place to their kids. The waitress's parents still own the place on paper, but she took over running the place for the most part a couple years ago. I figure that they will officially retire soon, leaving her the restaurant. In the kitchen... her brother and cousins do all the cooking. This is a completely family owned and family run business."

"Aww, that's a nice story."

"Yeah, they are the poster family for the American dream."

"Zeke? You said that they didn't have the money or power to fight the government?"

"Yeah."

"Your family was able to keep their home and land... So, does that mean that your family... ?"

"Yeah, I guess we had both. My family wasn't rich by any means but lived comfortably. There was power behind the Miller name though. Not many dared to cross the Miller's, the government included. They asked, of course, but when they were told no, that was that. My family couldn't be intimidated, and it would have been harder to crush us financially than others."

Roxie grinned at Zeke. "You talk with intense involvement and pride when you talk about your family's history."

"It's my family; why shouldn't I?"

"Yeah, it's your family, but it was a couple generations ago. I don't know. I guess it's just that you have such intensity when you talk about it, you sound like you were personally involved, like you were there."

"Oh, that's... uh..."

"Crazy, I know." Roxie dropped the subject as the waitress reappeared with their food.

"Mmm, this smells good." The plate was piled up with spaghetti and massive meatballs. Looking across the table Roxie noticed that Zeke's plate had less pasta but double the meatballs.

"What? You're smiling like someone with a secret," Zeke accused.

"Nothing, I just realized why you are so fond of this place," Roxie answered gesturing to Zeke's plate. "They know exactly what you like... meat, meat, and more meat."

Zeke grinned. "Is this going to turn into another lecture about eating my vegetables?"

"No, how often do you come here?"

Zeke laughed heartily. "Not as often as you must think. Our families have been close since the couple first moved here from Italy."

"Oh? So, your family was already here?"

"Yes."

"How long has your family been here?"

"As far back as records show, probably longer." Zeke answered as Roxie took a big bite of spaghetti. "How's your spaghetti?"

"Mm, great! How are your meatballs?"

"Just the way I like 'em."

The rest of their meal was spent in companionable silence as they both ate. When the bill came, Zeke insisted he pay, claiming it was the least he could do in return for all the hospitality her family had shown him.

When the waitress returned, she had written a little note on the receipt. She stood by the table waiting expectantly like she was waiting for a response. Zeke nodded once, and the waitress walked away.

"Bye, Zeke," the waitress called as Zeke and Roxie made their way back out the door.

"Bye, Isabella. I'll see you soon. Tell everyone hi for me?"

"Sure!"

What was that about? Roxie was positive that she had seen a deeper meaning on Zeke's face when he told Isabella he would see her soon. What could he have meant? She had to be at least twenty years his senior. Was Roxie simply reading too much into it, and why did she feel jealous of all things? Even if Zeke was hers, which he wasn't Roxie mentally scolded herself, there couldn't possibly be anything going on between Zeke and the waitress; she was much too old for him.

"What was all that about?" Red asked as they pulled out of the parking space.

Zeke wished he knew. Isabella's message was very vague. We've had trouble. It could have meant anything. He had tried to make it clear that he would be back as soon as possible. He could only hope that Isabella had understood. "What do you mean? I told you that our families are close. I've known Isabella her whole life."

"You mean your whole life."

"Oh... yeah." He risked a peak over in Red's direction. She looked frustrated, and her breathtaking blush was back. "Are you ok?"

"Fine."

Not fine. She was upset about something, but what? What had he done to upset her? Was she... jealous? No, if only, if only! There was nothing to be jealous of anyway; Isabella did not begin to compare to Red. He had never felt anything more for Isabella, not that her grandfather would allow it if he had.

Zeke pulled into the drive and put the car in park to let Red out. "You're not getting out?" she asked.

"No, uh, I've got to head back into town to take care of a few things, but I'll see you Monday?"

"Yeah, thanks again for lunch."

"It was my pleasure." Zeke watched as Red got into her car. She was still tense. Whatever was bothering her, Zeke knew he wouldn't be able to rest easy until he knew she was ok, but right now Isabella and her family were the more pressing issue.

Chapter Eight

Zeke got back to the restaurant as quickly as possible.

"Zeke, thank heavens!" Isabella breathed on a sigh as he walked back in the door.

"What is going on?"

"Grandpa would kill me if he knew I was telling you."

"Your grandpa never fully trusted my family."

"I know, but I've never known your family to be anything but kind. I know I didn't know your parents, but I know you and have heard my parents talk about your family."

"It's ok. You don't have to explain anything to me. Your grandpa has his reasons, but my family made a pact with yours back when your grandparents first came here. Each one of us took a vow to protect your family so long as your family kept our secret. There has never been any bad blood between us, and that vow is one that I take very seriously. Your family has kept up their end of the bargain; I will keep up our end. Now, tell me what is going on."

"It happened last week. Some vandals broke in. They didn't take anything; they just broke some stuff."

"You put in security cameras like I suggested?"

"Yes, the police took the tape with them, but they aren't doing much about it since nothing was actually taken… It wouldn't have been that big a deal, but I just worry. What if one or more of us had still been here? We work late a lot. We were lucky this time; we may not be so lucky next time."

"Did any of you get a good look at that video feed before the police took it?"

Isabella shook her head solemnly.

"Ok, that's alright. Isabella, listen to me. You don't need to worry. I will keep your family safe. It's possible that this is connected to a group that I've been keeping an eye on anyway. I'm going to do some patrol around here for a while. Tell your family, if they see any big dogs around, don't shoot; just go about your business. Ok?"

"Yes, yes, I will, and Zeke, thank you."

Zeke slunk through back alleys around the restaurant that night in wolf form, keeping his eyes open and listening out for any sound out of the ordinary. He did not really expect the vandals to come back a second time, especially after the police had been called, but stranger things had happened. Chances were that the vandals were from the gang that he had been tracking since coming back home. If not, he was certain that the gang had either sent a message of their own or flat out murdered the vandals. That was the thing about gangs; they called themselves territorial, but they didn't know jack about true territorialism. That was one lesson Zeke was going to be sure they understood before he was done with them.

It had to be close to four in the morning, and the smells from inside were just beginning to fade into the night. Nothing had happened all night long, and it had been a very long night making rounds in a deserted area. Zeke was preparing to call it a night. Nothing was going to happen if it had not happened already. He decided to make one more round before returning home for some rest. He crept along the back wall to the east side of the building when he heard footsteps making their way down the front sidewalk. It wasn't unheard of for one of the family to come in early to get a fresh start on the morning, something about pasta making. Still, better cover all the bases.

Zeke took a deep breath in through his nose as he casually made his way to the front of the building. He could smell two new and very distinct scents, but neither scent was one that Zeke recognized. He was quite familiar with the family and knew this was not one of the family members coming in for an early start. Zeke picked up his pace as he listened intently to pick out voices. He could hear low mumbling, slurred speech. He couldn't make out what was being said, but the two voices were most definitely inebriated.

Zeke turned the corner stealthily, but his effort was for naught. The two drunks were intently staring into the front glass of the restaurant and laughing as they planned out what all to break this time. They would not have noticed Zeke despite how much racket he made.

"This is the best part of the job," one man with a shaved head cackled. His voice was hoarse; he must have been a smoker as well as a drunk. The smell of cigarettes was burning Zeke's nose.

The second man smelt like he had not bathed in a couple days. His head bobbled up and down in agreement, throwing his long, dirty, blonde hair into a disheveled mess. He smelled strongly of BO, and his mouth hung open. "Yeah, wonder how long till they get the idea," he slurred.

This gave Zeke pause. He didn't want to give these two Neanderthals the chance to do any further damage to the restaurant; however, he did want to get down to the root of the problem. It wasn't feasible for him to spend the foreseeable future doing patrols each night. He had problems of his own to take care of. Someone had sent these two, and Zeke wanted to know who.

"Yep, the faster they get the picture, the faster we get moved up. We'll be running the gang soon," the blonde fantasized. "We should do more this time," he added lifting a bat overhead.

Zeke had heard enough. He let rip a menacing growl then leapt forward catching the two jerks by surprise. He was too late to stop them from crashing through the front window, but they did not get the chance to do anymore damage. Zeke knew the family would not understand if he killed the two intruders. He would save that task for a later date if they didn't wise up and get away from that gang as fast as their sluggish legs could carry them.

The blonde would have to be taken by ambulance to the hospital. Just because Zeke wasn't going to kill them tonight didn't meant that they were going to get off free and clear. Zeke racked his claws across the man's chest and bit through the man's thigh with his powerful jaw and sharp teeth.

When Zeke turned his attention to the second man, the bald one, he was slumped up against a wall and was clutching at his chest. It figures that the coward could dish out violence but couldn't take it when the violent tables were turned on him. It served him right.

Alarms had started going off as soon as the glass window shattered. Zeke did not know when Isabella had installed a security system, but he was glad for it now, knowing that the police would be here soon to take out the trash. He trotted off toward home satisfied with a decent night's work. He would swing by tomorrow to have a word with Isabella. He had taken care of these two, but Isabella needed to know that this would not be the end of it. She also needed to be assured that he was taking care of the bigger problem and not to give up hope.

◆◆◆

There was already a man measuring the pane for a replacement window by the time that Zeke got to the restaurant around noon. "Zeke!" Isabella's relieved voice cried. She rushed over and threw her arms around his neck. It was an odd feeling. Most of her family was leery of him but not Isabella. She had always counted him a friend from what he could tell.

"I'm sorry about the window," he whispered lowly into her ear so not to be overheard.

"Don't be silly! The two men who did this are safely behind bars now and spouting off some wild tale of a huge dog," she said with a wink.

"Yeah, can we talk somewhere a little more private?" Zeke asked glancing in the glass repairman's direction. For his part the repairman seemed engrossed in his work, but Zeke still didn't want to take any chances. He followed Isabella further inside to a back corner before continuing. "Listen. Vandalism won't keep those men behind bars for long, and the people who sent them won't stop just because they got attacked." He paused to be sure that Isabella was paying attention. "I am working on stopping them, but they are a large gang. It is going to take some time short of trapping everyone involved inside somewhere and killing off the whole bunch."

"Oh, Zeke, don't say stuff like that," Isabella whined.

"I don't want it to come to that, believe me, but these men are hurting other people. They have killed innocents and have no intentions of stopping. I can't stand by and let that happen. If they leave me with no choice, I will do what I have to do... I just wanted you to know that this thing is far from over. You know you can call me at any time. I'll do whatever I can to help. Don't hesitate to call me. Please, I'm begging you. Your family are good people, and I don't want to see you give up or lose everything that you've worked your whole lives for because of this gang. That won't happen if you'll trust me and let me help."

"Of course we trust you. Thank you. I don't know how we can ever repay you."

"You've already done more for me than you'll ever know. Your family has kept my family's secret for generations, and you are the few people who I don't have to worry about hiding from. It is I who is in your debt. I'm sorry it came down to this, but I won't let you down. That's a promise."

"I know you won't, Zeke, but please be careful."

Zeke nodded once then left Isabella to deal with her broken window and the mess that still needed tending to.

Chapter Nine

The weekend flew by in a blur, but the only thing that Roxie could think about was Zeke and that woman from the Italian restaurant. What did he say her name was, Isabella?

Roxie walked into the office Monday morning not in the best of moods. "Morning," she mumbled as she walked past Lucy's desk.

"Uh-oh," Lucy sympathized and followed Roxie into the office. "What happened?"

"He gave me a tour of his home then took me out for lunch." Roxie did not try to explain who "he" was, because Lucy would already know.

"And, that's bad?"

"No, at least it wasn't. His home is beautiful, and he hand made all the furniture in his bedroom. Luc, you have to see it! It's beautiful! The place he took me to is an Italian place within walking distance from here. I didn't even know it was there, and the food was amazing! Mmm, you've got to try that place!"

"It sounds amazing, so what is the problem?" Lucy asked clearly confused.

"Well, Zeke knew the family who owns the restaurant. It is a family owned and family run business. He told me their story. It was a powerful story; he called them the poster family for the American dream. The woman who runs it now is the third generation. She is middle aged, not bad looking. She is rather beautiful, but I just keep thinking she has to be so much older than Zeke. When she brought the receipt back to the table, she had left a note on it. On our way out, Zeke told her he would see her soon."

"So?"

"It was the annotation that went along with it. The message was clear; he would see her soon. Then when we got back to the house, he let me out of the car then left to go who knows where."

"And you're jealous." It wasn't a question. Roxie knew it wasn't a question.

"Well... yeah. It doesn't make any sense, I know. He's not mine. He can't ever be mine, but all the little innuendoes drove me crazy."

"Maybe she's like some cougar that you hear so much about," Lucy suggested conspiratorially.

"That's ridiculous, and even if she is, it's none of my business. Their relationship is none of my business."

"You are impossible, Roxie. Seriously, Rox, I love you, but you're being stupid. Here you've got this major hottie flirting with you. You spend every weeknight together, and he appears to be ok, no serial killer tendencies. But... you refuse to seek out a relationship of your own with this guy, because he is friends with your brother. If anything, that means that he has already been approved by your brother. Kris spent years in the military with this guy, and they are close, close enough that Kris invited him to your mom's. I don't think your brother would invite some guy over to your mother's house if he did not think the guy could be trusted."

"Zeke does seem to be a pretty good guy. Kris trusts him I guess, but there is a difference in trusting him enough to invite him home to meet your family and allowing him to date your baby sister. You don't have an older brother, or you would understand that."

"Eventually both your brothers are going to have to get over their aversion to their baby sister dating. That being the case, wouldn't it be easier to accept if they already knew and trusted the guy?"

"You would think so, but that is against some universal bro-code or something. I don't know. All I know is that Kris would see it as some kind of betrayal, and Michael would probably fire him. I can't get the man fired!"

"Oh, Rox, you're hopeless. If you aren't willing to take a chance on that fine piece of man, you're just going to have to accept that other women are willing."

"But she is so much older than Zeke," Roxie continued to protest. "Let's go eat there for lunch. You'll see what I mean."

"Great Italian food within walking distance of here? Sounds like a great plan, but Roxie... you don't even know if there is anything going on between Zeke and this woman. You are jumping to conclusions, and it is driving you nuts."

Lucy and Roxie walked inside the Italian restaurant at exactly noon. Isabella was once again hosting in the front section. She recognized Roxie right away. "Oh, hello! You're Zeke's friend! You were in here with him Saturday! I'm sorry I don't think I caught your name."

"Uh... I'm Roxie. This is my friend, Lucy."

"Would you believe that we work less than three blocks from here and never even knew you guys were here?" Lucy jumped in to save a stuttering Roxie. "Roxie was telling me how good the food was here, and I just had to try it for myself."

"I'm Isabella, and I'm so glad you're here. It's always nice to hear that our food is appreciated. Follow me, and I'll get you a booth."

Lucy followed Isabella eagerly with Roxie trailing behind. They both ordered water. Lucy decided to try Chicken Parmesan while Roxie had a Three-Cheese Ravioli. "Mmm, you were right," Lucy moaned around a bite of chicken. "This food is amazing."

"Yeah, it is good."

"Stop it, Roxie. You're sulking, and besides it appears that Isabella already has a significant other of her own. Look behind you."

Roxie turned slightly and stole a glance over her shoulder. Isabella sat at a booth on the same side with a man roughly her age with salt and pepper hair. They were flipping through what looked like a book of house plans and talking animatedly.

"Ok, so I read too much into it... Thank you, Luc. I don't know what I would do without you."

"Drive yourself batty." Both women laughed and enjoyed the remainder of their lunch.

Zeke drove down the road trying his best to keep his eyes open. He had stretched himself thin over the weekend. In a sense he was trying to be everywhere at once. He couldn't let anything else happen to the restaurant; he had made a vow, but at the same time he knew he shouldn't just give up on his own pursuit of the gang invading his territory. To top it all off he couldn't keep Red off his mind. That was no surprise. Lately he was never able to keep her off his mind for very long, but this was more specific. She had seemed upset about something. He didn't know what, but he knew he couldn't stand the idea of her being upset, especially if she were upset at him.

By the time he parked his car out front of Red's apartment Monday he didn't remember any of the drive over there, and he was earlier than usual too. Zeke made a mental note to pay more attention when he was driving. It was no doubt unsafe for him to be out there driving that fast on auto pilot. Zeke gave himself a mental shake to try and clear his head and knocked on Red's door.

Red opened the door with a slightly panicked look. "You're early!"

"Yeah, I made really good time."

"Come on in. I haven't been here long. I haven't gotten started cooking yet, but I'm sure I can find something fast."

"Is there anything I can do to help?"

Red eyed him suspiciously. "I thought you were a lousy cook?"

"I am."

"Then I'm probably better off without help," she teased with a friendly smile.

Zeke nodded his head. "Yeah, you're probably right... I see you're in a better mood."

"What do you mean?"

"I thought you seemed upset about something when I dropped you off back at the house the other day."

"Oh... I guess I was. It was just some silly thing that came up. Lucy put it all in perspective for me."

"Lucy?"

"She's my secretary and best friend. I don't know what I'd do without her. She really is great. Oh hey, we ate lunch at that Italian place you showed me."

"Oh yeah? I should charge them an advertising fee."

"Ha, ha. How was your day?"

"Long."

"Did something happen?" Red wondered.

"Nah, I'm just tired. I guess it was a long weekend."

"Well, if you can make it just a couple more weeks, you'll have the perfect opportunity to rest."

"Right, the big camping trip."

Red smiled at him and said, "No one is twisting your arm."

"No, I'm looking forward to it."

"Me too. I'm so excited! Our family camping trips are always so much fun, and I could really use the break. It's nice to get to spend that much quality time with my family too. We don't see as much of each other anymore."

"I imagine you see more of Kris now than when he was in the military."

"Yes, those were some hard years for my mom. She wouldn't admit it, but I saw her wince every time the phone rang. She was scared she'd get a call telling her that her son wasn't coming home."

"I guess that would be hard on any parent. I never had to deal with that aspect of the military life. By the time I joined up, it was just me on my own. There wasn't anyone back home to call, so no one to scare."

"That's awful. I'm so sorry."

"What? That I didn't scare anyone?"

"No, that you had no one to come home to. I would hate to think of Kris in that situation; I would hate to think of anyone in that situation."

"Aww, I'm used to it."

"Still, didn't you have any friends to miss you?"

"No... all my friends were military."

"What about that family? The ones who own that restaurant?"

"Oh... well, I guess Isabella might could care a little if something were to happen to me."

"Of course she would. What is the deal with you two anyway?"

"What do you mean?"

"You just seem really close friends for there to be such a wide age range between you."

"Yeah, she's easy to get along with, likes everyone."

"Is she seeing anyone?"

"I don't know," Zeke answered hesitantly. "We don't really talk about her personal life. Why?"

"Oh, no reason. I just thought I saw her with someone today is all, but I don't remember seeing a wedding ring the other day."

"I guess it's possible; she's a nice girl."

"A nice girl? You talk about her like she's a child when she must be what, almost double your age."

"Do I? Is that all?" Zeke asked indicating the large pot on the stove. Red appeared to be through with preparations, and he needed a chance of subject.

"Hmm? Yeah, it wasn't what I was planning, but it was quick prep and takes even less time to cook."

"I hope you didn't change your plans because of me."

"It's fine... um, assuming you eat it."

"I'm sure it will be delicious," Zeke said politely.

"Steamed cabbage and sausage?"

"I like sausage."

"And cabbage?"

"I eat cabbage."

"When you have to?"

"When I have to," Zeke reluctantly admitted, "but you're right about vegetables. They're good for me, and I really should eat more."

The next two weeks flew by in no time. Zeke felt like he was always on the run, like he had the weight of the world on his shoulders. That was over dramatic, and he knew it. What he did have was the weight of his family's territory on his shoulders. This wasn't the way it was meant to be, but the whole of the responsibility fell on his shoulders alone. Wolves are pack animals. He wasn't supposed to be alone in this, but everyone was gone now. It was all him. There was no other option but to succeed, but he was running himself ragged in the process. The only slight reprieve he got were meals at Red's apartment. He lived for those brief couple hours each weeknight. Red had quickly become the only thing keeping him grounded.

Zeke knew it wasn't a good idea to leave the area for an entire week. There was no telling what harm that gang could do in a week unguarded, yet he couldn't make himself stay. He needed the break desperately, and frighteningly, he found himself desperate to follow Red anywhere. He knew he had gotten too attached. He couldn't do anything about it, and it wasn't fair to anyone involved.

Red was a normal girl, a successful woman; the last thing she needed was some lone wolf pining after her. It wasn't fair to Kris. He had been a good friend, and he was fiercely protective of his family. He didn't deserve to have to defend his baby sister from an animal who was supposed to be a trusted friend. Finally it wasn't fair to himself. Zeke had sworn off romantic relationships a long time ago. How had this girl come into his life and completely turned his world upside down. He had done his duty to his country, and now he was back to do what was right by his family. What had he done to deserve to yearn endlessly for someone he could never have?

There were countless reasons why he should not go camping with her family, but there wasn't a single thing that could stop him. He was in deep, and it could only lead to trouble in the end. Despite any trouble he might cause, plans were made.

Zeke was going to stop by to pick up Red since her apartment was on his way to her mother's. They would all meet up at Ms. Gardner's and go from there. The sun was just coming up, and Red was already standing in the parking lot with all her stuff waiting when Zeke pulled in.

"Good morning," Zeke greeted cheerfully as he popped the trunk open to help her load her stuff.

"It's a great morning!" Red exclaimed. She was all but jumping up and down in excitement, and Zeke could not hide the smile that she brought to his lips.

He shook his head as they started to load everything that Red had sitting out on the curb. "Did you pack enough?" he teased lightly.

"Go on, and laugh, but when you boys aren't prepared, you'll be glad I packed so much."

"Sure," Zeke stood back and looked at everything; it filled his trunk completely. "I don't know how we're going to get all this down there."

"We'll have to take two cars, I'm sure. Mom packs like I do. She's got a Tahoe, and I'm sure that Kris and Michael are already outside arguing about the best way to pack everything inside."

"Thanks for the warning."

"Oh, I'm so excited! Come on, Zeke, get fired up!" Red exclaimed with a soft punch on his arm.

"Come on, Red, get in the car. Let's get you down to the lake before you wriggle right out of your skin."

"I can't believe you're not more eager to hit the road," she added after they were both in the car. "You've been drained lately, and don't try to deny it."

"No, you're right. I've got a lot on my plate right now."

"Promise me, Zeke. Right now. Promise me that you'll have fun on this trip no matter what. Promise."

Zeke grinned at the serious look on her face and said, "I promise, Red. I promise to have fun no matter what."

"Good, now let's hurry up and get to the lake!"

Chapter Ten

Red's energetically good mood was contagious. By the time they made it to her mom's, Zeke was beginning to get excited too. Why shouldn't he? This was the first vacation he had afforded himself in almost a half century. He had earned a little fun in his life.

Everyone was outside when Zeke pulled into the drive at the Gardner residence. Kris met them at the car as they got out. "How's all her crap looking?" he asked nodding his head in Red's direction.

"I couldn't fit another thing in my trunk."

"Yeah, sounds about right. We've already got Mom's Tahoe at maximum capacity as it is, and we've still got one more cooler to pack. Since you've already got her stuff packed up, would you mind driving?"

"No problem, where's the last cooler? I'll throw it in the backseat, and we'll be ready to hit the road."

Roxie watched Zeke slide a bright red cooler into the backseat of his car as if it weighed nothing at all. Mom always packed the food in one cooler and drinks in the other, and she always used the same cooler for each so that everyone would know without having to open it to see. The bright red cooler was the drink cooler. Roxie knew that cooler was anything but light. It would already be packed full of drinks and ice spilt into every nook and cranny, yet it was no trouble at all for Zeke. Roxie had gotten hints here and there of the muscles hidden beneath his shirts, but he must have been even more muscular than she had previously imagined.

Kris was probably the strongest person she knew, although she would never admit that to Michael, but even Kris would have showed at least a slight strain when carrying that cooler. It was the biggest cooler any of them owned. It was a huge, hulking cooler that had to be filled to the brim! She couldn't imagine why Zeke would need to be that strong or how he had gotten that strong for that matter. Next to sports, working out was Kris's favorite past time, yet Roxie was beginning to realize that even Kris had nothing on Zeke.

Lucy had commissioned Roxie with relaxing and having fun on this trip and reporting back every detail. One detail in particular that Lucy had been especially interested in was how Zeke looked in nothing but his swimming trunks. Roxie had found herself thinking about that a few times after Lucy had put the idea in her head. The early morning temperature started heating up rapidly as Roxie imagined how very well defined his muscles would look stretched taught across his bare chest, and she resisted the urge to fan herself.

"Come on, let's hit the road!" Michael's voice boomed breaking up Roxie's delicious daydream.

"So, I guess you're riding with me?" Zeke questioned her.

"Guess so," and she hopped into his car before either one of her brothers could say anything to the contrary. She caught Zeke smiling after her like a Cheshire cat but decided not to draw attention to his smile not daring to believe that Zeke would actually prefer her to either of her brothers.

Her own heart was beating like crazy. If she didn't know better, she would be worried that she was having a heart attack, but she knew from her last check up that her heart was perfectly healthy. There was a tightness in her chest to go along with the racing heart, but there was no pain involved. Her stomach was full of butterflies. It was silly to think she would get so excited and nervous to ride in the car with Zeke. She ate with him five days a week, yet this was closer quarters. For a ride that was every bit of four hours long, Roxie would be close enough to feel the heat rolling off of him.

She watched him ease into the seat like it was nothing out of the ordinary to be riding around with her. Roxie could not help but think about the first ride she had taken in this car. Would this trip feel as intimate as that lunch had? Of course her brothers' presence would not allow for too much intimacy, but here, in the car, she was free from their scrutiny.

Zeke cranked the car up and backed out into the road and back just far enough for Mom's Tahoe to back out in front.

"So, Michael was saying the campground isn't too far from here?" Zeke inquired.

"It depends on who is driving and how much Mom has had to drink."

Zeke laughed and stared intently at the Tahoe backing out before adding, "It looks like Kris is driving. I take it that means the drive will be over sooner rather than later. At least I hope that Michael doesn't drive any faster than Kris."

"No, Michael is the more dependable driver. He would get us there in about four hours. Kris on the other hand..."

"Drives like he is in the Indy 500, I know. I've ridden with him before."

Roxie chuckled and asked with a tease, "Do you think you can keep up with him?"

Zeke gave her a sly smile. "I had my wild and more reckless years; I'm sure I'll manage."

Roxie laughed loud and clear before settling into the seat for the long ride.

A little over an hour into the drive, Red undid her seatbelt and leaned between the seats into the back seat. "Do you want something to drink?" she mumbled with her back still turned.

"Hmm?" Zeke responded as he turned his head briefly in her direction. When he turned his head he got an eyeful of Red's butt that was up in the air. Her butt was right on his eye level the way she was leaned into the back seat. Zeke caught himself staring as heat washed over his body. He turned back to the road quickly and turned the air up a bit.

"You want something to drink?" Red asked again. "I see sprite, Dr. Pepper, coke, and water."

"Oh, water, please."

"I don't have any snacks," she apologized as she handed him a water and sat back down in her seat with a water of her own. "I'm sure Mom has a large bag full of snacks in the other car, but they don't have anything to drink. If I had thought about it, I would have grabbed us some snacks. Kris and Michael put the drink cooler with us on purpose, I'm sure. Mom has to go to the restroom more than the rest of us. As long as she hasn't had anything to drink since last night, we should be good for at least half the drive. I'll grab us some snacks when we stop."

"Oh, this is good," he said indicating the bottle of water.

Red got quiet again, but only for a few minutes before starting up conversation. "Did you know there is a full moon this week while we're up there?"

"Is that so?"

"Yep, are you going to be on the lookout for crazies?"

"Mmm." Zeke was not at all comfortable with this conversation. She was too close to the truth.

"I should give you fair warning before we get up there. Kris and Michael revert back to children while we are camping." Zeke didn't try to add anything, so Red continued on undeterred. "I mean, nothing serious, they are just having fun, but it is like they let go of every responsibility they have ever had."

"Zeke? Hello, earth to Zeke… Are you ok?"

"Hmm?"

"All I said are that Kris and Michael act childish while we are camping, and you look like I just delivered a devastating blow."

"I was just thinking about… uh… I…" he did not really know what to say, so he just let his words trail away unfinished.

Red laid her hand on his upper bicep. The muscles directly underneath her flesh tensed and burned with sensation, but the rest of his body instinctively relaxed. "Do you want to talk about it?" she asked softly.

"No, I'm fine, really." He reached up with his right hand and took her hand off his bicep. He instantly regretted the loss, but gave her hand a reassuring squeeze anyway. He laid her hand in her lap, and he realized with a leap of his heart that she was not going to pull her hand out of his. When he glanced her direction again, he saw that she was relaxed in the seat watching out the passenger window. If she was content to ride along in companionable silence with only the radio for background noise and hold his hand, he was not about to break the spell. It would take a stronger man than him to pull his hand from Red's, and he was grateful for the connection. One hand on the wheel was a small price to pay to hold onto Red for as long as she would allow it.

They rode hand in hand for two more towns. Zeke cursed silently when he saw Kris turn on the blinker indicating they were stopping for gas and probably a restroom break. It would feel good to get out and stretch his legs, but Zeke would have given almost anything to have stayed right there and held Red's hand. He didn't give up his hold on her until he pulled up beside a pump right behind Kris.

Zeke did not try to hold her hand again after getting back in the car. It was disappointing, but she was glad for the time she had. Roxie smiled as the thought crossed her mind. It was ridiculous. She felt like she was back in junior high, getting all excited over holding a boy's hand. Then again Zeke was hardly a boy; he was a big, strong, muscle-toned man with a heart of gold. Man, she was falling for him fast. If she didn't get herself in check soon, this whole thing, whatever it was, was going to end in heart break. She tried to remind herself that Zeke was Kris's friend. Even if Kris was cool with it, which he most certainly would not be, he still saw her as Kris's baby sister. He saw someone to protect and love like a sister not like a woman. Then again, he was the one who had taken hold of her hand. Was she reading too much into it? Could he see her as more? Was it possible that he could be as fascinated with her as she was with him? No, she was nothing more than a plain Jane business woman. Still, it did not stop her from admiring him, and there was so much to admire on him, she thought with a delicious grin.

Roxie studied him as he drove. His skin had a natural glow to it like he spent a lot of time outside in the sun. His eyes were trained on the road ahead as he worked to as safely as possible keep up with Kris burning rubber. In this natural light, she could finally see the grey of his eyes. With any less sunlight, they looked almost black, but today they looked like a smoky grey, mysterious and deep. He held the steering wheel with an easy two handed grip. She knew from experience that those large hands were calloused and rough. There were so many more experiences she would like to have with those sturdy hands.

Sinewy muscles ran from his hands all the way up his arm and beneath his T-shirt. The T-shirt he wore today was slightly snug and showcased all those strapping muscles that he kept hidden. Would she get to see more of those impressive muscles this week, or was he the type to swim without removing his T-shirt? So much to look forward to this week!

Dressed in jeans and a T-shirt this was the most comfortable she had seen him since that first meal they shared at Mom's. Was it possible that it had only been a month since that lunch? She felt like she had known Zeke for years, all her life. He had become a comforting and constant in her life. Would she ever be able to go back to life without him?

As they pulled into the campground's main parking lot, Roxie was taken again by the beauty of the area. They came here to the same campground each year, yet every time the natural beauty took her breath away. "It's go gorgeous here," she mumbled on a sigh.

"Yes, it is," Zeke said staring at her. It may have been crazy, but she had almost forgotten that he was there. She smiled at Zeke's awed look at the same beauty she was just marveling at before turning her attention back to the scenery.

Roxie jumped when Michael knocked on Zeke's window. "Sorry, kiddo, I didn't mean to scare you." Turning his attention back to Zeke he said, "I'm going to run in the office real quick to grab us a couple of parking decals and find out what site numbers we have. I'll be right back."

"Should I go with him?" Zeke asked after rolling his window back up.

"Nah, he'll take care of it. It won't take long."

"Doesn't it cost something? I could take him some money. It's not fair for your family to pay it all."

"No, no we have a lifetime membership here. Don't worry about it. Nobody is paying anything for the sites today."

"Still, I should give your mom something for it."

"Zeke, don't. Seriously, it will only insult her; besides, the membership has already paid for itself many times over. No one is being cheated, and if you start trying to shove money at people, it's just going to cause unneeded unrest."

"Ok, if you're sure..."

"I'm sure. Lighten up and enjoy yourself."

"Sure," Zeke responded with a big goofy grin.

He had his eyes trained on her as she continued to smile. He was studying her. Although she wanted to know desperately what he saw there, all she said was, "They're moving."

Chapter Eleven

It took no time to get the tents up, one for the boys and one for the girls. The tents went up faster than usual with Kris and Zeke involved. Roxie, helping to unload the back of the Tahoe, pulled out one of the tents. Kris already had the other in hand.

Zeke walked up close behind Roxie and put his hand over her hand that was holding the tent. He tilted his head down next to her ear and whispered, "I got this." Roxie turned back to look at him. Zeke was looking at Kris with a mischievous grin. "Hey, Kris! You game," he called.

Kris smirked at Zeke, and replied, "You're on. You're going down, Mills!"

Before anyone else had any idea what was going on, Kris and Zeke were standing opposite each other at the two sites. Kris said, "Go!" and they both took off in a whirl putting up the tents. It became quickly apparent that they were racing to see who could put the tent up faster. Shockingly both tents were up and secured in less than five minutes.

Roxie turned back to the Tahoe and continued helping her mom to unpack and set things up while the two grown men trash talked each other all in good fun.

"You saw us, Red!" Kris said walking her direction. "Who won?"

Roxie shook her head without replying. Kris, undeterred, moved on to Mom for confirmation as Zeke continued walking towards Roxie. "You know, when I warned you that my brothers acted childish, I wasn't encouraging you to join them," she scolded.

"Aw, we were just having a little fun. We used to do it all the time. If those had been government issued tents, we could have had them up in two minutes flat."

"Show off."

"It's only showing off if someone is impressed. Here, let me get that for you," Zeke said taking a large bag of groceries. "Where is this going?"

"You can just put it on the table for right now."

"This place gives the illusion of seclusion, doesn't it?"

"Yeah, it's great. It's like that just about anywhere you go. You feel like it is just you and nature. That is one of this place's great qualities. I love it up here. It's so different from living in the middle of a big city. That's one of the things I miss the most being in my apartment. You've never lived anywhere but the middle of the city, huh?"

Zeke hesitated before answering, "I moved around a lot with the military."

"Oh yeah, I guess so. I didn't think about that."

"So, it's true what they say then?"

"What's that?"

"You can take the girl out of the country, but you can't take the country out of the girl."

Roxie was not sure what exactly he meant by that comment. Was it meant to be an insult? She never got the chance to ask, because Michael and Kris called Zeke to go help them gather firewood.

In some ways spending time with Kris and Michael out here, gathering wood, was like being back with his unit. True Michael had never been a part of that unit, but the camaraderie and horsing around was the same. So what that Red called them childish? It was good, clean fun; no one was getting hurt, and no one was going to get hurt. And, it felt so good to just let go like that and have fun. He never got to feel carefree like this anymore. Sure, he had responsibilities during his military career, but it was different. Back then he wasn't in charge. He wasn't the one giving commands, and most importantly he didn't have to carry all the weight on his own shoulders. At home, he did.

Michael as it turned out made a mean campfire. Zeke couldn't have done better himself. It was a nice sized fire, not to big, not too small, and it burned bright. Everyone was sitting around cooking hotdogs over the campfire. He had to admit, there was something about this that was both soothing and enjoyable.

The boys sat on one side while the girls sat on the other. Red sat directly across from Zeke, and he could see her clearly as night descended. Her face glowed in the firelight. Her hair, that was indeed the same color as the flames waving between them, danced around her face like it was an extension of the campfire itself. Her curls bounced around, like a tease meant to torment him.

The heat from the fire was giving her skin a becoming flush, making her freckles stand out begging for attention. He wanted so much to kiss each and every one of those tantalizing freckles. Having Kris and Michael on either side, certainly served as a reminder that Zeke had to remain on his best behavior.

Nevertheless, it did not keep him from staring. She was laughing. Her perfect smile was infectious, and Zeke found himself smiling and even laughing for no other reason than for the joy of seeing Red laugh and smile. Her laugh chimed through his head, the most melodious tune he had ever heard. He could die happy having heard it, and yet, he knew unexplainably he would die if he were denied that laugh now. Her smile, her laugh, it was like a drug to him now. He couldn't live without it, without her.

Zeke shook his head. He was being a drama queen. He'd die without her? It sounded ridiculous, but deep down, something he would not admit even to himself, he already knew it was true. Now that he'd found her, he needed her like he needed air. He ran his hand over his face and paused to rub his eyes.

When he opened his eyes again, his focus was still trained on Red. He couldn't take his eyes off her. Some time while they had been gathering wood right through sunset, the girls had changed clothes into their night clothes. Red wore a snug tank top and short shorts. If this was what he was going to be exposed to night after night, Zeke was not going to last a week out here, but ah, sweet torture, what a way to go. Watching those long legs kick around and squirm had Zeke mesmerized until another gut wrenching, belly laugh caused her breasts to bounce up and down like a couple of rubber balls.

He knew his dreams would be haunted all night long, but any dream involving Red was a good one.

Kris popped up, rummaged through one of the many bags of food, and returned with marshmallows, chocolate, and graham crackers. Red locked eyes with Zeke. He winked at her, trying to communicate that everything was ok. He knew his limits with chocolate. He wasn't a masochist for Pete's sake. Red shook her head at him almost imperceptibly. Zeke smiled and pretended not to notice her warning.

Red stood up and made her way around the fire. "Scoot," she ordered Michael as she sat down so close to Zeke that another inch and she would be in his lap. "Zeke and I have already talked about this. He's never made s'mores. I promised I'd show him how it's done," she lied easily, nudging Zeke with her elbow.

Kris passed everything around, and they all started roasting their marshmallows. Red pretended to walk him through step by step, but when it came to the chocolate she snatched it out and popped it into her mouth before anyone else noticed what she had done. Zeke gave her an accusatory grin and dug into his marshmallow and graham cracker.

"Alright, I'm beat. I'm getting too old for these long days," Ms. Gardner said. "I'm turning in for the night. Whoever is the last one to bed, be sure you put out the fire."

They laughed and talked for another two hours. Either Kris and Michael did not notice that Red still sat so close to Zeke, or they just didn't care. Zeke reveled in the sweet friction caused by their arms brushing against each other. He could only wish that he had, had the foresight to wear shorts that morning so that he could feel the silky smoothness of her perfect legs against his own.

"Ok, I think I'm going to head to bed too," Red announced.

"Yeah, we should probably all hit the hay," Michael agreed. Zeke sort of got the impression that Michael had stepped up into his dad's shoes after their dad died. Even on vacation when they visibly let loose, Michael was still the more responsible one. There were little things here and there, where he kind of stepped up and demanded the others listen, and they did. Without any argument, Kris stood up, slapped Zeke on the shoulder, and headed for the boys tent. Zeke knew that Kris was more of a night owl, but apparently it wasn't worth the argument with Michael.

Normally Zeke would have no problem turning in himself. Tonight, however, the full moon was only a night away. It wasn't true what some werewolf fanatics said about the moon controlling werewolves. Wolves neither had to turn on nights of a full moon, nor was it the only time they could change. Zeke could shift any time day or night that he wanted. The only effect the full moon had on him was to make him antsy. In fact, as far as Zeke new, the myth of werewolves was not at all true. Lycanthropy was supposed to be a virus of sorts. You had to be bitten by a werewolf to be infected. The transformation was unnatural and painful, and the werewolves had no control when in wolf form.

No, Zeke was not a werewolf. He was a shifter. He had not been infected with anything; rather, he had been born a shifter like his parents before him and their parents before them. Although some thought him unnatural, Zeke had never thought of himself that way. He was human… maybe just not pure human. Unlike non-shifters, he aged slower and would live longer. He had a few more animal like tendencies than others, but they were all subtle.

There were more people out there with the shifter characteristics in their DNA than one would think. There were considerably fewer who showed active, outward signs of the trait. For most, the trait was an inactive part of their DNA, like a sleeper cell in a way. Zeke's brother had once believed that if they were to become aware of that trait and actively chose to awaken it, they could do so. Zeke was not so sure about that, but his brother had been more medically minded.

Zeke felt a pain in his heart, knowing that his brother never got the chance to test that theory. Zeke could not carry on his legacy in that respect. It made very little sense to him, and he would be unable to test that theory even if he did find it ethical. Of course, he did not find it ethical, a sore point that he and his brother had debated many times before his family's death. Zeke knew that he would not want someone to take away his sifting abilities as part of some test or experiment. It was a part of who he was, a part of himself he was not willing to forfeit for an idiotic experiment. On the flip side, how would pure humans feel being given shifting abilities? They had lived there whole lives without that. Would it feel foreign and wrong to them? Wouldn't it be as much a violation to them giving them sifting abilities as it would be to take his?

Zeke waited until everything was quiet. Kris and Michael were asleep. Zeke slid silently out of his sleeping bag and exited the tent. Very few creatures were stirring. Animals had a way about them. They could sense danger in a way. Even though Zeke was not an actual danger, wolves normally equaled danger. The whole forest emptied for him. It was a sort of lonely feeling, but it left him with run of the forest. He hid behind a clump of trees, shed his clothes and shifted into wolf worm. Then he let go.

Zeke's wolf ran free. The wind whipped through his fur as his muscles pulled and stretched. Leaping over fallen trees and dodging in and out between trees still standing, he ran his energy out. The smell of the forest filled his nostrils, the bark of the trees, the damp soil, fragrant flowers. Running on instinct more than anything else, the forest was a blur of plants and wildlife hiding from the big bad wolf. His paws lightly touched down while he ran lithely, barely leaving a trace. By morning there would be no sign that he was ever there. He ran until his muscles all burnt from use, and he was close to falling asleep on his feet.

Zeke eased back into camp where everyone was still sleeping. No one would know that he had snuck out or why. Better than that, no one would wonder what had gotten into him tomorrow when he couldn't be still for thirty seconds at a time. Thanks to his midnight run, he would be able to control his energy abundance... until tomorrow night.

Chapter Twelve

Mom woke everyone bright and early for a morning hike. Mom loved to hike, but she liked to hike early before it started to get too hot. They really should have thought about that last night before they stayed up so late. Poor Zeke looked absolutely exhausted. Roxie felt bad about that; he had not known about Mom's early hiking habits. She and her brothers did; they should have said something or at least suggested that they go to bed earlier.

"Here, I made some coffee, while everyone was getting dressed," Roxie said handing Zeke a mug. "It's instant, but it's better than nothing this early in the morning."

"You're a life saver, Red."

It took a mile into the hike before everyone really woke up and started to pick up the pace. Not surprisingly, Kris and Zeke took the lead. They set a pace that was perfect for them, slightly challenging for Michael, and downright tiring for Mom and Roxie.

"You go getters want to slow down a bit?" Mom called up ahead to the boys. "Your sister and I aren't the athletes that you boys are."

Zeke seemed to slow up casually, but Kris and Michael shared a look that Mom and Roxie knew all too well. Here came the childishness.

"Come on," Michael instructed, turning his back to Roxie and squatting down.

He couldn't be serious, could he? Did he really expect Roxie to hop onto his back and ride through the woods piggy back? She had not done anything like that since junior high, and that had not ended well. She had been goofing off with friends. She and a couple of girl friends had gotten onto the shoulders of some of the boys and they were dancing when both Michael and Kris walked in and caught them. The whole thing had been completely innocent, but that wasn't the way her overprotective brothers saw the situation. She was mortified. Kris and Michael had yelled and carried on so much that the guys were scared to come near her ever again.

"Hop up, Mom," Kris joined.

"Boys, this is ridiculous," Mom argued.

"Come on, we got you," Kris encouraged.

"Kris, I am too old to be riding piggy back."

"You're in great shape, Mom. You can do this. Come on. Hop up. It will be fun, and you're perfectly safe with me carrying you."

Mom looked over to Roxie and shrugged. Was she really going to give in? Yes. She was hanging Roxie out to dry. Mom climbed onto Kris's back.

"Your turn, Red. Up you go!" Michael ordered, but Roxie was not going to be ordered around.

"No, go on. I'll keep up."

"Red, don't do this to me," Michael whined. "You're going to let them show us up? Hurry up, Red!"

"I am not going to ride your back just to show off or whatever it is you're trying to do."

"You know how the boys are," Mom tried to smooth over. "It will be easier and faster if you just get it over with."

"I know how they are? Do you mean that I know how childish they are? Maybe you mean that I know how much they like to show off how strong they are, or maybe you mean that I know how stubborn they are?"

"Oh forget it, Red!" Michael ground out. "We all know how self righteous you can be, so save us all the trouble. I wouldn't want to make you do anything you don't want to do."

"Red, come on, honey, if I can do this, you can too. You are a lot younger than I am. Michael won't drop you, will you, Michael?" Mom tried to negotiate.

"She knows I won't drop her. Just let it go, Mom. Red, isn't going to play unless it was her idea," Michael continued as he started to walk away.

"If it is going to start a fight, just come back and let's do this," Roxie gave in.

Michael came back and kissed the top of Roxie's head before turning around for her to hop on his back. She was the self righteous one? Who just played the guilt card here?

Roxie climbed up onto Michael's back, and he took off after Kris who was right on Zeke's heels. Zeke, who was leading the pack, had not said a word in all this. Roxie wondered what his take on this little game was. At the same time the arrant thought rushed through her head that it was too bad Zeke had not been the one to offer his back. She would have hopped on his strong back without hesitation. Bet Kris and Michael wouldn't have been so fond of their little game then.

Roxie was getting bounced around mercilessly on Michael's back from the rushed walking. It was a good thing that she didn't get motion sickness, or she was sure she would have already thrown up all over Michael's back. Ah, another opportunity lost. That would have served him right. She hoped that Kris was being easier with Mom.

Soon Michael had caught up and overtaken Kris. Kris, not to be outdone, sped up. They both progressed into a slow, but far from gentle jog, and surpassed Zeke. Now Kris and Michael were in the lead but hardly paying attention to where they were headed. The only thing they had on the brain was hiking along faster than the other.

"Kris, where are we headed, Man?" Zeke asked in a tone that was slightly amused, slightly irritated.

Both Kris and Michael slowed up and turned back to look at Zeke. Then they looked around the path that was headed up a steep hill. Roxie was sure they had never been that way. There were not many trails here that they had not taken at least a dozen times, but Kris and Michael were careful not to take her and Mom on the hardest trails. Sometimes they would go out on their own on the hardest trails just for a little challenge, but they always said that she and Mom would not like them. Roxie suspected that was their polite way of saying that she and Mom could not handle it.

"I think we missed the cut off. It's not too far back. We'll just back track a little ways," Kris said.

"What cut off?" Roxie asked. There were several "cut offs" they had found by leaving the beaten path and discovering new places. There was one that lead to a clearing where Mom liked to picnic.

Obviously they were not going to the clearing since no one had packed a lunch. There were a couple cut offs that lead to cliffs with breathtaking views, and one that lead to...

"The fall's cut off," Kris answered as if should have been obvious.

"If you had told me we were going to the falls, I would have worn my swimsuit," Roxie scolded her brothers.

"No one did," Kris pointed out. "We just thought it would be fun. 'Sides, Zeke hasn't seen them yet. You can get in like you are."

"You want to see the falls, don't ya, Zeke," Michael asked.

Zeke looked over Michael's shoulder at Roxie, and he looked nervous about how to answer or even to answer.

"I didn't say I didn't want to go," Roxie protested.

"Then let's go!" Michael said before heading back the way they had come.

This "cut off" was a pretty well worn trail that had been taken by many of the hikers over the years. The falls were a very popular place to hang out and go swimming. It wasn't hard to follow the trail while carrying someone on your back, well, at least not hard for two guys as strong as Kris and Michael. So, Roxie continued to bounce along on Michael's back, Mom on Kris's back. Zeke remained quiet as he had for most of the hike.

The water was crystal clear as usual, and it rushed down into white foam at the bottom. The regular rhythm of the waterfall was relaxing. Everyone took their shoes off and waded into the shallow end of the water. The water was freezing, ice cold. Of course, the two biggest kids immediately start splashing one another and everyone else by default.

"Boys! Take it somewhere else," Mom ordered in a high pitched voice.

Kris and Michael dove into deeper water and began rough housing. Mom found a large rock to sit on with her legs dangling in the water. Zeke waded his way to Roxie as she continued wading into deeper water.

"Sorry about that back there," Zeke offered.

"For what?" Roxie asked.

"I wasn't expecting them to put me in the middle of that back there, whatever it was."

"Oh, don't worry about that. They both claim that I am a hot headed drama queen, but the truth is they will do whatever they have to in order to get their way."

"Speaking of your brothers, where did they go?"

Roxie looked around. Sure enough, neither of her brothers were anywhere in sight. "They must be diving off the falls. We found a secret passage when we were little; at least that is what we called it at the time. It takes you out of sight for a while, but it's the safest route to the top. Everyone else takes the direct route. It's faster but slippery and dangerous. I can show you if you want."

"Absolutely!"

Roxie stifled a laugh at Zeke's enthusiasm as she made her way over to the falls. Making the trek to the top, Zeke asked, "So, you dive off the falls?"

"I haven't in years, why?"

"I just can't picture you the type to dive off falls like that."

"Oh."

"So, why haven't you done it in so long?" Zeke continued questioning.

"I'm not a kid anymore. It sounded like fun back then, but now it just sounds..."

"Dangerous?" Zeke finished for her. "You are such a girl," he teased giving her a poke in the arm.

"What about you, Mr. Big and Bad? Are you going to dive?"

"Sure, why not? I'd hate to think we came all this way for nothing."

"Well, here we are put your money where your mouth is," Roxie challenged him.

Looking over the falls it was further than she remembered. She couldn't believe that she used to dive that far without a care in the world. Kris and Michael were already back at the bottom laughing and cutting up. Michael spotted Roxie at the top, and he nudged Kris pointing to where Roxie stood.

"Hey, toss her down!" Kris called up to Zeke. Kris and Michael watched Zeke with eagerness and smiles that stretched from ear to ear.

She looked to Zeke, who was watching her intently. Was he seriously thinking about throwing her over the falls?

"I won't do anything you're not comfortable with," he whispered barely moving his lips. "It's your call."

"You won't hear the end of it."

"I can handle your brothers."

Was he serious? "It's too dangerous."

"I wouldn't do anything that I thought put you in danger. I won't let anything bad happen to you, but the choice is yours."

Awe man! Talk about peer pressure. His eyes were smoldering. It felt like his eyes were boring right through her. It wasn't like he was trying to look through her to the other side. No, his eyes were burning a hole straight through to her soul. How did he do that? The better question was how was she supposed to say no to that. She couldn't. She couldn't deny him anything when he looked at her like that. Still, she tried.

"Are you sure?"

"Yeah, it is plenty deep enough."

"I know. It's not that. The cliff wall is so close."

"I wouldn't just push you over so that you could hit every rock jutting out like a rag doll. I'll throw you out far enough that the cliff wall isn't a factor. Don't you trust me?"

Did she? Did she trust him with her life essentially? "Yes, but be careful."

Zeke could not believe that Red had just agreed to let him toss her over a water fall. He saw the fear in her eyes when she talked about going over. This was a big deal, the trust she was giving him. He smiled at her as excitement bubbled just underneath his skin threatening to explode.

Red did not smile back. Her lips were pressed together in a straight line. Determination was etched across her beautiful face. "What do I do?" she asked tentatively.

"Just enjoy the ride; I'll do the rest." She gave him a grim nod, and Zeke bent forward to pick her up. He placed his right hand on her back and his left behind her knees. Her skin was as smooth as silk, soft and pliant underneath his grip. Internally Zeke rejoiced that Red had chosen to wear shorts that day at the same time that he cursed how briefly he would be allowed the exquisite feel of her skin against his own.

He swooped her off the ground and held her close to his chest. Her arms instinctively wrapped around his neck. She clung to him like she was clinging to life, and something about it felt right. "Are you ready," he breathed.

Red was staring straight into his eyes, and for a minute Zeke was caught up in the intensity of that moment. She nodded without taking her eyes off of his. "On the count of three?" She nodded again, and he started counting. "One... two... three!"

Zeke threw Red out and over the falls on three. It was harder than he thought it would be. It felt wrong on a very deep level to be letting her go. Kris and Michael were whooping and hollering as Red fell through the air. Kris was, as usual, the loudest cheerleader around. He had kept a lot of them going during the toughest assignments.

Zeke dove after Red before she hit the water, trying to calm an internal need to be where she was. By the time he came back up out of the water, Red was laughing. Letting her go for only a brief moment in time was worth it to hear her laughter, but now he wanted her back. He wanted her in his arms where she belonged. He would have to fight the need, because Red was not his no matter how much he wanted her to be his.

They made it back to the campsite roughly an hour before sunset. Ms. Gardner made sandwiches. Everyone ate like a ravenous pack of wolves. Zeke smiled to himself. This felt more like family than anything he had known in a long time. After eating, they took chairs out to the lakeside and watched the sunset.

"Alright, that was beautiful," Kris announced. "I say we start that fire back up and make some s'mores."

"We just had s'mores last night," Red pointed out.

"So?"

"Well... you don't want to get burnt out on them."

"Yeah right. You don't have to eat them if you don't want to."

Red looked at Zeke like a mother would look at a misbehaving child. The message was clear, you tell them, or I will.

It didn't take long to get the fire going. There was still plenty of wood left over from last night. Tonight Ms. Gardner sat between her two sons, and Red squeezed in between Kris and Zeke. Like last night, she was practically sitting in his lap, she was so close. Zeke had no objection to the proximity; if he could slip his arm around her and pull her closer without drawing unneeded hostility, he would.

Red's brothers, it seemed, did object. Kris was looking at Red like she had grown an unexpected appendage. Michael said, "Red, I think he gets the idea. S'mores aren't that hard a concept."

"I know. I... I was just..." Red was floundering for an excuse, and her brothers were still waiting expectantly. Zeke couldn't leave her hanging out there by herself.

"She is trying to cover for me," Zeke fessed up. "I'm allergic to chocolate. I didn't want to be rude," he told Ms. Gardner, "so I didn't mention it before. I told Red that I'm fine as long as I don't eat too much of it, but she is trying to intercept any chocolate that comes my way."

"Oh, well, just don't eat it, man. It's not that big a deal," Kris said. Michael and Ms. Gardner nodded their agreement.

Red cleared her throat and moved to Zeke's other side putting ample room between them. Zeke resented Kris and Michael's interference. He was mourning the loss of Red's body heat.

Zeke had roasted marshmallows while the others had s'mores. Red hardly lifted her head to look around. For the most part she kept her head down, her face hidden in the shadows. The rare moments that she looked up, Zeke saw anger there and... embarrassment. He had done that. He should have already said something to the others. He knew she was not going to feel comfortable with him eating chocolate knowing he was allergic. He had inadvertently left it resting on Red's shoulders, and that wasn't fair to her. It wasn't fair, and worse, it had embarrassed her. He wanted more than anything to take it all back, but it was too late for that now. All there was left to do was damage control.

Unfortunately, Zeke was clueless on how to do damage control. Give him a military action, a business transaction, a dozen other situations, and he could easily do damage control. When it came to women and relationships, he was perplexed. He was still trying to puzzle it out when everyone headed to bed. No one stayed up nearly as late as they had the night before. Whether it was because they were beat after the day's revelry or feared another early morning to follow, he didn't know.

Once again, Zeke waited for Kris and Michael to fall fast asleep. Everything was quiet when Zeke slipped out of the tent and into the woods.

Chapter Thirteen

Roxie opened her eyes. Everything was still pitch black. Great. It was the middle of the night, and her bladder was full. Roxie patted the ground around her sleeping bag, looking for her phone. 3:49, it would be at the very least two hours before anyone began to stir. No way was her bladder going to wait that long. She slid out of her sleeping bag resolute with the fact that she would have to walk to the bathhouse alone.

Roxie grabbed a flashlight and started her trek. They were not too far from the bathhouse, but it was far enough. It was three campsites away, and the girl's side was on the backside. It wasn't visible from any of the other campsites. Roxie did not think that it had been well designed at all. There was a wonderful view of the lake from the entrance to the girl's bathroom, but it was not safe for the women's side to be so secluded.

Although Roxie did not mind walking to the bathhouse alone during the day, she rarely did. After dark, though, she detested walking alone to the bathhouse. Besides the threat of wild animals that would not ordinarily come out during the daylight due to the abundance of human activity, there was also the threat of unsavory characters lurking in the dark with the intent to do harm. She knew Mom would have walked with her, but Roxie hated to wake her in the middle of the night. Her brothers would have a conniption if they knew she walked to the bathroom alone after dark. They did not even want her and Mom together going without one of them after dark, but that was just too bad. It was bad enough that she had to get up in the middle of the night and walk all the way to the bathhouse and back; she wasn't about to ask anyone else do the same.

As she washed her hands, Roxie wondered what Zeke would think of her walking to the bathhouse alone after dark. He probably wouldn't much care for it since he didn't want her walking from her office to her car alone after dark. He would probably be willing to get up and walk with her too... She would not wake him at this unruly hour either. She dried her hands and started back to the comfort of her sleeping bag.

She had barely made it out of the bathroom when she spotted a wolf. She froze. The wolf was running around the lake. It looked like it was playing and having a good old time while unsuspecting humans slept all around. The wolf had not spotted her yet, but she knew she would not make it very far before it saw her, certainly not halfway to the campsite. Then it happened.

The wolf turned its head slowly suspiciously as if it somehow sensed her there. Roxie made eye contact with the wolf, yet neither of them moved. Something was not right about that wolf, but Roxie could not put her finger on what it was. She didn't want to stick around to find out what it was. Should she try to run for the campsite? She would never make it. Should she scream for help? That might frighten the wolf, causing him to attack. Should she dash back into the bathhouse to hide out? There was no telling how long she would be trapped in there, but it was less likely that the wolf would wonder in after her.

Before she could make a move back into the bathhouse, the wolf turned and darted back into the woods. It had just run away. Roxie stood there for a long while waiting to see if the wolf would come back. She did not want to be caught between the bathhouse and the campsite with nowhere to run. The wolf didn't return though, and Roxie moved cautiously but swiftly back to the campsite.

Her heart was racing a million miles an hour by the time she snuggled back down inside her sleeping bag. Amazingly she had managed not to wake Mom. She felt more at ease; it was not likely that the wolf would attack the tents. If it was from around here, it was surely used to sleeping campers. If he, and Roxie could tell this time that it was a he, was from around here. That would be the million dollar question. Roxie wasn't so sure it was from around here. It looked just like the wolf from her attack. It had to be the same wolf from the night she was attacked. Obviously it had the same color fur and was the same size, but the unusual eyes were the exact same. Those dark, mesmerizing eyes were exactly the way that Roxie remembered them. His eyes were as dark as the night around him, so strange for a wolf. And, what kind of wolf runs away after making eye contact. Eye contact is usually seen as a threat or challenge in canines, and Roxie was unquestionably not a threat. Why would he just run away, and what were the odds that two wolves who looked exactly and uniquely alike would both run away at the threat of someone so weak.

No, it was the same wolf. He was so beautiful, and there was just something about his eyes, something familiar. Twice he had the chance to attack her, and twice he had run away. Once he had attacked her attacker. Could that have been purposeful? Was he protecting her? Either way, this wolf was really beginning to stir Roxie's interest, and now that she had seen him, she could not find sleep again. All she could think about was the wolf. All she could see when she closed her eyes was the wolf.

Mom woke around 6:30, and Roxie helped her start breakfast. Together they fixed a big breakfast of sausage, bacon, eggs, and toast. There was a lot of food. It smelled great, yet even that was not enough to wake the boys. Mom spread some strawberry jelly over a piece of toast and went to sit out by the lake to eat it. Roxie fixed her plate and followed Mom.

"I saw a wolf last night," she casually mentioned.

"What are you talking about, sweetheart?"

"I went to the bathhouse around four this morning, and on my way back I saw a wolf playing down here by the lake."

"Why on earth did you go to the bathhouse at four this morning?"

"I had to use the restroom, but mother are you listening?" Roxie asked having expected more of a reaction to the wolf.

"Yes, I'm listening. Why did you not get one of us to go with you or just wait?"

"I couldn't wait any longer, and I didn't want to wake anyone that early. Mom, I saw him. He was running around. A lone wolf was just running around playing, and it was the same wolf."

"The same wolf?"

"Yes, from my attack. It was the same wolf that saved me."

"Red, honey, can you hear yourself? This whole thing is starting to sound fantastical."

"What does?" Michael asked walking up behind them.

"I saw a wolf last night," Roxie answered.

"In your tent?" Michael asked skeptically.

"No, of course not, I'm not delusional no matter what any of you say. I saw him down here by the lake."

"What were you doing down here by the lake last night?" Michael inquired.

"I wasn't! I had to go to the bathroom!" Roxie was losing her temper now. She knew it; she could hear it in her voice but couldn't seem to rein it back.

"So, go to the bathroom. Who's stopping you?" Kris reacted as he walked up with Zeke hot on his heels.

"I don't need to use the restroom!" Roxie snapped.

"Whoa, calm down. What is going on?" Kris asked.

"Red thinks she saw a wolf when she went to the bathroom last night," Michael filled him in. He sounded like he didn't believe a word of it. Roxie could feel her face flush in anger.

Kris shrugged his shoulders as if the situation was simple. "Who went with her?"

So now she needed a witness to be believed!? Roxie leapt to her feet ready to take on both her brothers.

"That's my point," Mom jumped in. "No one went with her. She went alone. What was your sister doing walking to the bathhouse alone in the middle of the night?"

Everyone's eyes turned expectantly to Roxie. "I did not want to wake anyone up in the middle of the night just because I could not hold it! I did see a wolf, and it was the same wolf that attacked my attacker. Furthermore, I did not realize that I was so untrustworthy that I would need witnesses to corroborate my story!" She was yelling now. She did not try to hold it back any longer, because she just didn't care.

"No one said you were untrustworthy," Michael tried to console.

"Maybe not in those words, but no one believes me!"

"Red, it's unlikely that a wild wolf would come this close to civilization. It was more likely one of the camper's pet dog," Michael reasoned.

"I know what a wolf looks like, Michael," Roxie growled. Now her temper was getting dangerous, and Michael was getting dangerously close to the wrong end of her temper.

"Let's say, just for arguments sake, it was a wolf. A wolf is not going to travel that far for no good reason. It couldn't have been the same wolf," Kris pointed out. It was obvious, however, that he still didn't believe it had been a wolf.

"Well, it doesn't matter. Everyone is safe. Whatever it was is gone. No one goes to the bathhouse alone after dark again. Now, sit down and eat your breakfast, Red," Mom instructed.

Roxie tossed her plate into her chair. "I'm not hungry." She stalked away from her family towards the peer. She slipped her flip flops off, sat down at the end of the peer, and plopped her feet into the water. The water was so calm; there was not a ripple to be seen anywhere. It was always unnerving to see how calm everything and everyone around her could be when she was in turmoil. It was crazy, and it drove her crazy. How could everything else be so calm when she couldn't?

One tear escaped and rolled down her cheek before she even realized she had teared up. Conceding to one tear opened up the flood gates. Roxie could not hold back the tears that streamed down her face. She folded her arms across her middle and let herself cry.

She had lost control. It hurt that she had lost control like that, but it hurt more that no one believed her.

Roxie didn't know how long she sat there crying, but she couldn't face her family right now. The longer she sat, the longer she cried. Her eyes burned, but still she cried on until her eyes were dried out. Eventually her eyes did dry out. Now they were burning and itching. She sat staring at the calm water and took deep breaths trying to calm her still frazzled nerves.

Someone sat down next to her on the peer. They were close enough to touch, but they didn't. They didn't say anything either. Roxie did not look up to see who it was; she was not ready to face her brothers or mom. Whoever it was stayed silent like they were waiting.

Finally, Roxie peeked to the side to see who was sitting next to her without speaking. Zeke's eyes slid over to hers. He picked the sides of his mouth up in a slight smile. Great. Roxie had forgotten that Zeke had been there to see her erupt.

"Are you okay?" he asked.

"I'm fine. I just... I saw the wolf."

"If you say you saw a wolf, then you saw a wolf. You understand, though, why it is so unlikely for it to have been the same wolf, why your family is having such a hard time with it... They've been worried about you... You've been over here for a while. Kris said you needed time to calm down."

Roxie nodded her head. She turned back to look for her family, but she could not see the campsite from the end of the peer. They couldn't see her from where they were either.

"Red?"

"Why do you call me that?"

"I thought..."

"No one but my family calls me Red. I didn't introduce myself as Red, but that is what you call me."

"Do you not like it?"

"It's not that. I don't mind that you call me Red. I was just curious why."

"Honestly?" Roxie nodded. Zeke reached up with his left hand and ran his hands gently through her hair. "You have beautiful red hair that grabbed my attention the first time we met. I knew that I had heard Kris call you Red. Then that first afternoon we ate at your mom's, I realized you had an appealingly red blush that almost matches your hair. I knew then that I would never be able to think of you as anything but Red. I've noticed since then that you blush often."

"Oh." She could feel that blush he was referring to creep up her cheeks.

"Do you have any idea how beautiful you are when you blush like that?" Zeke ran his fingers across her cheek in a barely there caress. He leaned in and ever so slightly touched his lips to hers. Roxie sucked in a breath. She needed Zeke to kiss her, now. She needed his kisses like she needed air. Agonizingly slowly his lips began to slide across hers in a tender kiss. He ran his tongue along her bottom lip. She parted her lips on a sigh. Zeke's tongue plunged inside her mouth, and his hand pushed back into her hair as he deepened the kiss.

Roxie forgot about everything else as their tongues tangled together in a dance older than time. The taste of Zeke was better than anything she had ever tasted before. She couldn't get enough, and she knew instinctively that she was addicted to him already. His right hand connected with her hip and pulled her closer. Roxie went willingly as Zeke pulled her right into his lap.

Changing their positions gave her a better angle on his mouth. Roxie moaned into his mouth as they continued their exploration. When Roxie did pull back she was huffing and out of breath. Zeke was equally as winded.

"Zeke?"

"Mmm?" he responded before stealing another quick kiss.

Roxie smiled unable to remember what she had been about to say. Zeke took the opportunity to kiss her again. This time she gave in, returning his long, lingering kisses. She had no idea how long she sat there in his lap eagerly, hungrily kissing him. All she knew was the agitation she felt when Kris called her name.

"Red... are you still down here?" Kris's voice was getting steadily louder. He was headed their way and not at a slow pace either.

Zeke picked Roxie up off his lap and sat her back down on the dock and cleared his throat. They both took a quick swipe at their lips with the back of their hand before Kris came around the corner.

"Are you seriously still down here pouting? You know we didn't mean any harm... Anyway, Mom, wants you to come eat lunch; she sent me to find you two," Kris said.

Zeke hopped to his feet and held his hand out to help Roxie up. Kris stared at them as they walked his direction. His expression was neutral, but then he was better at hiding his emotions than Michael. Finally, he turned and walked with them back to the campsite where Mom and Michael were already sitting at the picnic table. Roxie took a seat next to Mom.

Kris saddled up to Zeke's left ear before he sat down and whispered something into his ear. Zeke did not respond, and they both took a seat with Kris on Roxie's other side. Did he suspect what she and Zeke had been doing down by the lake? Would he handle it quietly so that it did not effect Zeke and Michael's working relationship? More importantly what would Kris do to handle it? Surely he would not try to fight Zeke; he was more mature than that now, wasn't he? Had she already cost Zeke and Kris their friendship? She had not meant to cost anyone anything. What had she been thinking?

She had not been thinking. All she had thought about was kissing Zeke. How he tasted. The feel of his lips on hers. No, she couldn't get lost in those thoughts right now. She had created enough trouble. After lunch, Roxie could not have told anyone what she ate. She never noticed the food. She moved mechanically as her thoughts were consumed with possible damage she had caused. All day long, Roxie worked to keep a respectable distance between herself and Zeke while keeping an eye on Kris.

Chapter Fourteen

Zeke could feel Red's eyes on him, but she was still avoiding him. She had avoided him all day since they had returned from the lake that morning. He may have pushed too hard this morning. He would have to back off some. Today would be a big step backwards he would have to overcome.

Everyone was sitting around the campfire again, but there were no s'mores tonight. Idle chit chat and laughter filled the air. To anyone outside the situation, everything would seem normal. Everyone sitting around the campfire appeared happy and relaxed, but Zeke's mind was in turmoil. Red was purposely not looking in his direction, and it was eating him up inside despite the facade he wore.

Michael was the first one to go to bed with his mom close behind. Kris being the night owl that he is, stayed up much later. It wasn't hard for Zeke to stay up with Kris keeping the conversation flowing. He was used to late nights. It was obvious, though, that Red was struggling to outlast them. Kris didn't seem to notice the discomfort any more than anyone else, but then again, he was trained well to be covert when needed.

Eventually Kris went to bed too claiming that he was getting too old to be sitting out all night shooting the bull. Red watched him into the tent then just stared at the tent for another minute or two. Zeke did not have the slightest clue what she was doing or how he should handle their own situation. If she were avoiding him, why not go to bed herself before Kris or at least when Kris went to bed?

Red scooted a little closer and whispered, "Are you ok?"

"I'm fine," Zeke replied confounded by what might have triggered her line of questioning.

"What did he say to you?"

"What?"

"This morning at lunch, I saw Kris whispering to you. Was he horrible?"

"No, it wasn't even aimed at you, honest. Your brothers had both warned me this morning that is was better to leave you alone to work through your emotions alone. They thought because I had been gone so long that I must have caught backlash trying to approach you. All he basically said was told you so."

"I thought..." Red stopped, took a deep breath, and started again. "I thought that Kris had guessed what we had been doing down by the lake."

Zeke was starting to catch on to why she had been avoiding him, but still, he wanted to know her take on it all. "And, that would be a bad thing?"

"Well, yeah, I've told you how overprotective my brothers are... I just don't want anything to happen to your friendship with Kris."

Zeke closed the remaining distance between them, wrapped his arms around Red, and pulled her into his lap for the second time that day. "I don't see that being a problem, but how about you let me deal with that?"

"I just-"

"Red," Zeke interrupted in a scolding tone. She gave a strained nod and kissed him. Zeke took a minute to enjoy kissing her before he pulled back and added, "If it makes you feel better, we don't have to tell your family until you feel comfortable doing so."

Red graced him with a breath taking smile. "Thank you," she breathed.

A few more shared kisses hidden in the darkness of the night and they too called it a night.

The remainder of the camping trip rushed by with fun and friends and a stolen kiss or two here and there when he and Red could catch a moment alone. Everyone was great to make Zeke feel like one of the family. Of course he was already as close to Kris as he was almost anyone these days from their time in the military, but that time he spent in the military was the last time he felt a sense of family... until now.

"Well," Michael said as they packed up on Saturday afternoon, "I don't guess there is any reason for you two to have to make an extra stop at Mom's. We have plenty of room in the Tahoe for both coolers this time. It always amazes me that we go home with so much more space."

"It's because you and Kris ate all the food, bonehead," Red jabbed.

"Ha, ha. Seriously though, I don't see any sense in you coming back to Mom's before going home."

In the end no one argued with Michael, and they all piled into the cars to go back to the real world. Zeke was sorry to see his time with the Gardner's come to an end, but at the same time he was psyched to get more time alone with Red. As soon as they were out on the road, he took her hand in his and brought it to his lips. "You ready to go home?"

"Yeah, it was fun, but all good things must come to an end."

"That, and it will be easier to sneak around behind your family's back when they are not within shouting distance."

Red laughed and pulled his hand down into her lap to hold with both of her own hands. They rode like that for almost three hours before stopping for gas and a bathroom.

Kris and Michael got out laughing when their mom got out and took off in search of a bathroom. "Don't give her a hard time," Red scolded.

"Hey, we didn't do anything," Kris said throwing his hands up in the air.

"I pulled over as soon as she said something," Michael explained. Michael was driving back home instead of Kris. It made the ride a little longer with Michael's considerably slower driving. He wasn't incredibly slow, but he did do the limit. It gave Zeke more time with Red, and he didn't have to focus so much on his own driving.

Kris walked up behind Red and put her in a loose fitting headlock. "So, this is it. You are free of us," he teased.

"Thank heavens! You and Michael should only be taken in small amounts."

Kris laughed and let her go then added in Zeke's direction, "Watch this one, man. That sharp tongue of hers has been known to make the toughest men cry."

"And, by toughest men, I assume you are not including yourself," Zeke shot back.

"Oh, cute, Miller. I've got yours. Come on," Kris egged on with a clearly amused smile.

"Break it up, Kris, and let's go," Ms. Gardner rebuked as she returned quickly from the bathroom and climbed back into her Tahoe.

"Better run along, Gardner. I hear your mommy calling," Zeke taunted in a voice low enough that Ms. Gardner could not hear from inside her car.

Kris pointed a warning finger at Zeke letting him know that this was far from over, and Zeke smiled at the promise of more to come. Zeke capped the gas tank and got back into his car where Red was waiting.

"What is it with you men? Don't you ever grow up?" Red asked.

"No, what would be the fun in that?" Zeke gave Red a playful smile and poked at her hand and added, "Besides, I was under the impression you kind of liked me the way I was."

"Ugh," she groaned and allowed him to take hold of her hand, "what are we, thirteen years old?"

"Why? Are you feeling as giddy as a school girl?"

"Really? I don't think my brother is a very good influence on you."

"Mmm, I agree. I don't know why I let Michael talk me into some of this stuff."

Red reached across with her right hand and playfully slapped Zeke's shoulder. "You're awful!"

The ride from that point on only took another forty-five minutes back to Red's apartment. "I didn't realize that not going by your mom's would cut out fifteen minutes of drive time," Zeke commented as he helped Red get her stuff out of the trunk and lug it up the stairs to her apartment.

"Yeah, it is sort of out of the way. It would cut out a lot more time for Michael, but we've never entertained the idea of starting from a different point. I guess we've all become creatures of habit."

"Nah, I think it's nice that you meet at your mom's. It's a sign of respect, and it is more convenient for her."

"I had never thought of it that way... You want to come in?"

"Sure." It was far from the first time that Zeke had been inside Red's apartment, but his heart skipped a beat anyway. He grinned at the irony; now who was as giddy as a school girl?

He followed Red inside and followed suit as she dropped everything next to the couch. "I'll be right back," she excused herself as she darted off to the restroom. Zeke sat down and made himself comfortable while he waited for Red. He had been in this same apartment enough times that he should be more than comfortable, but he was nervous now.

Red came back grinning ear to ear. Zeke smiled back and pulled her down into his lap. Red giggled and planted a warm, wet kiss on his lips. He stayed for as long as he could stand her sweet torture. "I should go," he forced out his lips as he pulled away from Red.

"Do you have to?"

"Yeah, it's getting late. Tomorrow?"

"Yeah."

"Good, I'll see you tomorrow," Zeke said and gave her another chaste kiss.

Zeke did not go straight home. He had been gone for a week, and it was time for a little recon. He parked his car in the usual spot, but did not get out right away. Something wasn't right. He wasn't alone. This area was usually deserted this time of day. It might still appear that way to most people, but Zeke was not most people. He could hear people hiding in the shadow could feel their eyes on him. Zeke pulled back onto the road to return his car home. He would come back after dropping off the car.

Sure enough, when Zeke returned he found a whole team doing their own reconnaissance, if you could call them a team. They were not very organized and didn't seem to have any sort of communications method if they had run across trouble. And, they would run into trouble. Tonight was not the night though. Zeke knew he needed to figure out what was going on before he made his next move, but soon, he would make sure they ran into trouble, a whole boatload of it.

Zeke wondered around a bit. There were men set up all around the surrounding area. Luckily for Zeke they were none too bright. They wouldn't have spotted a tank out here unless it ran them over. Too many of them were young and playing on smart phones or other devices. Didn't they realize that brightly lit screen gave them away, or did they just not care? There were only a handful of men out tonight taking the surveillance seriously. The biggest question Zeke had was, what were they watching for?

Zeke continued on until he got to the building that the gang had been using as their base of operations. It seemed that they had been recruiting while he had been away. Their numbers had doubled. What had happened to cause such an intense increase?

"None of the scouts have spotted anything, and no one has been hurt in at least a week. Maybe the dog has moved on, or maybe it's dead already," one man inside suggested.

"You don't seriously believe that do you? It's more likely that the dog just got full on its last victim. He'll be back. It's got to be close to feeding time now," another man responded.

"Good! I'm ready to get this problem taken care of. I don't like the idea of letting some wild dog run around killing people," yet another man chimed in.

It was starting to make sense now. All those scouts were watching for him. They were looking to kill themselves a wild dog. What did these people think they had gotten themselves into? Some kind of neighborhood watch? There were two things that Zeke knew for sure. One, it was going to take more than the untrained idiots he had seen so far to take him down, and two, he was going to have to be more careful from now on. Now there were innocents involved. He would have to be proof positive that he aimed his offensive at the right men and not ones who did not know what they were doing.

Perhaps it would be best to take another few days reprieve to come up with a new game plan, but this would not stop him. Nothing would stop him until this area was safe again.

Chapter Fifteen

After church all Roxie could think about was seeing Zeke. Maybe he was right. Maybe she was acting giddy as a school girl. She had just spent a whole week with him, yet here she was anxious to see him again. She had the urge to start jumping around when her phone started to ring.

"Hello."

"Hey beautiful, what ya' up to?"

"Not much, just sitting around dreading work tomorrow."

"Can I come by to see you?"

"Of course."

"'Kay, I'll be there in ten."

"Ok."

If Roxie thought she was antsy before, she was absolutely hyper now. She had already unpacked. The house was clean. Lunch was over. It was hours before supper. There was nothing to do but wait. Roxie tried to sit still, but it was a losing battle. She was up and down. When she managed to stay seated she was wiggling around like a young child confined to one spot. Every noise she heard had her running to check the peep hole on her front door.

Finally the last time that Roxie peered through the peep hole she saw Zeke. He was still a good eight to ten feet from her door, but she threw the door open anyway. He smiled at her, and she could not hold back any longer. She closed the space between them and launched herself into his arms. Zeke caught her like she weighed no more than a child.

"I missed you," she mumbled against his lips as she gave him a very eager, very juicy kiss.

"Mmm, I bet I missed you more," Zeke replied when he managed to pull away from Roxie's overzealous kisses.

Roxie started to respond to his claim, but stopped short, startled to see that they were already back into her apartment with the door closed behind them. Zeke lumbered over to the couch and dropped down with Roxie landing in his lap. He slipped his hands up to burry one in her hair, which was wild and all over the place, the other slid along her cheek bone and held her steady as he took his fill of her lips.

Zeke grumbled something against her lips that sounded like "too much wasted time." Roxie pulled back to ask him about what he meant, but Zeke pulled her back demanding a barely intelligible "more."

Eventually they had to stop to breathe. "What did you do this morning?" Roxie wondered.

"Church, lunch. You?"

"Same, Michael didn't make it. He was probably tired. I know I am."

"You go to the same church as Michael?"

"Yeah, we all still go to church with Mom where we grew up."

"Wow, that's quite a drive."

"Tell me about it. Michael and I have talked about finding churches closer to our homes. Michael has visited a couple other churches, but hasn't found a good fit yet."

"And you?"

"No, I haven't been anywhere else. There aren't many churches around this area. If I'm going to have to drive that far anyway, I might as well go with my family. Where do you go?"

"It's a small church about ten minutes from my house."

"That's close."

"It's the opposite direction, about twenty minutes from here. There are a couple churches closer to you, but I don't think you'd like either one. They are both pretty liberal. They have some uh... interesting beliefs."

"Still twenty minutes isn't so bad. The closest I've found so far is an hour, little more from here."

"Hmm, I can show you some a lot closer than an hour."

"Maybe I'll visit your church next Sunday."

"I'd like that. Stop off at the house and we can ride together."

"It's a date."

"Speaking of, Friday do you want to go out?"

"What did you have in mind?"

"I haven't decided yet. I just thought we should make this thing between us somewhat official. Do you have any preferences?"

"No. So, are we official?"

"I guess that's up to you. I want us to be."

"I want that too."

"We're official then, as official as we can be not telling your family."

"I'm sorry. Are you sure you're ok with that?"

"For now, but eventually we do need to tell them. Kris is my friend."

"I know. That's why I don't want to tell them. Kris and Michael have never liked anyone I dated. If they didn't end up in a fight it was because their threats were good enough to get the guy to run for the hills."

"I'm not going anywhere," Zeke soothed.

"That doesn't make it any better. Because you aren't going anywhere, based on my brothers' past history, I'm afraid that is going to start something. I don't want you and Kris to lose your friendship, and you work with Michael. How uncomfortable could that be?"

"You're an adult now, and so are they. I can understand that you want to wait to tell them until you are sure this between us is going somewhere, but eventually... Red, we have to tell them sometime. I'll give you time; I just want to make sure you're thinking about it."

Roxie nodded not wanting to further the conversation. Zeke wasn't that sure of them already, was he? How could he be? She hadn't given any thought to telling her brothers. Not only did she not want to ruin those relationships, she didn't want to ruin or strain what she and Zeke had this early on. It was selfish on her part. Obviously, Zeke was not going to let her get away with not giving it any thought. It was time she gave this some serious thought before Zeke started helping her think it through.

Pity, though, she had been in such a good mood before the conversation of her brothers came up. Where she had been on fire, the conversation had doused her with cold water. She was no longer in a light, kissy mood. Roxie grabbed the controller from next to Zeke and turned the TV on. It was on one of the movie channels. Roxie didn't care what was on; she wasn't watching it anyway.

She had managed to twist and turn inside the circle of Zeke's arms until she was lying across his lap facing the TV. Zeke leaned back in a very relaxed sitting position. He slowly, nonchalantly ran his hand through Roxie's hair over and over.

"You should wear your hair down more often," Zeke mentioned lightly.

Roxie turned her head to look up at him. "Are you kidding me? It's everywhere."

Zeke smiled. "It's wild and beautiful. I like it this way."

"Wow, no need to get all dolled up for you, huh?"

"Mmm," Zeke hummed before pulling Roxie around for another thought clearing kiss. Zeke kissed her thoroughly quite a while before giving in to the need for air.

Roxie turned her attention back to the movie, needing a chance to catch her breath and her runaway thoughts. As it turned out, she barely caught either before falling fast asleep curled up snuggly in Zeke's lap.

"Red... Red." Someone was whispering her name. Whoever it was their large, rough, warm hands felt heavenly rubbing along her arm and back. It felt too good to be real; she must have been still dreaming. "Red?" Those marvelous hands moved into her hair. Her whole body was alive with tingling sensations. If she were awake, she would be worried.

"Red... Red, are you awake?" Of course she wasn't awake. What sort of question was that for a dream to ask? She snuggled deeper into her bed. A deep chuckling echoed through her dream and vibrated her entire body.

"Red?" the voice called again. There was something familiar about that voice. It was a safe but exciting voice that she could not quite put her finger on.

"Red, wake up." This time she felt lips press against hers. She could feel herself starting to wake up, and she moaned in protest. This was a confusing dream, but none the less delightful.

"Red?" The mystery lips, that felt so perfect against hers, pressed to hers again. This time she caught the taste. She knew that taste and that voice.

"Zeke?"

"There you are. I wasn't sure if you were coming back to me or not."

"I'm sorry. I must have dozed off."

"I need to go."

"Don't go. I'm awake now." Roxie could hear the pleading in her voice and it wasn't a pretty thing.

"I'm not leaving because you fell asleep. I'm leaving because we both have to work tomorrow."

"What time is it?"

"Ten o'clock."

Zeke lifted Roxie off of his lap and sat her back on the couch. He stood up, and Roxie jumped to her feet and followed him to the door. "I'll see you after work," Zeke said.

Roxie nodded sleepily, and Zeke leaned in for a kiss goodnight. Her body was still tingling with his nearness, but when his lips met hers, something exploded. She didn't see fireworks, but it was definitely an explosion of some sort, and a potent one at that. She was still reeling from the foreign sensations as Zeke walked away.

The next morning, Roxie did not make it through the door good before Lucy was on her. "Welcome back! How was it? Wait, I know that look! Oh, Rox! What is it? What happened? And, don't tell me nothing, because we both know better!" Lucy demanded in a high pitch of excitement.

"Something happened all right," Roxie replied with a teasing grin. "We'll talk at lunch?"

"I don't think so, girl! You get back here, and start talking," Lucy insisted following Roxie into the inner office.

"Don't you have work to do?" Roxie continued to taunt.

"Not nearly as much as you who was off playing for a week."

Roxie looked at her in-box and sighed. She threw herself into her chair. "I'm not going to get out of here on time today, am I?"

"So ambitious."

"I'll have to call Zeke at lunch to let him know I'll be running late," Roxie thought aloud to herself.

"So, he's still coming to your apartment to eat?" Lucy pushed.

"Yes, he has to eat."

"Oh, and he was starving before he met you? Come on, now. What happened? Did he kiss you?"

"Are you asking me to kiss and tell?"

"Of course. So, he did kiss you?"

"Maybe."

"Maybe, nothing. He did kiss you! How did your brothers take it?"

"They don't know. We aren't telling them yet. I don't think Zeke likes the idea of sneaking around behind their backs, but he's giving me time."

"Well, I'm sure he doesn't, sweetie. Don't you think they would take it better that their friend, who they approve of and respect, was interested in their baby sister than the friend they had trusted has been sneaking around behind their back?"

"I hadn't thought of it that way. It does sound bad when you put it that way."

"Yeah, it does," Lucy said sympathetically, "but tell me more about you and Zeke. There is something to hide from your brothers, so it was more than just a kiss?"

"Lucy, stop. We aren't hiding it from my brothers; we just haven't told them yet."

"Yeah, yeah, haven't told them what exactly?"

"That Zeke and I are dating." Roxie could stop the massive smile that spread across her face if she had tried. She knew that was exactly what Lucy wanted to know but would not come out and ask.

"So, it's official?"

"Yes, Lucy, we talked about it last night. We are officially dating. He's going to take me out Friday."

"Well, good, it's about time you had a life."

"Hey!" Roxie reacted defensively but Lucy just laughed as she walked out and left Roxie to her work.

Roxie knew there was no feasible way that she was going to catch up on all her work in one day, but she was certainly going to try. She did not take long for lunch, only long enough to call Zeke.

"Hey," Zeke answered chirpily, "you on lunch?"

"Sort of. I've got a lot of work piled up that I've got to get caught up on. You may beat me home tonight. I'm going to be a little late leaving."

"No, I'll come meet you there."

"It's not that big a deal. I'll try not to be too long."

"Are you seriously going to tell me you're thrilled about walking to your car alone after the last time?"

"Well, no, I'm not thrilled about it, but I'll be fine."

"Of course you will, because I will be there to walk with you to your car."

"Zeke-"

"Don't bother arguing. You won't win. Just stay put until I get there."

"There's no sense in you having to come out of your way."

"I can ask Michael if he thinks it would be a waste of my time, if you think that's best."

"You wouldn't," Roxie challenged.

"You're out numbered, Red."

"Fine."

"Thank you. I'll see you after work. Have a nice lunch," Zeke said in a too sweet tone.

"Uh-huh," Roxie grumbled and hung up. She swore she could hear Zeke chuckling as she hung up.

It was hard, but Roxie managed to put Zeke out of her mind so that she could focus on her work. She was really in the zone, when Lucy walked in and said, "It's quitting time. Can I take it you aren't leaving?"

"I've got some more I want to finish up before I leave today."

"Sure, do you want me to wait?"

"No, I'll be fine. Zeke insisted in coming to walk me out to the car like a child."

"Good for him. You hang on to him. He sounds like a good one."

"He does, doesn't he?"

"Mm-hmm," Lucy nodded and turned for the door.

"Lucy?"

"Yeah?"

"Thank you."

Lucy smiled and said, "I love you, Rox."

"Love you too, Luc."

Roxie immersed herself once again in her work. She jumped when her phone went off. She hadn't realized how late it had gotten.

"Hello."

"Hey, beautiful. I'm outside your building. Are you about done?"

"Not really. It will take me days to catch up, but I am done for tonight. Just let me clean up, and I'll be right there."

"Ok."

Roxie opted for the stairs wanting to get to Zeke faster than what the elevator would carry her. She slowed down considerably when she got to the lobby. The walls were all glass windows, and she could see Zeke waiting for her just outside. He was leaned against the glass with his back against it. He looked casual and comfortable, like it was nothing unusual for him to be waiting for her outside her office. He was already so intricately woven into her life, it was like he had always been there. She felt like she had known him all her life not a matter of months.

Roxie opened the door and smiled as Zeke turned to face her. "Hey," he returned her smile and kissed her before sliding his arm possessively around her waist. "How was your day?"

"Busy. Yours?"

"Same, but it's looking up now."

"Has that tired line ever worked?"

"You'd be surprised," Zeke returned with a conspiratorial smile and a wink.

Roxie slapped him playfully on the chest. "I retract the question. I really do not want to hear about your sorted past."

"I'll tell you mine, if you tell me yours," Zeke said as he waggled his eyebrows. "Seriously, you want to pick something up, so you don't have to cook?"

"You don't mind?"

"Nah, I'll give Isabella a call, put in an order to go." Zeke got on the phone and had dinner ordered in less than two minutes.

As they walked up to her car, Roxie snuggled in against Zeke's chest not wanting him to let her go yet. She was rewarded by Zeke wrapping his second arm around her and pulling her tighter than before. He held her there for one glorious minute. Then he kissed the top of her head and ruined the moment by saying, "I'll pick up the food and meet you back at your apartment."

"Mmm, ok."

Zeke must have been driving like a maniac, because he pulled into the parking lot before Roxie got her key turned in the lock. She left the door opened and walked back to the bedroom to take her shoes off. She returned thinking she'd find Zeke; instead, a bag with to go boxes sat on the table, and the door stood wide open. Zeke was nowhere to be seen. Roxie walked outside a step or two and looked both ways. Zeke wasn't anywhere she could see. That was weird. Where would he go in such a hurry without saying anything? He was usually such a stickler for locking the door.

Roxie turned back into the apartment to get her phone and call him. She zeroed in on her purse and kicked the door shut behind her. Suddenly her feet flew out from under her, and the world all around her began to spin. Roxie tried to scream for help, but her lungs couldn't take in enough air. She could feel arms, strong as steel, locked around her body. Then without warning she was falling. She couldn't make sense of what was happening. Who was in her apartment? What did they want? Did they hurt Zeke?

Roxie bounced, her back against something soft. Abruptly everything came to a screeching halt. Everything was still and black, and there was a weight on top of her. It took Roxie only a second to realize that she had squeezed her eyes shut out of fear. She opened her eyes and found Zeke hovering above her on the couch. She sucked in a massive gulp of air and focused on continuing to take air in and out of her lungs.

"I thought you weren't going to leave the door unlocked anymore, much less standing wide open for anyone to walk in," Zeke accused austerely.

"Zeke!" Roxie screeched finally finding her voice again. She started slapping at his shoulders with everything she had left in her, which wasn't much. The unexpected fear and brusque relief had drained her. "You scared me to death! I thought someone had come in and hurt you!" She was screaming hysterically now, but she didn't care. "I thought something horrible had happened to you!" she let him have it, hitting him to punctuate each word.

Zeke didn't try to stop her from hitting him, and it didn't seem to faze him either. "That is exactly what I worry about each and every time you leave that door unlocked or worse open."

"You didn't have to scare me like that!" Roxie was still worked up, still out of breath, and mad. Oh boy, was she mad! She wasn't seeing red, but then she never did when she lost her temper. She had tunnel vision. All she could see was Zeke, and all she could feel was anger.

"You obviously weren't listening before. Talking didn't work. What else was I supposed to do?"

"Not try to kill me!"

"I wasn't trying to kill you. If you would calm down, you would realize that you are not hurt."

"Calm down? Not hurt? Are you serious? You just scared me to death! I thought you were dead, and I thought I was next!" Now he had done it. In a rush, her anger ebbed back into fear, fear that completely paralyzed her. Tears started streaming down her face like a waterfall. Her vision blurred. She couldn't move, and she couldn't stop her body from shaking.

"Ok, shh, shh, that may have been a bit extreme."

"A bit?" Roxie shot back but without much force.

"Shh, Red, I would never hurt you."

"I-I didn't know it was you," she blubbered.

"Yes, I heard you. I just... ?
her head in his chest.

Zeke held her there for a
important. Are we moving to

Roxie sat up to look at Z
just that you scared me tonigh

"I said I was sorry for that

"I know you did."

"I was thinking too much
just wasn't thinking. It won't h:

"Zeke, can I be honest?"

"I wish you would."

Roxie took a deep, calmi
"I'm scared of us sometimes, a
fast. We aren't moving too fas
at times."

"What do you mean?"

Roxie took Zeke's hand i
him to see. "This, skin to skin
It floods my whole body with
normal. It's..."

"Wrong?"

"No, not wrong. It's-" Rox
focused on the feeling. "It feel
warning of something bad to
sounds crazy."

"I know. I'm sorry. I won't do it again."

"You better not. My brothers are going to kill you, you know."

Zeke sat up on the couch, pulling Roxie along with him and right into his lap, wrapped tight in his arms. "I'm sorry," he whispered soothingly against her temple. "I just got so irritated when I saw the door. It scares me to think something could happen to you. I wanted to get my point across somehow. I shouldn't have done that."

"No, you shouldn't. And-and, I only left the door open because I saw you parking the car. I knew you were right behind me."

"That isn't good enough. I was downstairs. Anything could have happened before I got up here."

"You're really paranoid, you know that?"

"I know. Just humor me, please."

"You are in no position to be making demands. I'm still mad at you."

"I know you are." He reached up and wiped the tears from her face. "Let me make it up to you."

"No!"

"Come on, Red, please. Tell me what I can do."

Roxie shook her head vehemently, not trusting her voice to stay steady.

"You're not going to forgive me?" he asked running his lips back and forth across hers and giving her big, pleading puppy dog eyes.

"Stop. Stop trying to distract me."

"Is this distracting?" He kissed her softly.

"Mmm-hmm."

Elizabeth Lee Sorrell

"Sorry, how about this?"
behind her earlobe.

"Mmmm."

He kissed along her nec
wake. "Still mad at me?"

"For what?" Roxie asked
neck. He sucked gently and t
soft lips.

"Hungry?"

"Yes," Roxie answered loi

Zeke stood up hastily dr
said with a seductively wicke

"What?"

"You said you were hung
on the table. "We should eat

"I... you... what?" All the
She let Zeke guide her to the

Zeke threw away the tras
couch, and sat her down in hi
serious."

"No, Zeke, no more toni
take anymore tonight, really."

"Do you think we are mc
her resistance. "I mean I know
scare you off. So, are we movi

"What?" she asked stunr

"Red, are you even listeni

"Your body is warning you about me? You're right; it sounds crazy." Zeke kissed her long and hard. "So, what do you want to do about it?"

"I don't know," Roxie answered honestly.

"You're sure we're not moving too fast?" Zeke asked again.

"I'm sure. Are we moving too fast for you?"

Zeke smiled a smile that lit up his entire face. "Absolutely not, I don't think we could move fast enough to make me nervous."

"Wanna' bet?"

"Red," he said softly, "that's a bet you would lose." He caught a stray hair from around her face and tucked it back behind her ear, letting his fingers trail down her neck and across her shoulder. "We could get married tomorrow, and it wouldn't be too fast for me. I'm already sure, but you need time. There is a lot to get used to."

Roxie's breath stuck in her throat, and she didn't know what to say.

"I better be going. It's late, and it would be difficult to explain to Michael that I stayed out to late with his baby sister without telling him about us." He kissed her good-bye shifted her to the couch and let himself out. "Don't forget to lock this door."

Zeke was a whirlwind of emotions. He had made so many mistakes tonight. He was too harsh with Red. His demonstration was too much over the top. He'd made her cry, and it was terrible. He'd never get that image out of his mind, watching the tears that he caused flow down her beautiful cheeks. She just didn't know. She didn't need to worry about her brothers killing him; he was beating himself up enough.

Then if he hadn't upset her enough, he hit her with a discussion of their relationship. He did want to know if they were moving too fast. He wanted to know her thoughts on their relationship, but more than anything after his little stunt over the door, he wanted to know where he stood. He'd upset her, that much was clear, but she was so easily distracted from the whole ordeal. There was no denying the lust in her eyes, but was that enough. He had to know if he had blown it. After she starting talking about her tingling and it being a warning. He knew. It was a warning alright, a warning that her mate was there. She was his mate; of that there was no further denying.

Still, just because he knew, didn't mean he should have put it all out on the line like that. He was going to scare her off. She wasn't a shifter. She didn't know about mates. She didn't know how it felt, how pure, how rare, how perfect. That's what it was, perfect. Their love was perfect. They'd make mistakes; he'd proved that tonight, but if she gave him the chance, they'd be happy together. He just couldn't do anything to run her off.

Chapter Sixteen

Zeke pulled up to the only traffic light that he passed between Red's apartment and his house. It was on a timer and stopped him despite the fact that the road was deserted other than himself. As his car came to a complete stop a man walked up and tapped on Zeke's window. Zeke rolled the window down to find out what the man wanted. He was somewhere in his mid-fifties. His salt and pepper hair was disheveled, and he was dressed warmly enough that Zeke got the idea the man planned to be sitting outside rather late when the temperature began to drop.

"You headed home? It's late to still be out," the man said.

"Yes, it is," was the only response that Zeke offered.

"You be careful wondering around out here this late. There have been sightings of a wild dog, big rascal, been known to attack for no reason," the man warned. Zeke resisted the urge to smile at the man's bogus claims. Sightings indeed. Roxie was the only one who had sighted him and lived to tell the tale, and Zeke was confident that she had not talked to this man.

"Is that right?"

212

"Yeah, it's a violent monster. Don't let it catch you out here unarmed."

"That's kind of strange for a dog to attack for no reason. Usually there is a reason, even if it is as simple as extreme hunger or territorial protection," Zeke pointed out.

"Look, there is an attack on record at the police station. I'm out here tonight to try and hunt the creature."

"Is that legal?"

"What are you, one of those nature loving yuppie tree huggers?"

"Nah, I just know the person who called the police to make that report. I'd say that dog had a reason. It saved her life."

"It could have killed your friend. She's lucky to be alive, and we are going to make sure she stays alive."

"We? How many of you are hunting for the dog?"

"Enough."

"Ok, well, good luck." They're going to need it, Zeke thought as he pulled away. It wasn't luck against him that they would need; it would take a lot of luck to keep them alive now that they have chosen to side with an aggressive gang.

After he got home, Zeke decided to take a little walk, have a look around. He wanted to know just how close these so-called hunters were coming to the house and to Red's apartment.

They sat in trees, on the ground, on stands. There were all sorts of men out tonight waiting in all sorts of places. Some even had night vision goggles sitting to their side. No doubt they were waiting to hear the slightest sound before grabbing up their goggles to survey the surroundings, but none of them had strong enough hearing to notice Zeke's stealthy wolf body slipping through the shadows.

The hunters were considerably closer to Red's apartment than they were to his house, proving that they had no idea what they were doing. Any normal wolf in the wild would stay in an area less populated, not to mention that his house was closer to the parking garage where Red had been attacked. Were these men really that stupid? What had they been told about the wild dog? At least tonight proved that the hunters were not all that big a threat if he was careful; however, he really did not want armed and ignorant hunters camped out that close to Red.

Zeke knew he had to get them out of there before anyone got hurt, including themselves. They had no idea what they had gotten themselves into. They needed to be as far away from the hostilities as possible. It was nothing new for him, but for them, it would be war the likes of which those hunters had never dreamed of. He could find a way to scare them off, but that would be a last resort. He decided this may be a battle better fought through legal paperwork. He would call Kris in for reinforcements tomorrow. He wouldn't have thought of bringing Kris into his problems before, but now it involved Red. Anything threatening Red was a mutual foe.

Lunch was an easy time to slip away for a minute to make a phone call. Plus, by waiting that late, it would ensure that Kris would be up.

"Yeah," Kris answered on the third ring.

"Hey, remember that wolf that attacked Red's attacker?" Zeke started off with no preamble.

"Not you too, man. The likelihood that a wolf would come that far into the business district and defend Red is astronomical. The only reason a wolf would be around civilization like that was if it were desperate for food, in which case the attacker's body would have been desecrated and Red would have been attacked too."

"Look, it doesn't matter what it was or why it did what it did. The reason I'm calling is because I ran into a hunter on my way home last night. He said they were out hunting for a wild dog that had been attacking for no reason. It wasn't just the one who I spoke with either. The area is crawling with hunters eager to kill what they deem a killer, and they are way too close to Red's place for comfort."

"What'd you do?"

"Nothing yet."

"Ok, just hold off. I think I know a couple of guys who can help us out on this one, but keep an eye on my sister, will ya.'"

"No problem. Thanks, Kris, I owe you one."

"You don't owe me anything. We were trained as a team, and we'll always be a team."

"Right."

"I'll talk to you later, after I've worked it out."

"Bye."

Zeke got to Red's as fast as he could that evening. He didn't want her to be alone at her apartment any more than absolutely necessary. Red opened the door almost immediately following his knock. Her breathtaking smile was the first thing he noticed.

"You're early," she enthused.

"Are you keeping your door locked?"

Her enthusiasm deflated and fell into a look of wariness. "Yes, don't go all psycho on me again."

"I am sorry about that. I spoke to a hunter on my way home last night. He was only one of dozens. He said they were out here hunting for a wild dog." Zeke waited for understanding to seek in.

"Dog? The only dogs around here are pets. Why would they be hunting them?"

"Not domestic dogs, wild dogs. Like the wolf from your attack."

Red's eyes widened. "But why would they be hunting him? He hasn't done anything!"

"He did attack a man," Zeke pointed out cautiously afraid that Red might take the hunter's side.

"That man was holding me at gunpoint. If that wolf had truly wanted to attack just for the sport, he would have turned and attacked me too. He... there was just something about him. They can't kill him Zeke, they just can't." Her voice was cracking. Maybe telling her hadn't been the right thing. He wanted her to be on alert with those hunters on the loose, but he did not mean to hurt her.

"Hey," he said pulling Red against his chest. She wrapped her arms around his waist and leaned into him. "You said you saw him at the campgrounds, right?"

"Yeah, but what if he comes back? It could happen, and there's just something special about that wolf. You must think I'm crazy."

He thought her to be an incredible blessing but not crazy. She had no idea how special that wolf was. The fact that she felt anything out of the ordinary toward Zeke in wolf form was encouraging. "No, you're not crazy. It's not the wolf I'm worried about though. If he has survived this long, it sounds like he can take care of himself. It's you I'm worried about. They are vigilante hunters, and they are stationing themselves very close to the apartments. I want you to be careful, ok? People like this aren't always playing with a full deck when they get this obsessed. Promise me you'll be careful."

"I promise, but the wolf..."

"I've already got Kris working on that problem. He said he thought he knew some guys who could help. He'll call when he hears something more."

"Kris is helping to save a wolf he doesn't even believe in?" Red asked skeptically.

"He believes there was a canine of some sort there that night, but no, you're right he isn't helping to save your wolf. He's doing this to help protect you."

"Ok, I haven't finished supper yet, so make yourself comfortable." She turned toward the kitchen, but Zeke heard her whisper, "My wolf," as she walked away like she was trying the words out to see how they felt on her lips. He smiled at her retreating back. She just had no idea, definitely her wolf.

Zeke sat down on the couch and found an action movie on TV. Soon he was engrossed while Red worked away in the kitchen. She had been in there for a while, but he hardly noticed. Finally Red came into the living area with two bowls in her hands. She handed one to Zeke and sat down snuggling into his side.

"We're eating in here?"

"I thought it would be a nice change. You're watching a movie, right?"

"Yeah." He looked down into the bowl and saw notable hunks of meat in his own bowl that seemed to be missing from Reds. He gave her a quizzical look.

Red gave him an impish smile and said, "Don't look at me like that. It's vegetable soup, so don't skip the vegetables. And, don't try to hide them either." Zeke leaned in to kiss her meaning it to be anything but a chaste kiss, but Red pulled back. "Stop, you're going to make me spill the soup." Zeke took the bowl from Red's hands and sat them both on the coffee table. He turned to hover over her and backed her down until she was lying underneath him on the couch before covering her lips with his own.

It was all over for Roxie. She was done for. In her head she knew that she didn't have time for a serious relationship, but her heart said too late and was singing na na na na boo boo. She would do anything for this man, go anywhere and be anything. It didn't matter that she had spent so much time and effort fighting her way to the top in the business world. She would give all that up without a moment's hesitation if Zeke asked her to. That's how hard and fast she had fallen for him. She had never believed before that someone could fall in love so fast, but there was no arguing what she felt at this point.

"Mmm, I love you," Roxie panted, pulling away to catch her breath.

Zeke pushed away a loose strand of hair that had stuck to her face. "I love you," he whispered.

"You want to have dinner at Mom's Friday night?"

"Sure."

"I'll call her tomorrow and tell her about us. I want to tell Kris and Michael Friday."

"Are you sure?" He was giving her a way out, but she saw the way his eyes lit up at the prospect. This was something that would make him very happy, and Roxie wanted so badly to make him happy.

She laid her hand on his cheek and ran her thumb over his lips. "I am very sure."

Zeke gave her a heart melting smile and a slow seductive kiss. "Thank you."

Roxie did not know how to respond to that. You're welcome seemed a bit conceded, but what else should she say? She settled for changing the subject. "You better eat your soup before it gets cold."

Zeke sat up again, pulling Roxie into his lap. "Let it get cold. It's a small price to pay for you agreeing to tell your brothers. What changed your mind?"

"Nothing, I always knew that if things worked out I'd have to tell them eventually. It's time."

"Is this your way of telling me that you think we are working out pretty well?"

Roxie took a deep breath, swallowed down the lump in her throat, and prepared to put it all out there on the line. "I think we passed right by working out well. If someone had told me even a month ago that it was possible to fall in love this fast, I would have believed them fools, but we went straight from just friends to very serious."

The smile that stretched Zeke's face taut fell, and he looked at her very thoughtfully. "Do you think you and I could ever have been classified as just friends?"

Roxie gave it a minute, mulling it over in her mind. "Maybe, that first day we met in my office."

Zeke laughed and said, "I couldn't believe that Kris forced me on you like that."

"Me either, but I'm not sorry."

"Why? I high tailed it out of your office as fast as my legs could carry me. It wasn't until Kris forced me on Michael that our paths crossed again."

"True, but I was drawn to you from the first time I saw you. It's your eyes. It's cliché, I know, but a person really could get lost in your eyes… I think that's why I'm so fascinated with the wolf. That's it! That was what was so familiar about the wolf's eyes. He really does have your eyes! You don't think they'll really kill him do you?"

"Kris will take care of it. Don't forget your mom's part in our relationship. Do you think she really was trying to push us together, or did she just want to make sure I ate?"

"Knowing Mom, both… Kris and Michael will know something is up. Mom won't be able to hide it."

"You think she'll tell them?"

"No, she'll wait and let me do that myself, but she won't be able to hide that something is up."

"You must get that from your mom."

"What!?"

"Your emotions are written all over your face."

"Oh, is that right?"

"Yes, that's right. You're lucky everyone was too immersed in the fun of the trip for you to give us away on the camping trip."

"No, no one knew."

"No thanks to you. You could not have been more obvious avoiding me the way you did."

"What was I supposed to do? I really did think that Kris had threatened you when we got to the table."

"Kris? Not a chance. He knows better. He's seen me fight, and he knows he wouldn't stand a chance."

Roxie couldn't help the giggle that escaped her throat. "You know? I always wondered what kind of guy could survive my brothers. It figures I'd fall for someone just as violent as them."

"And, I'd tried so hard to hide that side," Zeke teased.

Chapter Seventeen

Roxie called Mom on the way to work. She knew that Lucy would be able to tell something was up and would not stop until she had dragged it from her. Mom had been kept in the dark long enough. She deserved to hear it first.

"Mom, do you think we could all have dinner together Friday night?"

"Sure, sweetheart, what's up?"

"I'm going to bring Zeke... We've been seeing each other."

"That's wonderful. He is such a sweet boy. How long?"

"Well, technically nothing started until the camping trip, but it's already serious. I don't know how much longer I could hide it from Kris and Michael, and I don't think I should."

"They'll be fine. It's time they accepted you aren't a baby anymore."

"I know. I'm just scared it will jeopardize the relationships they have with Zeke."

"What does Zeke think?"

"He never liked the idea of hiding it."

"Your brothers are adults now. It will be fine; just you wait and see. I can't wait. Is there anything special you would like me to cook?"

"No, anything you'd like. Are you sure you don't mind? I mean we can all go out somewhere if you don't want to cook."

"Don't be ridiculous. This is a big occasion."

"Mom," Roxie whined, "it's not like we are engaged."

"Maybe not yet, but this is the first boy I can ever remember you bringing home to meet your brothers."

"Maybe that's because they would beat up anyone who showed any interest."

"Oh, they were just over protective, but they've grown up. Give them a chance, sweet pea."

"Ok, we'll see. I'll see you Friday. Thanks, Mom. I love you."

"I love you too, sweetheart. Bye."

Lucy's reaction was not at all what Roxie had been expecting. She had expected some more of that rousing excitement Lucy had been sporting up until now.

"Oh, Roxie, I'm all for telling your brothers, but are you sure you should be taking things so serious this soon?"

"I thought you'd be happy for me."

"I am, Rox, I just want you to be careful. I wanted you to get out there and have a little fun, live a little. I didn't mean that you should hurry up and settle down. If anything you're already too responsible."

"How can you be too responsible?"

"You know what I mean. You need to lighten up."

"I am. I'm more carefree when I'm with Zeke than I have been in years. I'm telling you, you wouldn't recognize me."

"If you're sure, I just hope you know what you're doing."

Zeke drove to Mom's on Friday night. It was a good thing too. Roxie was too anxious to focus; she never could have driven like that. She knew it was time. Mom and Zeke both thought that it would be fine. Roxie only wished she could be that calm about the whole thing. She was imagining every horrible thing that might happen.

Michael might fire him. Maybe Kris would call Zeke out. Would they go to the backyard to duke it out? Would Michael join the fray? Would they really gang up on Zeke like that, two on one? What would she do to stop it? What could she do? What if Mom tried to stop them? Mom could get seriously hurt stepping into the middle of such a disastrous encounter. Kris and Michael were both strong in their own rights, but Roxie had a feeling she was only beginning to scratch the surface on how strong Zeke was. Would she have to call the cops to come break it up? Could she call the cops without pressing charges? Was that allowed? She didn't want anyone getting in trouble, but she didn't want anyone getting hurt either. Would they need an ambulance?

"Red, calm down. Everything is going to be fine," Zeke said breaking through her thoughts.

"I can't help it. Nothing like this has ever turned out well with my brothers."

"That's because you never brought me home before," he said with a cocky grin.

"Ok, we'll see, but don't say I didn't warn you."

Zeke and Roxie were the last ones to arrive at Mom's, and nothing appeared out of the ordinary. The only sign of the extraordinary was the frantic beating of Roxie's heart.

"It's about time you two got here, I'm starved," Kris welcomed them.

"Oh, Kris, hush, and use your manners. I know I taught you some," Mom scolded. "Everything is on the table, sweetheart. You two come on in and sit down.

Roxie eyed the spread on the table. Mom had gone all out, and Roxie was not the only one who thought so. "So, what's up, Mom?" Michael asked. "And, don't say nothing. This much food doesn't say nothing."

"Sit down, Michael. We'll get to that later," Mom said firmly.

Michael and Kris shared a look then looked at Roxie, who tried to school her face and give them no reaction. If they weren't suspicious before, they certainly were now. If Roxie knew Kris and Michael, the curiosity would eat at them until they knew exactly what was going on. The boys didn't disappoint either. They were only five minutes into the meal before they started pushing for answers; except, this time Mom was through covering.

"Ok, it's later," Kris announced. "So what's going on?"

"Yeah, is it serious?" Michael pushed.

"That is something you'll have to ask your sister," Mom said simply.

Roxie took a deep breath. It was now or never. "I asked Mom to have this dinner tonight. I have something to tell everyone." Roxie took another deep breath. This wasn't getting any easier, but then she never expected it to. Zeke reached underneath the table and gave Roxie's hand a reassuring squeeze. "Well ..."

"Just spit it out already, Red. You're starting to scare me," Michael ordered.

"Yeah, is something wrong?" Kris asked.

"No, it's nothing like that. Something is right. This is good news." That seemed to relax Kris and Michael a bit, but they were still anxiously watching her. "It's... um ..."

"Do you want me to tell them?" Zeke whispered.

"No." Roxie took another deep breath. Isn't that what people told you to do to calm down? Her heart was nearly beating out of her chest it was flying at such a rapid rate. Was it possible to be scared to death? Could it actually give you a heart attack? She took a deep breath and tried again. "Zeke and I are dating," she said in a rush.

Michael picked up his glass of water and looked down to his plate like it held the secret to life. He took a slow sip of water and placed the glass back on the table without moving his stare from his plate. He moved to pick up his fork, but his movements were slow and robotic.

Kris stared at Zeke. Roxie couldn't judge the emotions she saw on his face. Was it anger? Betrayal? Confusion? He shifted his glace to Roxie, and she felt like his stare was burning a hole straight through her. He looked back to Zeke. Then he returned to his meal but silently this time.

Neither Kris or Michael were reacting at all. That was certainly not what Roxie had expected. Was this somehow worse? She was left sitting there waiting for them to explode or implode or something.

And here came Mom to the rescue. "The two of you make such a cute couple. How long have you been dating?" Mom knew the answer. She had already asked all these questions. None of this was for her benefit. She was trying to get the conversation moving again and ask the questions that Kris and Michael could not find a voice to ask.

"Officially, since the camping trip," Roxie answered.

"Officially? How long unofficially, and what exactly does that mean?" Mom asked kindly. Roxie had to admit it was a lot easier getting grilled by Mom than her overgrown brothers.

"It's been a long time coming. I guess really from the first day we met," Zeke answered glancing at Roxie for confirmation. Roxie nodded her agreement before Zeke continued. "It all just came to a head at the camping trip."

"At the camping trip, dear, or after?"

Uh-oh! Why did she have to ask that? How would Kris and Michael react if they find out this whole thing got started right underneath their noses?

"That depends how technical you want to get. It all came to a head on the camping trip. I guess it wasn't so hard to talk to Red when she is upset after all," Zeke replied. Oh, Zeke, don't take a jab at Kris right now, Roxie thought. "We did not really get a chance to talk it through until we got back. That was when we decided to make it official."

"Why didn't you say anything before?" Michael finally spoke up.

Zeke shrugged his shoulders. "Red wasn't ready."

Kris and Michael's heads both snapped up in Roxie's direction in a cold, hard, shocked glare. Way to throw me to the wolves, Zeke! "Well, what would you have done in my situation? Y'all don't have the best track record for meeting my boyfriends."

"What boyfriends?" Michael asked.

"Exactly, boys have always been too scared of you to come near me!"

"So, is it serious?" Mom interrupted.

"Yes," Roxie declared matching Kris and Michael glare for glare.

Kris glanced at Zeke who gave a sight nod. Kris seemed to visibly relax. His shoulders slumped into a more comfortable position rather than rigid and stiff. He let his face fall into a normal expression, and he leaned back in his chair. Kris started eating like it was just a normal family meal. What was that some kind of secret code he and Zeke shared? Roxie looked quizzically at Zeke, but he just shrugged.

Michael was still floundering, trying to grab hold of something stable. "How serious?"

Roxie looked again to Zeke. This time they both shrugged. "Very," he answered.

"You've been in a serious relationship with my sister and came into work every day this week and never said anything?"

"It wasn't my place," Zeke answered intently. "I always knew that Red would tell you when she was ready."

"A week? How serious can you be?" Michael continued.

"It's like Zeke said; it has been a long time coming," Red provided.

"Yeah," Zeke agreed, "we have been steadily moving toward serious long before we made anything official."

"So, you're dating?"

"Mm-hmm," Zeke and Roxie answered together. Michael gave a thoughtful nod. Then with a single quick raise of his eyebrows he too returned to his food like everything was a done deal, case closed.

"Kris, you haven't said too much. What do you think?" Mom inquired.

Roxie held her breath and waited for Kris's reply.

He shrugged then added, "They're adults, none of my business... I had to go after the guys who were interested in Red in high school. They were all stupid jerks who wouldn't have treated her the way she should be treated," he explained like it should have been obvious. "Zeke, knows how to treat her. This was bound to happen one day. Red wasn't going to spend the rest of her life alone. I never wanted that for her either. I know and trust Zeke... with my life. She could do a lot worse than him." He looked up at Roxie. "You did good, kid," he said with a wink.

Roxie smiled. She couldn't believe that it had all gone so well. Kris had even given his blessing. Was this all a dream? She looked at Zeke who was smiling right at her. He gave her hand a more congratulatory squeeze this time. He looked so proud, and he had been right. Kris and Michael had taken it quite well. She decided to press her luck by leaning over and giving Zeke a kiss. It was not an indecently long kiss, but it was still more than a quick peck.

"Oh yeesh," Kris cried throwing a napkin in their direction. "Just because I approve doesn't mean I want to watch the two of you make out. I'm trying to eat over here."

Zeke and Roxie just laughed.

There had been a decrease in hunters since Kris had started talking with his political buddies. Still, there were too many. It had only been a few days. Zeke knew he should give Kris some more time, but Kris understood as well as he did that sometimes time just isn't a luxury we are afforded. Zeke loped around the shadows. The hunters who were left weren't smart enough to spot him if he walked right in front of them. It certainly wasn't his safety he was worried about. He was worried about the hunters... and Red.

Dinner with her family had gone well. She was much more relaxed on the drive home, and happier. Zeke was glad too that he had gone to pick her up rather than meeting her at her mom's. It was out of the way to backtrack, but she really did need that extra support.

The only thing that really upset Michael was that they had hid it from him. Zeke figured that would be an issue, but had figured it would be an issue with both of Red's brothers. He knew that Red was more worried about Kris. She cannot see how much he has matured since they were kids. They saw a lot of things in the military. War will mature you real fast. Kris is more capable than Red can imagine right now. He is a good man, and Zeke was proud to call Kris a friend.

Zeke settled down in the shadows near a couple of hunters who were whispering back and forth.

"Can you believe what that lawyer is trying to pull?"

"Too dangerous to hunt within the city my tail. It's a lot more dangerous to let that dog keep roaming around attacking people."

"Yeah, I heard people are rallying behind that lawyer though."

"Nah, no one can get together that kind of support that quickly."

"Maybe not, but I've got a wife and two kids to think about."

"Like I don't? I don't want my family attacked by some wild animal, and I don't want them afraid to set foot outside our door either."

"I don't want that either, now, but I don't know what my family would do if I get arrested. We don't have that kind of spare change lying around for a rainy day. Not to mention bail bond to get me out, I heard that court fees alone will eat you alive."

"Are you telling me that you're going to let one little old lawyer make your decisions for you?"

"It's not one lawyer. It's two lawyers, both from big law firms. They got a lot of pull."

"Go running home to your family then. Not me. I'm going to stay right here and make this town safe again."

"Have you seen any dogs?"

"No, but it's attacked people."

"There was one report on record with the police. I asked. No one has been able to give specifics on any other attacks. If they really happened, why can't anyone tell us about them? Besides, I haven't seen a single dog, domestic or wild. I hate to say this, but it sounds like someone caught wind of the first attack and made this whole thing up. I'm starting to think we've been had... Maybe the police already found the dog from the attack, huh?"

"Well... I haven't seen anything except a few squirrels. Maybe you're right, and maybe you're wrong. What happens if we all go home thinking we've been had, and it turns out to be true?"

"One attack is all I've been given any proof of. It was at night. So what if that dog is still lose? This place is deserted after dark. We're the only fools out here this late. If that dog is still out here attacking people, it is more likely one of us is the next victim. I'm done after tonight."

Zeke liked this guy. He was a little more reasonable than the others. Much smarter to protect your family on the home front than from a distance. You can't do anything to protect them if you aren't there when the unthinkable happens. The errant thought gave Zeke pause for a moment. He wasn't with Red right now either with careless hunters all over the place. No decent hunter would be sitting in the middle of the business district with a gun, and hunters who think they know more than they do, are the ones who cause accidents.

Should he be closer to Red's apartment? She wouldn't care for him camping out there all night, every night, but she liked him in wolf form too. Would she object if her wolf kept hanging around? How long would it take to clear out all these hunters? No, Red was tucked safely in her bed. What were the odds that something would happen to her in bed? Zeke yawned and decided that bed was where he should be too. There was nothing more he could do here tonight, and he had promised Red he would come by tomorrow.

Chapter Eighteen

"Hey, beautiful," Zeke greeted as Red opened the door.

"Hey yourself, handsome."

Red was dressed casual in jeans and a T-shirt. Her hair was pulled up in a loose ponytail. She was dressed to stay in, and that sounded good to Zeke. It had been a busy week, playing catch up at work, keeping an eye on the hunters, and telling Red's family about their relationship. Zeke was ready for a little down time, and spending a relaxing afternoon with Red was just the ticket.

Zeke grabbed Red by the hips and pulled her to him for a kiss. Their lips molded together perfectly. Had it really only been a week since they had taken that next step? One week had felt like a lifetime of bliss.

"I went by Redbox and rented some movies. You interested?" Red asked.

"Sounds perfect. What have you got?"

"One action and one romance."

They settled in on the couch. Zeke was lounged across the length of the couch, and Red was snuggled into a ball in his lap. They watched the action movie first. Zeke was almost asleep by the end of the movie. He knew he was tired, but he had not realized he was that tired. Red looked up at him and said, "You too, huh?"

"I guess so."

"It's been a long week...but good."

"Definitely good," Zeke agreed accompanied with a long, slow kiss.

When they came up for air, Red said that she would put the next movie in, but as she got up to do so, Zeke slid the rubber band from her hair. All her wild, fire red hair cascaded down her neck and shoulders and tickled her back.

"Hey!" she cried, but Zeke paid her disapproval no attention. He held her wrist and pulled her back down in his lap.

After kissing her soundly he told her, "I like it down."

"I haven't even brushed it today."

"I don't care. It's perfect this way. It's wild like the fire it resembles."

"That's just another way of saying out of control."

"Yes, out of control like an all consuming wild fire."

"There is just no arguing with you."

"Not on this." Zeke ran his fingers though her hair a few times. "It is mesmerizing like a flame, but it's cool to the touch. It's soft, like you."

"Zeke? You really have a thing for red hair, huh?"

Zeke tried to focus in on her face as she spoke, but he had not been kidding when he said her hair was mesmerizing. All he could see was the silken, smooth flame of her hair dancing around her face. He gave his head a shake trying to knock himself out of the daydream. When he finally tore his gaze away from her hair, he was zeroed in on her lips. He leaned down for what he meant to be a quick kiss, but it wasn't. Was it ever with Red? He just couldn't seem to get enough of her. They sat there wrapped around one another on the couch and kissed until his lips were numb, yet he wouldn't trade a second.

Roxie fell to sleep in Zeke's arms as he slowly and lightly ran his fingers through her hair. It was nice falling asleep in his warm, safe embrace. This was the second time. She had better be careful, or she would get used to this.

She woke up to find that Zeke had also fallen asleep. Somewhere along the way it had gotten dark outside, but she couldn't muster enough concern to care. She turned her head deeper into his chest and went back to sleep.

"Red?" Zeke whispered her name and pressed his lips against her temple. This was the best wake-up call she had ever received, and she hadn't even opened her eyes yet. "Red? I think we fell asleep."

"Mmm, what time is it," she asked as she stretched out her stiff body.

"Ten."

"That's not so bad. Let me sleep just a little while longer before you leave."

"Red, it's ten in the morning, not at night."

"What? I never sleep that late." She finally pried her eyes open and stared wide eyed at Zeke.

"Neither do I, but we did today."

"Wow, I guess I was tired."

"Yeah, me too," he agreed. "This week has felt like a month."

Roxie knew what he meant, and it wasn't all the work she had to catch up on or even the stress of telling her brothers about her and Zeke. No, it was more than that. It was Zeke. She felt like she had known him all her life, and it felt like they had been together for years, not just a week. Everything with Zeke was so familiar and comforting. Maybe it had only been a week, but she could never go back to life without him.

"I love you," she told him tenderly.

He smiled and ran his fingers across her lips. "I love you too." He gave her a quick kiss and then continued. "Thank you."

"For what?"

"Just for being here, and being you."

"I don't know that, that is something to thank me for."

"It is, Red, it is…Hey, that's the first time we spent the night together."

"Ha, ha, you're-" Zeke cut her remark off and her air, but she wouldn't' dare complain as long as he was kissing her so thoroughly.

"How about I make us some breakfast?" Roxie asked when she finally caught her breath. She got up and started for the kitchen.

"Sounds good. I'm starved; we slept through supper."

"Yeah, and had popcorn for lunch. That's not very healthy. Don't get used to it."

Zeke wrapped his arms around her waist from behind. "Too late." He kissed the side of her neck and continued, "I don't guess Kris and Michael would take the news well if I moved in here to hold you while we slept at night, huh? That's the best sleep I've gotten in a long time."

"No, I don't guess they would," Roxie laughed. They had already said they were serious, but that was the first time Zeke had said anything like that. Was he seriously talking so flippantly about moving in with her? He couldn't be even remotely serious. No, he wouldn't leave his family home. Still...time to change the subject.

"I don't guess we'll make it to church today."

"I'd say that's a safe bet."

"I was going to go with you this week."

"I'm sorry. Next week?"

"Yeah, next week."

"I promise to be more responsible. I'll make sure we make it next week."

"You talk like it is all on you to get us both up and ready for church."

"I was the one who stayed over. If I had gone home when I should have, you would have slept in bed and probably been up a long time by now."

"Oh, stop it. You were asleep. It's not like you did it on purpose. Besides we both slept on the couch, remember. I didn't wake you up to go home any more than you did."

"Still, it isn't right. What would your brothers think if they knew I slept here last night?"

"You know exactly what my brothers would think. That's why we are never going to tell them you slept here. Now, grab the eggs. I'm going to make a meat-full breakfast to make up for all the meals you missed yesterday."

Instead of getting the eggs, Zeke spun her around to face him. "I don't deserve you," he whispered before devouring her lips. By the time he stopped kissing her silly, Roxie forgot all about refuting his claim even though she was pretty sure she was the one who didn't deserve him.

Zeke left Red's early Sunday night. There was no sense in tempting fate twice. Her mother had already called earlier that afternoon to make sure she was alright after missing church. Zeke didn't need to be around late that night if Kris, on some crazy whim, decided to come by and check on Red. Kris did keep some odd hours after all, but then again, Zeke was not one to talk. After all he was on his way home to drop off his car and set back out in wolf form.

Most of the hunters were gone. Only a few remained. It was amazing what Kris could do with some high profile contacts and a handful of days. The few that remained were not all that sober, and Zeke was sure that a couple of them belonged to the gang before the hunters showed up. Zeke was relieved that the hunters were gone. He wouldn't have to worry about Red as much, and he could get back to business as usual. However, he still worried about the hunters' safety. What would the gang do to deserters, even deserters who never knew about the gang?

Surely the gang leader had better sense than to start killing off that many hunters. It would most assuredly attract attention, and then Zeke would not be the only one after this gang. He wasn't sure if the extra help would be a good thing or if they would just be in his way. Either way, though, it wasn't worth risking anyone's lives.

Zeke headed in the direction of the last known head quarters. It was possible that they had moved locations while he was busy with camping trips and ignorant hunters. It was a starting point, though, and he really wanted to know what if any danger the hunters were in.

Zeke was somewhat surprised to find the gang had not moved locations yet. Were they really that stupid? All the lights were on inside, and Zeke could see movement through the windows. He curled up and got comfortable next to the building underneath a cracked window. Tonight was all about reconnaissance, and with his enhanced hearing, a cracked window was all he needed.

"Well, that's that. All the hunters are gone except three, and those three are raging alcoholics who couldn't hit the broad side of a barn, much less spot a dog the size of a black bear."

"It isn't the size of a black bear. I'm telling you, no canine gets that big."

Zeke mentally rolled his eyes. He wasn't the size of a black bear, but the first guy had not been too far off. Most black bears did not get much bigger than he was in wolf form. He was a rather large wolf, and black bears are a rather small bear.

"It doesn't matter how big it is. It's a nuisance. It is picking us off one by one, and someone needs to kill it."

"Are you suggesting that we are being targeted by a dog?"

"What other explanation do you have? The only attacks have been on our members. No one else has been attacked. What about that girl at the parking deck? The dog left her standing there."

Zeke tensed when he heard them mention Red. He did not like these lowlifes talking about Red.

"Yeah, what about that girl? Why did the dog not attack her?"

"Maybe she's like some kind of dog whisperer."

"That's enough. I want eyes on this girl. I want to know who she is and what she knows about this dog, and if she is stupid enough to walk alone again, I want her taken care of."

Zeke jumped to his paws with his hackles raised. His blood was boiling, his adrenaline was pumping, and he was seeing red. He stood up on his back paws and placed his front paws on the window pane. Looking inside, it wasn't hard to figure which one had threatened his Red. All the men were looking at one man and nodding their assent.

The man was tall and bulky. His dark hair looked like it had not been washed in a couple days and not brushed in a week. He had dark skin hidden beneath his baggy clothing. His brown eyes were anything but warm; they appeared cold, and Zeke was sure he could see murder in those vile eyes. Zeke quickly memorized his features for future use, and his most prominent feature was the big bull's-eye that Zeke had painted across the lowlife's chest. Zeke made a vow then and there that the man who had ordered Red's death would be the next to die.

"How did everything go with your brothers?" Lucy asked.

"Shocking. Michael had a few questions, but in the end he was ok with it. Kris took it even better than Michael did."

"Hon, that is wonderful!"

"Yeah, I guess so."

"You guess so. Rox, what are you talking about? This is what you've been so worried about. This was the reason you were hesitant to go ahead with Zeke, and you guess it is wonderful?"

"No, it is. It's wonderful. I think I'm still just a little shell shocked...Lucy, what do you think about everything? Do you think we are moving too fast?"

"Do you think you are moving too fast?"

"No, it feels like I've known him for years. I haven't though. Are we rushing things?"

"Roxie," Lucy said softly, "no one can answer that for you. My parents knew each other for barely two weeks before they were engaged. It wasn't a long engagement either. They've been happily married for thirty-two years and counting. My brother dated the same girl all though high school and college. They got married right after college and were divorced a year later. Only you and Zeke know if you are moving too fast."

Roxie nodded her head. She had heard both those stories before. Lucy's parents' story was an especially romantic one. It sounded like it came straight from a fairy tale. She and Zeke certainly weren't engaged two weeks after meeting for the first time, but could she be more like Lucy's parents? Roxie was starting to understand why they were not scared out of their minds going into a marriage with someone they barely knew. Logic says that she and Zeke should barely know each other, but she was pretty sure that she knew Zeke as well as anyone else. He must feel the same about her.

Could Roxie see herself engaged sometime soon? Yes. She knew that if Zeke asked her, she would not hesitate to marry him no matter how short a time they had known each other. The more Roxie thought about it, she realized that if Zeke had asked her during the camping trip, the same day as their first kiss, to marry him, she would not have hesitated then either. She thought about it, wracked her brain, but she could not figure out at exactly what point she had given him her heart. How early on would she have agreed to marry him? She had always felt some sort of unspoken connection with him. Before she knew anything else about him, she knew he was special.

"Earth to Roxie," Lucy sing-songed.

"What? Sorry."

"I lost you for a while. You were daydreaming. You've got it bad, girl. I'm going to get back to work."

Roxie attempted to get back to work as well, but she simply could not concentrate. It was taking a toll; none of the numbers were adding up right for her. Finally after her third goof up, she stopped, took a deep breath, and forced herself to focus on the numbers in front of her. Again, the numbers did not add up correctly. It wasn't her lack of concentration that was the problem. The numbers just didn't add up. Someone had made a mistake, a mistake that never should have made it all the way up to her. Looking over all the figures yet again, Roxie began to notice that it wasn't just any mistake, it was a well hidden mistake, and it gave her a very dreadful feeling deep in her gut.

Roxie pressed the intercom button and called out, "Lucy, could you set the auditors up to evaluate the Chicago company."

"Sure, should I tell them it's a routine check-up?"

"No, have them on the lookout for fraud."

"Will do."

How long had this been going on? How long had it taken before Roxie had caught on? She pulled up Chicago's records for the last five years and settled in for a long day.

It was nearly twelve-fifteen before Roxie took a breather, and if her phone hadn't started ringing, she would not have slowed down then.

"Hello," she answered without taking her eyes off her computer screen.

"Hey, you sound distracted," Zeke's voice came from the phone.

"I am."

"I'll make it quick. I was thinking about leaving a little early and meeting you at the office when you get off."

"Oh, Zeke, I've run into some trouble. I'm probably not going to make it out of here on time tonight. I'm so sorry."

"That's ok. I'll be there to walk you to your car whenever you get finished."

"You really don't have to do that. I don't know how long I'll be. It might take a while."

"All the more reason for me to come your way when I get off. You're not walking to your car alone," Zeke insisted.

"You're being ridiculous. What are the chances that something like that would happen again? I'm already nervous enough about it without your paranoia making it worse."

"Whether it is likely or not, your nervousness is reason enough for me to come walk you to the car." His voice was starting to take on an agitated tone. Roxie knew his agitation would only grow until he became authoritative, and she did not have time for that today.

"Ok, Zeke, that's fine, but I can't tell you how late I'll be."

"That's ok. I don't mind. See you then."

"Alright, thanks, bye."

Lucy was the last one to leave out of their building leaving Roxie alone. Lucy had waited as late as she could, but she was adamant that she was not going to walk over to the parking deck after dark. As a matter of fact, she didn't like the idea of Roxie staying so late. She had begged Roxie to leave when she did. Roxie flatly refused, and the only reason that Lucy had relented was because Zeke was on his way to walk Roxie to her car.

Roxie nearly jumped out of her skin when no more than two minutes after Lucy walked out of the office, Zeke walked in.

"Oh my goodness! Zeke! You nearly scared me to death. How did you get in here?"

"I ran into Lucy downstairs on her way out. She let me in."

"Oh... I'm not ready to go yet."

"I'm not trying to rush you. You go ahead and work." Zeke pulled a chair up and made himself comfortable, so Roxie focused back on her work.

Finally Roxie finished going through the Chicago records for up to nearly thirteen years before the inconsistencies ended. "Ok, well, I'll probably be playing catch up for the remainder of the week, but at least I've found the extent of damage done for now."

"Is there anything I can do to help?"

"Not unless you can catch a crook and make them pay back all the money they've cost the company for me."

Zeke gave her a conspiratorial smile and said, "I've had tougher assignments through the military."

"Ok, tough guy, that won't be necessary. I'll tell you what you can do though. You can walk me out to my car." Roxie picked up her purse and briefcase and started for the elevators with Zeke hot on her heels.

"I think that's doable," Zeke responded as he wrapped his arm around Roxie's waist.

"Thank you. I really do appreciate you coming to walk me to the car. I know it's silly, but I do actually feel better knowing that I have a big, strong protector holding on to me tight."

"I know." Zeke leaned his head down and kissed the top of her head. "It makes me feel better too."

Red just had no idea how much better it made him feel to be here and hold her all the way to the car. If she knew what he knew, she probably wouldn't leave the apartment. He didn't blame her. He would love nothing more than to tuck her away somewhere safe until this whole thing blew over, but how would he tell her he got his information?

No, it was better to offer to be the sweet boyfriend and come walk her to the car. If he had his way, she wouldn't be driving to or from work alone, but he would have a hard time convincing her to allow him to drive her. It made him nervous not walking her inside in the mornings; however, the way he understood it, most people arrived to the office at the same time in the mornings. Red walked inside with a group of people each morning.

That would have to be good enough for now, but Zeke would need to take care of the underlying problem as quickly as possible. He wasn't going to be comfortable with Red walking around while there were people gunning for her, and he wouldn't be satisfied until the person who ordered it had been made an example of.

Red was walking as close as she could without tripping over each other's feet. No matter how tough she tries to act, she was still very frightened to be walking alone. He couldn't blame her. The night that she was attacked was one that he would never forget either.

He didn't understand then why her safety was so important to him, so much more important than just any innocent. He understood now that Red is his mate.

He had parked next to Red's car, so he could keep her in his sights as they pulled out. He wasn't going to take any chances in a deserted parking deck. Red had not changed much of her routine. She parked a few spaces down now from where she was attacked. She still parked on the same level. Her car still looked exactly the same. She wouldn't be hard to spot, especially leaving late like tonight.

As they got closer to the car, Zeke could smell something out of place. He pulled Red closer out of instinct. The closer they got the more sure he was that there was someone out there, waiting and watching. He scanned the area, but whoever was out there was hiding. Their smell was all around like they had scoped the area out, but it was strongest off to their right. Zeke turned his body slightly to add a little extra shielding for Red. He didn't know if their spectator would attack with him there, but he wasn't going to take any chances.

The sound of movement was the first warning Zeke had that attack was eminent. He turned to face the attacker head on, pushing Red further behind himself at the same time. His whole body was vibrating with rage. The attacker stepped out of the shadows making him clearly visible. Red gasped.

"Get in the car," Zeke warned.

"Stay right where you are, or I'll shoot pretty boy here," the man threatened. "If you do what I say your boy doesn't have to get hurt." It was a lie. Zeke had seen him, could identify him. This lowlife had no intention of leaving either one of them alive, but that was going to backfire on him.

"Zeke?" Red cried out in a whisper. This guy was scaring her, and Zeke was not going to let that go.

"Get in the car," he repeated.

"It's up to you, girly. Only one of you has to die tonight. Come on over here, and your brave boyfriend lives to fight another day."

Red twitched behind him like she was seriously debating stepping around him. The criminal smiled like he had already gotten his way, and that was all it took for Zeke to snap. His vision went completely red except for the black silhouette of the threat in front of him. Zeke didn't think after that point; he only acted. He was acting on instinct, completely out of control.

Zeke did not come to again until he was standing over the attacker's mutilated body. His clothes were in tatters all around the area, and Red was standing frozen next to the car with silent tears cascading down her cheeks.

Zeke had to report the attack. People would come across the body. Who knows, maybe the police would turn out to be helpful. Thankfully he had an extra set of clothes in his car. It was always a good idea for a shifter to keep a set handy, and he was certainly proving that now. He grabbed his clothes and called the police before going to Red.

She was still standing in the same spot, same stance, staring at the dead body. "Red, look at me." Zeke held her face in both his hands and forced her gaze on him. "Red, the police are coming. I had no choice. I promise I'll explain everything later, but for now, you've got to leave what you saw me do out of your story...Red? Red, look at me. Red, please snap out of it. You're scaring me."

Sirens blared in the not too far distance. They were close. "Red, the police are almost here. Please, talk to me."

The first police car came on the scene. A cop jumped out of the passenger seat. "What happened?"

"That man came out of the shadows with a gun pointed at us. I put my girlfriend behind me and told her to get in the car, but the guy was after her. He told her that he would kill me if she got in the car. I couldn't get her moving. Then some big canine came out of nowhere and attacked the guy. It ravaged the body and just ran off."

"Again?" the officer said. Obviously he must have been one of the cops on scene the first time.

"Yes, my girlfriend was the one involved last time."

"Is she ok?" the cop interrupted.

"I don't know. I can't get her to respond. I think she's gone into shock or something."

"Ma'am, are you ok?" the cop spoke slowly and clearly as if speaking to a child.

"Wolf," was all that Red said.

"Ok, what were you doing here?" the officer asked Zeke.

"She had to work late. I didn't want her to walk to her car alone after what happened last time, so I came to walk her out here."

"Good call. What's your name?"

"Patrick Miller."

"Her name?"

"Sallie Gardner."

"You said this guy was after her?"

"Yeah, I told her to get in the car, and he told her he'd shoot me to get to her. She didn't move, so I told her again to get in the car. He told her that only one person had to die tonight if she cooperated. That's when the wolf, or whatever, came from that area." Zeke gestured to the area to the right behind where he and Red had been standing. "It was after the wolf ran off that I remembered to give you guys a call."

"Your first response wasn't to call the police?"

"No, my first reaction was to assess and deal with the situation."

"Military? What branch?"

"Marines, special forces."

"Alright, is she going to be ok? We could call in an ambulance; the ME is on the way anyway. You live around here?"

"Yeah, about five minutes from here. She lives about fifteen."

"Leave your addresses and stay close. Then you can get her out of here."

Zeke scribbled his address and Red's on a paper the cop handed him. "If I'm not at home, I'll be at hers."

"Thanks."

Zeke helped Red into the car and buckled her in. He left his car in the parking deck until he could come back for it. Red's reaction was scaring him to death. He wanted to get her somewhere where he could talk to her in private, try to talk her down. He needed to get her out of there before she said something he couldn't explain.

She stayed in her trancelike state the entire ride, however short, to her apartment. Zeke opened the door and reached around Red to unbuckle her seatbelt, but she still did not show any signs of responding. Rather than struggle to get her up the stairs in her distracted condition, Zeke scooped her up in his arms and carried her upstairs to her apartment. She clung to her purse like a life line, and it swung awkwardly back and forth as they ascended the stairs.

Zeke found himself cooing in Red's ear as he walked, trying to calm her. "Shhhh, shh, shh, shh, it's ok. I've got you. Everything's going to be fine. Just hang on, Red. We're almost there."

He sat Red on her feet at her apartment door while he fished through her purse for her keys. Zeke knew it was an intrusion. He really should not be going through a woman's purse, but they couldn't stand outside her door all night. And, Red was not going to be finding that key anytime soon.

After unlocking and opening the door, Zeke picked Red up once again to carry her inside. He kicked the door shut behind him and went to lay Red down on the couch. He pried the purse from her arms and put it on the floor at the end of the couch. He tugged a blanket from the back of the couch to tuck around her then went to get a cool, wet rag. By the time he returned with the rag, Red had turned onto her side, but she did not seem any more alert.

He began gently wiping her face and neck down with the rag as he spoke to her. "Red, are you ok? Can you talk to me? Just one little word so that I know you're going to be ok? I can't imagine what must be going through your mind right now, how scared you must be. To be exposed to yet another attack would be traumatic enough, but...Red, I'm not going to let anyone hurt you...ever. You know that, right?...You saw some pretty unbelievable things tonight. I guess you probably want an explanation. If you'll come back to me I'll explain everything to the best of my abilities, and I'll answer any questions you might have...Where are you inside that head of yours?...Red, please, snap out of this. I've got to call your family to let them know what happened. It will be so much easier if I can tell them you're fine...Red...you're scaring me. If you don't snap out of this soon, I-I don't know. I guess I'll take you to the hospital."

Waiting another five minutes, Zeke's nerves hit an all new high. He dialed up Kris, needing someone.

"Hey, what's up?" Kris answered.

"Kris, there has been another attack. I was with Red this time. She's fine. That wolf was back. Red, has gone into shock or something. I've got her back at her apartment, but I can't snap her out of it. Kris...I'm scared." That was hard to admit, but Zeke needed Kris here.

"I'm on my way." That was all Kris said, and he hung up.

Zeke leaned in to kiss Red's forehead. "Hang in there, Red. Kris is coming. He'll know what to do." He pressed his lips against her head again and stayed right there. "I love you," he murmured against her skin. He sat there skin to skin for barely forty-five minutes when Red's front door swung wide. Zeke leaped to his feet ready to fight. He nearly crumpled to the floor with relief when he saw Kris, a worried expression etched on his face.

"How is she?"

"She's still not responding." Zeke was shocked at how frightened his voice sounded even to his own ears.

Kris knelt down next to Zeke to check on his baby sister. He picked up the rag that Zeke had been using on her face and gave it an incredulous look. "Get me a glass of ice water."

"Kris, are you sure?"

"Unless you've got a better idea, get me the ice water."

Zeke followed Kris's lead. It was true that he had no better ideas, and that was why he had wanted Kris here. Kris took the ice water and without hesitation dumped it right over Red's face.

Red jerked up into a sitting position and shrieked with a high pitched protest. "Stop!"

"Red!" Zeke reacted and immediately drug her into his lap. "Thank heavens!"

Red squirmed and pushed back from Zeke then unceremoniously pulled out a lone piece of ice that found its way into her shirt. Then the waterworks began. Finally, Zeke didn't like to see Red cry, but at least this was something he knew how to deal with. He tentatively pulled her back against his chest and whispered, "Ok, it's over now. Everything is going to be ok."

"Red, what happened?" Kris demanded.

"Wolf..." Red struggled to speak.

"Baby, don't. I can fill in the blanks for Kris. Just take it easy." Red nodded and collapsed against Zeke.

Kris scowled at Zeke. "Red, are you ok?" Red nodded her head against Zeke's chest. "Are you hurt?" She shook her head.

Kris sat there for a few more minutes before Red sat up and said, "Kris, I'm fine, honest. You can go. Tell Mom I'm ok, and Michael. I'll call you tomorrow; Zeke will stay." She gave Zeke a questioning look. He nodded.

"Are you sure? I ..." It was obvious that Kris was not used to being dismissed by his baby sister. Zeke was probably the first person she would lean on since her brothers. "Ok...Zeke, call me when you leave out, no matter how late it is, and you call me tomorrow. You don't need to work tomorrow either."

"I-I'll give Lucy a call."

"Ok, well...Zeke?"

"I'll take care of her. Thank you for coming so fast."

"No problem, she's my baby sister. Of course I'd be here fast as possible."

Zeke nodded and followed Kris to the door. Kris dropped his voice to a low whisper and asked, "Was she leaving late again?"

"Yes," Zeke whispered in reply.

"But, you were with her?"

"Yes, I was there to walk her out whether she left late or not, but... I won't let her walk out alone, no matter what."

"Good, I don't like that this happened a second time. What were the odds that she get hit twice? Was there anything you noticed?"

Zeke hesitated before answering. "Yeah, he was there for her specifically. He wanted her, and he was willing to kill me to get to her. He wouldn't have let me live anyway, but he kept telling her that if she would sacrifice herself I didn't have to die." Kris swore under his breath. "I wouldn't let that happen, but ..."

"But what?" Kris urged.

"That was when the wolf burst onto the scene."

"Did the police file a report? Was all that on their report?"

"I just got her out of there. With the way she was reacting, I thought that was best. I gave them an overview of what happened and left both our addresses and numbers so that they could get in touch with us to give a more in depth statement when she's doing better."

"Ok, you stay on them, and I'll make a few calls. I don't want them to let this go until they get to the bottom of it."

"I know, me either."

"Ok, take good care of my baby sister."

"You have my word."

Kris nodded and left. Zeke locked the door behind Kris and turned back to Red to find her standing with her legs spaced slightly apart, hands on her hips, and an accusatory expression that could kill.

"You. Are. In. So. Much. Trouble."

"Red, please, just let me explain."

"Oh, you better believe you're going to explain. I want to know exactly what I saw. How was that even possible? And, you! You let my family believe I was crazy! The eyes, I should have figured it out. I can't believe that you pretended not to believe me on the camping trip!"

"What? I took your side. I agreed that if you said you saw a wolf, then you saw a wolf."

"You said it was highly unlikely that it was the same wolf!"

"What was I supposed to say? Oh yeah, it was the same wolf. I'm sure it was, because it was me both times. Sure, that would go over well. They would have tried to institutionalize us both. As soon as they start to poke and prod on me they would find some interesting oddities."

"I can't believe this!" Red began pacing back and forth across the living room.

"Wait, wait, wait, let me get this straight. You're mad, not because I turn into a large, vicious wolf, but because I didn't back you up to your satisfaction."

"Yes!" she shouted.

"Can you please keep it down? You have neighbors, and I really don't need them overhearing any of this."

"Oh, don't you dare tell me to calm down, buddy!"

"Maybe you'd like me to leave!?"

Red gulped in a huge lungful of air and physically deflated as she let it out. Her shoulders slumped and her face fell. "What?" Red asked in a quiet defeated way.

"Do you want me to leave?" Zeke asked again in a much calmer voice.

"Please, don't leave me alone right now. Zeke, I'm still scared."

Zeke rushed to her and enveloped her in his embrace. Red buried her face in his shirt as an onslaught of tears overtook her.

Chapter Nineteen

Roxie did not know how long she had been crying, but after a while, Zeke sat down on the couch and pulled her down with him. He carefully swept her feet off the floor and folded her into his lap, and she burrowed her face into the space between his neck and shoulder. All she wanted to do was hide in his arms. She was so scared. So much had happened. Too much had happened. After the first attack she told herself that it was coincidence, being in the wrong place at the wrong time. It wouldn't happen again. Besides that, Zeke and her brothers wouldn't let her walk anywhere alone after dark.

But... it did happen again, and this time there was no question of her being in the wrong place at the wrong time. It had been no random mugging. No, that guy had wanted her; he wanted her dead. What had she done to make herself a target? Who was that guy? Why did he want her dead? He had been desperate enough to approach her even while Zeke was with her. Worse than that, he had been willing to kill Zeke to get to her. They could have both died tonight. She was scared. She had so many questions that it made her head spin, and that did not even begin to examine everything she had seen unfold from that point.

Zeke had stood in front of her to protect her. The guy had a gun pulled on them, yet Zeke had still put himself between them. He had been willing to die for her. That in itself was terrifying, overwhelming, and... spoke a great deal about their relationship. Then... it couldn't have been real. She had tried so many times to wake herself, but this was no dream. She was not going to wake up from this nightmare. It had all happened. Zeke had turned into a hulking, volatile wolf right before her eyes. He was a wolf. Not just any wolf, he was the wolf she had referred to as her wolf. Their eyes weren't just similar; they were the same eyes.

She had watched Zeke, in wolf form, kill their attacker. It was... vicious and bloody. He had not just killed the guy. He had ripped into him with fury. Blood and flesh had flown everywhere. The mangled carcass was barely recognizable as a human body by the end. It looked like something straight from a horror movie and just as unrealistic.

The questions she had about the attack were nothing compared to all the questions she had about what Zeke had become and what he had done. Right now, though, she wasn't ready. She couldn't even think about asking questions yet. Right now, she was still struggling to get her hysterical sobs under control. Her eyes stung. Her chest burned. She hurt all over, yet she still cried on. Zeke didn't try to stop her, and he didn't try to talk. He held her tight and rubbed her back. He was letting her get it out of her system. She loved him for that.

Eventually her tears dried up, and she was left with dry, silent sobs that racked her body. She still sobbed uncontrollably, but no more tears flowed. Her body shook violently with both her sobs and tremors.

◆◆◆

The next thing Roxie was aware of was sun coming in her patio doors and shinning in her eyes. She closed her eyes again and started to take inventory. She was curled up into a ball at a funny angle. She was certainly not in her bed since light through the patio doors had blinded her, but the surface beneath her was much too hard and warm to be her couch. Every muscle was tense and sore. Her head was pounding, and her eyes were burning. She moved her head and opened her eyes again.

"Good morning," Zeke's sleep roughened voice scratched. Roxie blinked a few times as last night came crashing back. "How are you feeling?" Zeke asked.

"Like I've been run over, but I'm finished crying if that's what you mean."

"Are you hungry?"

Was she hungry? Her stomach chose that moment to start growling.

"I guess that's a yes," Zeke said. "Why don't you sit tight, and I'll see what I can find."

"What time is it?" Roxie wondered.

"Ten, I've already called the office and talked to Lucy. She said to give her a call when you're feeling better. I tried to tell her you weren't hurt, but I don't think she believed me."

"She must be worried out of her mind. What about my family?"

Zeke chuckled. "I've already talked to each one of them individually. I've talked to Kris and your mom several times. I think your mom wants to come over to check on you. I kept telling her you were still resting, but I don't know how much longer she can hold back."

"Do you think we have time to talk before she shows up?"

Zeke paused and took a breath before answering. "I'll make us some coffee."

Ten minutes later they were seated on the couch with coffee and bagels with cream cheese. Zeke was visibly nervous. His back was rigid. He wasn't relaxed at all, and he wasn't making eye contact. Roxie stood up and pushed Zeke back on the couch before crawling up into his lap like a child. After he let a breath out in a whoosh, his body relaxed, and his arms encircled her, Roxie nudged, "Well?"

"You must have questions," Zeke noted shakily.

Roxie looked up at him thoughtfully and suggested, "How about you start from the beginning, and whatever questions I still have I'll ask when you get finished."

Roxie knew Zeke was holding his breath, but she wasn't sure how to make this situation any easier on either of them. Noticing a smudge of cream cheese on Zeke's top lip, she reached up to wipe it away with her finger, licked the cream cheese from her finger, and gave Zeke a quick kiss. She was stalling as much as he was, and she knew it.

Zeke gave her a weak smile. He took a deep breath and started. "I'm a shifter. Obviously, I shift into a wolf. I was born that way... a very long time ago. We don't age the same as those who don't shift, so we live a lot longer. It is a hereditary thing. I moved to America with my family not long after it was discovered. We came over here to form our own small, family pack. There were others, but we had nothing to do with them. I was away when my family was murdered in what basically equates to a turf war. Wolves are very territorial animals, and we are no different. I got home too late to help them. All I could do was defend our home. I... I ran the invading pack back. I haven't heard anything from them in generations. I don't know if they are still out there or if they all died out. We have to keep our existence secret for obvious reasons. If knowledge went public, the few of us left would be hunted down... They would try at least... Obviously, I do not own all the land around the family home as my family once did, but I still feel very territorial. I told you there has been talk of gang activity around this area. I have seen them. I've been keeping an eye on them and working to combat them. Um... oh, Isabella's grandparents knew our family's secret when they first came to America. They agreed to keep our secret quiet, and we promised our protection in return. There had never been need for that protection until now. A couple of the gang members targeted their restaurant... When I leave here each week night, I park my car at a spot between here and my house. Then I shift and do reconnaissance, prevent movement by the gang, whatever is needed. When I went after your first attacker, that was the first physical attack I had made against one of their men. You were a randomly chosen victim the first time, but now they blame you for the wolf attacks. They are specifically targeting you now. That's why, if you've noticed, I've been significantly more overprotective. I promise you, though, I won't let anyone hurt you, and I will get the one who put out the order."

Roxie nodded. "Is that it? Is there anything else I need to know?"

"Yes."

"Do tell."

"Wolves mate for life. I thought I had found that once, but... I never believed I would find a mate, but I did. I found you."

"What does that mean? You want to turn me?"

Zeke rolled his eyes. "That would be werewolves, and they are a myth. I can't turn anyone. It's... a lifelong commitment, much stronger than today's marriage. It's an unbreakable bond that runs deep, perhaps all the way to our DNA, who knows? That means that if you choose now or ever to leave me, I will still remain loyal, and you will always have my protection. There's no falling out of love, no irreconcilable difference on my part. You're it. You will always have my heart."

Roxie reached her arm around Zeke's neck and hugged him close then whispered, "It is a shame I'm all cried out, because that was very sweet."

"Red, I need to ask a favor," Zeke said, his face stone cold serious. Roxie sat up and listened intently. "You can't tell the police or anyone else about me shifting and attacking that guy."

"Well, of course not. Why would I do something so stupid? You've already said that you would be hunted and killed. As for anyone else... I suppose most people would think I'm crazy, but could you imagine if I entrusted that information to my family even? My mother would worry herself into an early grave, and my brothers would want you out of the picture. They'd worry you're too dangerous for their baby sister. No, I wouldn't tell anyone. This is our little secret. I'm still confused though. How is this even possible?"

"I don't know really. We were just always different. No one knew if it was like that from the beginning or if something happened to change our bloodlines. We didn't have DNA testing around back in the day, and since it is so obviously a hereditary thing, it wouldn't be wise of me to walk into a hospital for blood work."

"How did you get around that in the military?"

"I fudged a few papers. Bribed who I could. I couldn't very well tell them my real age or anything like that, so..."

"How old are you?"

"Are you sure you want to know?... Two hundred and forty-nine."

"Wow... you're really robbing the cradle," Roxie teased.

"That's rich coming from someone dating a guy old enough to be her ancestor," Zeke returned with a smile.

"Do you age?"

"Slowly."

"What will I tell my family in a few years?"

"Eventually we'll have to tell them the truth, but I'd like to put that off as long as possible if that's ok with you. Maybe..."

"Maybe what?"

"Maybe we won't have to tell them. There was a theory that when a wolf took a human mate, they would age accordingly. It isn't right to outlive your mate. I can only imagine how devastating that would be."

Roxie nodded. "Will you still want me when I'm old and wrinkled?"

"Did you miss what a mate is? No matter what you do or how you change I will always love you." Roxie nodded and laid her head back down on Zeke's shoulder.

"I can't believe you are taking this so well," Zeke marveled. "I was so scared to tell you. I knew I had to tell, and I had to tell you soon if we were going to have any kind of life together. But, I dreaded it so much."

"I may have more questions later," Roxie warned.

"That's fine. I imagine there are many unanswered questions right now. I'll answer any questions you have. I'm just so psyched that you aren't leaving me."

"I love you."

"I love you too." Zeke leaned in to kiss Roxie. It wasn't just a quick kiss like she had given him earlier either. It was a fiercely passionate kiss. He pressed his lips hard to hers, but just as he was starting to deepen the kiss, someone knocked on her door.

With a groan, Roxie pulled away and went to stand up. Zeke pulled her back to the couch next to him and said, "Let me." He was in business mode. This must have been what he was like in the military. Roxie was not about to get in his way. Zeke looked through the peep hole before opening the door wide. Roxie was surprised to see Mom emerge from behind the door.

"Mom! What are you doing here?"

"What do you mean what am I doing here? My baby was attacked. Of course I came to check on you! All Zeke would say is that you weren't hurt and that you were resting. Kris said you weren't doing all that great last night and that you didn't look very good when he left."

"I'm fine. I was just shaken up that's all. Zeke was here to look after me."

"And, praise the Lord he was! There's no telling what would have happened to you if he hadn't been there!"

Before Roxie could respond, Mom had crossed the room, closing the space between them, and encased her in a crushing hug. "Oh, my baby! I was so scared. I wanted to come with Kris last night, but he didn't think it was a good idea, said he could get here faster if I wasn't griping about his driving. I cringe thinking about the break neck speeds he must have flown. I think the truth is he was scared what he would find when he got here. You know how protective he can be. He didn't want me seeing you hurt or worse."

Roxie could feel big, fat, crocodile tears dripping on her shoulder. "Mom, I wasn't hurt. Seriously, he never got near me. Zeke didn't let him. I was just scared."

"Well, I guess so! How could you not have been scared?"

"It all just hit me a little hard. I was in shock or something, but I'm fine now. You can relax."

"You do look ok," said Mom, who was busily taking inventory of Roxie's body. "Michael is panicked. I'm going to call and let him know that you are ok."

"I told him that she was fine," Zeke interjected.

"I know, Zeke. I know, and it isn't that we don't trust you. We really don't mean any insult, but put yourself in our position. Wouldn't you want to see for yourself, with your own eyes?"

"I guess so."

"I wouldn't be surprised if Michael still comes by after work. That is why I'm going to stick around for a bit. I'm going to take care of meals."

"Mom, we just finished breakfast not too long ago. We don't need anything," Roxie argued.

"Good, I can focus more on dinner. I don't want you to worry about anything, and I know Zeke can't cook. Now, just let me take care of everything."

"Mom, what about Kris?" Roxie countered.

"I'm sure Kris will be around here long before dinner."

"Mom? I don't have room enough for everyone over here at once."

"Don't be silly, sweetheart. There's plenty of room. We'll eat in the living room. Maybe we could watch a movie while we eat. Zeke, why don't you take Red into town to rent a movie, get her mind off things?"

"Yes, ma'am," Zeke answered, the traitor.

As soon as they were out the door, Roxie asked, "What just happened here? Who pays rent on that apartment anyway?"

"She's just trying to take care of you the only way she knows how. Be glad you have people around you who love you so much."

"I am glad, but I told her I was fine. I don't need her to take care of me."

"Oh, come on, Red," Zeke goaded wrapping his arms around her waist from behind. He nuzzled her neck with little nibbling kisses. "You aren't the only one who was shaken up. I was scared to death when you wouldn't respond. I didn't know what to do, and I was frantic when I called Kris to come to the rescue," he whispered.

Roxie turned around in his arms and placed a kiss right on his lips, just a chaste peck. I'm sorry I scared you. It was a lot to take in all at once. I mean the idea of being attacked again, the idea that he was after me specifically, and then you... I didn't know what to think. I still don't know what to think. The only thing I know is that I love you enough to figure it out."

"I love you too. That's sort of the thing with mates; they're inseparable. No matter what, they don't give up on one another. I wasn't sure if that would apply to you since you're not a wolf, but..."

"Do you feel a weird tingling any time we touch, skin to skin contact I mean?"

"Do you?"

"Well... yes?"

"Wow, we've got a lot to talk about, later. Right now let's go pick out a movie before your mom gets worried."

<h1 style="text-align:center">Chapter Twenty</h1>

The night drug on, but at least Zeke wasn't the only one waiting for it to end. He had talked Red into renting a romantic comedy from Redbox just to drive Kris and Michael up a wall. It worked too. Neither of them said a word out loud, because this night was really about Red. If she wanted a romantic comedy, they'd suffer through it for her. Plus their mom was already excited going on about how she had been wanting to see that movie, but all that didn't stop Kris from giving Zeke a sidelong glance when Red first told them what they had rented. Both guys were barely keeping their eyes opened through the movie. Zeke didn't care for the movie much more than they did, but he had better things to occupy his attention with Red held fast in his lap.

Anytime he thought Kris and Michael were both oblivious, Zeke would kiss Red's neck with a barely there brush of his lips. He had gotten caught a couple times. Kris shot him a look that said, not cool, man. Kris might have been ok with Zeke's relationship with his baby sister, but that didn't mean he wanted it flaunted in his face. Zeke couldn't blame him really. He would have felt the same way if his sister had ever found her mate before...

The movie ended and everyone said goodnight. Red told them that she was planning to take at least one more day off work just to compose herself, and Michael insisted that Zeke take tomorrow off as well to keep an eye on Red. Red was actually doing a lot better now, but that didn't mean that Zeke was going to argue having a whole day to spend with Red.

They finally left. After shutting and locking the door behind them, Red turned and rounded on Zeke. She had a look of determination in her eyes, and Zeke did not know what he was in for. He braced himself for whatever onslaught came his way. His muscles tensed. He stood tense and wary.

Red threw her arms around the back of his neck and pulled his head down, fitting their lips together. They stood in the doorway kissing for several minutes before Zeke pulled back and asked, "What was that for?"

"I've been waiting all night to do that. You were driving me crazy with your lips all over my neck."

"What like this?" Zeke asked with a mischievous smile. Then he dove at her neck and covered it in chaste kisses. He moved so quickly that she squirmed and giggled at the relentless tickle at her throat.

"Quit!" Red chastised with a playful slap across his chest.

"Mmm, I really should be going," Zeke told her reluctantly.

"What? Why are you leaving so soon? We just got the place to ourselves."

"I know, and believe me I want more than anything to stay right here and take advantage of that fact. But... you remember that gang I was telling you about? I can't really afford to let them sit on the back burner. Besides, now it is more personal than a question of territory. They threatened my mate, and that I won't let go."

"Zeke... just be careful please."

"I promise." He leaned down and gave her one long, tender kiss. "But, you have to promise me the same thing. If you so much as hear a bump in the night, I want you to call me, ok? I'll find a way to have my phone with me even in wolf form. You call."

Zeke watched Red as a shiver ran down the length of her body. "I don't think I'm ok with this wolf thing yet," she admitted.

"It will take some getting used to. Just give me a chance?"

Red nodded. "Are you coming back tomorrow?"

"I'll be here beating down your door as soon as the sun comes up."

"Here, take a key," Red instructed reaching for her key hook next to the door. Zeke shook his head and started to protest, but Red rushed on. "In case I'm not up yet, or if you decide to come back when you get finished tonight?"

The last was asked with wistfulness in her voice. She must not have liked the idea of being alone after dark, even in her own apartment. Zeke hated himself for even thinking about leaving her, but it needed to be done. More than that, he hated the men who had given her reason to fear. "Red, I'm so sorry. I promise that I'm just a phone call away. I can be back here quickly. In wolf form I can run a straight path here; I don't have to stick to the roads... I could call Kris or Michael to come stay with you until I get back."

"No. No, I'm fine. You go on." She was putting on a brave face, and it was killing Zeke. "I don't understand, though, why the police can't handle this. Isn't that their jobs?"

"Yes, it is, but they are already stretched thin as it is. Not only that, but this is my family's territory to protect. It doesn't matter if there is one or a hundred of us left; we defend that territory. It's something that is ingrained in me, a part of who I am." Zeke wanted so badly for Red to understand where he was coming from, but it remained that she wasn't a wolf. She didn't think like a wolf, and that made it harder to understand. "They made their own beds when they started in on the people closest to me. Each member of my family swore and oath to protect Isabella's family. These thugs have broken into their place twice now. I gave that family my word; I will protect them. They have attacked you twice, and now they want you dead... How can I explain this?... You know that as marines Kris and I were willing to die for our country. The commitment to a mate is a thousand times stronger and more powerful."

Red bowed her head on Zeke's chest and whispered, "That's what I'm afraid of. I don't want to lose you."

Zeke rubbed both hands up and down Red's back in a soothing motion. "You're not going to lose me. I'm a little harder to kill than you think. Plus, I'm smarter than the thugs I'm up against, and I have a lot more stealth."

"But, accidents can happen."

"I know what I'm doing. You're just going to have to trust that I'm being careful."

"Are you?"

"Every minute of every day. The last thing I want is for you to get hurt. I can't stand to see you cry... I'll be back, ok? Why don't you go get a nice warm shower and go to bed? I'll be back before you even know it."

Red nodded, gave Zeke one more kiss, then watched him walk out the door. He waited to hear the lock click into place before walking away.

Zeke got in the car, and tensely started down the road. No doubt that the gang members would be gunning for Red even more now that the first one of them to get close to her was viciously killed by the same wild animal they all fear. Now... they had more to fear than ever before. Now, it was no longer a territorial thing, at least not for Zeke. Now, it was no longer about keeping an oath. Now, he wanted their blood, and he wanted it now. He couldn't think level headed. He didn't want to go in with a level headed plan to follow.

Parking the car, Zeke stepped out into the pitch black night and began stripping. He took his belt out of his pant loops and slipped it back around his bare waist with his phone still clipped to the belt. It was uncomfortable in human form. It would be barely tolerable in wolf form, but he needed his phone with him whatever it took. A large wolf sulking about with a belt strapped around its middle was sure to stand out, yet tonight there would be no one out whom he did not want seeing him.

Sticking to the shadows and back alleys, Zeke stealthily made his way to the last known headquarters. With any luck, they would still be stupid enough to be there. If they were, he would make them regret the decision.

Still ignorant and still there. Zeke snorted to himself. Now was his chance for a little immediate revenge, and he was so ready. One window on the east side was already shattered in its frame. Zeke backed up several yards and ran full force launching himself through the window. Glass flew in all directions as well as digging into his flesh. All eyes turned to him.

Some of the gang members retreated. Others reached for guns, but all reacted in fear. As they should. Zeke did not stop to acknowledge the pain from impaling glass shards, and he didn't stop to take inventory. Instead, he went straight for the closest man. He went straight for the throat. It was a quick kill, and he was on to the next. He continued like that as he dodged bullets, and he quickly lost count of how many he had killed. Although he had no idea how many, he knew their loss in numbers would be devastating.

Still he wasn't happy. They wanted Red's blood, and he wanted theirs. Gun clicks filled the air, empty. They were rapidly wasting ammunition. Many of the men who started out shooting were now running with their empty guns. Zeke continued to take down as many as he could. As the body count rose, so did the number of wounded who managed to get away. Still it wasn't enough. Zeke wanted their leader. He wanted the ugly thug who had ordered his mate's murder.

Soon the warehouse was void of all living besides himself. He had not gotten the leader. He had failed. He had failed, but had caused them significant damage. The cowardly thug may have won the battle, but he would not win this war.

Slowly Zeke limped his way back to his car. He was bleeding and sore. Not bothering to redress, he got in the car and drove home. After getting a quick shower, he dressed and cleaned all traces of blood from his car.

The sun wasn't up yet when he got back to Red's apartment. The truth of it was that he had only been gone a few hours. After all, it not been hard to find the gang, and even though during the heat of battle, it felt like forever, it only could have taken an hour itself, max. He had wasted no time getting himself and the car cleaned up. He let himself into the apartment and walked silently down the hall to check on Red.

She was tucked safe and sound in her bed fast asleep, or at least he thought so until she groggily called out, "Zeke, is that you?"

"What are you doing awake?"

"I was thinking about you."

"You should be sleeping."

"I was doing that too, a little. The police called after you left."

"What did they say?"

"They said that they are coming by first thing tomorrow morning. I told them you would be here. That made them happy; they can kill two birds with one stone. They also apologized for not getting by sooner."

"Yeah, I wondered about that. They've waited much longer than is advisable." Obviously the police were not going to be of much help. Someone in the department was probably being paid off, but Zeke wasn't going to tell Red that. He didn't want her any more upset than she already was.

"Are you staying?"

"Yeah, do you have an extra blanket anywhere? I'll stretch out on the couch."

"You could lay down with me unless you don't think you can behave."

Zeke chuckled. "You sound a bit too tired for any kind of mischief tonight."

"Aren't you tired?"

"I am actually," Zeke admitted. It was hard to lie to Red, and now that she knew all about him, he had no reason to lie. He went around to the other side of the bed, kicking his shoes off as he went. He crawled into bed and pulled Red's back flush against his chest. With his arm draped over her waist, he fell asleep in a matter of minutes.

◆◆◆

When Roxie woke the next morning, Zeke was still fast asleep, and she was secured tightly against his warm body. She closed her eyes again to just enjoy being with Zeke for a few more minutes. Before long, though, the bathroom became a necessity. Some coffee would be nice, and her stomach was beginning to growl.

She tried to carefully excavate herself from Zeke's arms without waking him, but as soon as she started to move, Zeke pulled her impossibly tighter and grumbled, "Mmm, morning."

"I didn't mean to wake you up." Roxie turned around in his arms and lightly kissed his cheek. "Go back to sleep, and I'll come wake you when breakfast is done."

"Sure?" he replied incomprehensibly.

Zeke loosened his grip so that Roxie could slip out of bed easily. She hurried about getting dressed, and cooking up a quick breakfast. Once she had breakfast and coffee on the table, she went back to get Zeke out of bed, which was easier said than done. Roxie called his name, but Zeke's only response was to grunt and roll over to his other side.

Roxie smiled at her stubborn man then walked around the bed to squat next to his face. She gave him a peck on the lips and whispered, "Zeke, it's time to get up. Breakfast is on the table."

In one swift movement that Roxie never saw coming, Zeke grabbed her around the waist and yanked her back onto the bed beside him. "It's too early, woman."

"It's almost nine o'clock," Roxie laughed.

"Really?"

"Yes, really. Now come on before the coffee gets cold." This time Zeke followed her out of bed and into the kitchen.

They had just sat down at the table when there was a knock at the door. Roxie had almost forgotten about the police coming this morning. She started to get up to get the door, but Zeke gave her a grave look and shook his head. Then he got up instead to answer the door.

"Mr. Miller, is Ms. Gardner home?"

"Yes, come on in." Zeke backed up, holding the door open wide, and four policemen walked into the tiny apartment space.

"I'm sorry we're interrupting your breakfast," one officer apologized noticing the meal on the table.

"That's fine. It's my fault. I couldn't seem to drag myself out of bed this morning. I honestly forgot that Red said you were coming by this morning." That was the first time that morning that Roxie really took in Zeke's appearance. His clothes were wrinkled everywhere, more like crumpled. Hair stuck up in every direction. One side of his face was still rosy where he had been laying on his side. Roxie knew that he had just rolled out of bed, and one look at him would tell the police the same thing.

"Is there somewhere that we could interview each of you separately?" another officer asked.

"Yeah, just let me grab a cup of coffee. Can we get you anything?" Zeke offered. The officers indicated that they did not want anything, and Zeke continued. "In that case, we can head back to the back bedroom, and you can talk to Red here."

The officer, who appeared to be in charge, nodded his approval. Zeke gave her a quick peck and whispered, "I'll be right down the hall if you need me." With that Zeke disappeared into the bedroom with two of the officers.

The two remaining officers walked casually over to Roxie. One was taller and thicker. He had thick, bushy brown hair that was unruly, looking as if it never laid down in an orderly fashion. The second man was short; he couldn't have been much taller than Roxie. He had a receding hairline. His slim build was deceivingly muscular. Warm, brown eyes smiled at Roxie as much as his big, goofy grin.

"Go ahead and finish your breakfast ma'am," the taller man said. "We can talk while you eat. It sounds like you have been through enough lately without us interrupting your breakfast like this."

"You're telling me! Oh, I mean-"

"No, that's ok. It's true. Please, go ahead and eat. We'll just have a casual chat while you eat. I'm sorry it's such a gory subject while you're trying to eat."

"Can you tell us about what happened the other night?" the shorter officer asked.

Roxie nodded and started in on her story, leaving out the part where Zeke turned into the wolf that had saved her life not once but twice now. Instead, she told them that the wolf came out of nowhere and that she was so scared she could not really tell from what direction it had come from. The officers were very nice about the whole thing, but they questioned her for what felt like hours. At one point they swapped with the two officers who had started out questioning Zeke. When both pairs of officers were satisfied with the answers they had rung from Zeke and Roxie, the officers thanked them for their cooperation and left.

"Well, that was tiring," Zeke commented after the police left.

"Do you think they are going to do anything?"

"I think if they had anything to go on, they would, but they have no leads."

"But you do?"

"Better than a lead, I know exactly who was responsible for that attack and why."

"Can you explain to me why?"

"Oh, Red," he soothed pulling her into his strong embrace. "You didn't do anything. It is all my fault. It's me they want. They just don't know who I am or how to get me, so they are using you. I swear, though, Red, I won't let them hurt you."

"I know. What did you do last night?"

Zeke took a deep breath and let it out in a loud sigh. "Last night is not something you want to hear about."

"I do. I hate to think about you out there night after night in danger. I want to know what you are doing."

"Last night was... not my normal MO. Believe me that's not what you want to hear about."

"Now you have me more curious. Was it dangerous?"

"It was stupid."

Now it was Roxie's turn to take a deep breath and sigh. She put her hands on Zeke's chest and ran them up around his shoulders to his neck before reaching up on tiptoe to kiss him. Although he tried to hide it, Roxie saw the way he winced at her touch. What was he trying to hide? She ran her hands back around to the front of his shirt with a barely there touch. Slowly she started to unbutton his shirt very carefully, not wanting to hurt him anymore. Zeke kept his eyes focused on her face as she worked at the buttons. There was no defiance in his expression or even a challenge of any kind. He simply watched her with a look of acceptance.

After the shirt was completely unbuttoned she slid it off his shoulders and let it fall to the floor. Roxie pulled his undershirt up, and Zeke helped by lifting his arms in the air. When she had lifted the shirt as high as she could reach, Zeke pulled it the rest of the way over his head and off. Roxie took the shirt and threw it across the back of a chair. She couldn't help the small gasp that escaped her lips when she saw Zeke's bare skin.

Scratches and bruises covered his torso. "Zeke, what happened?" she asked softly. She ran her fingers lightly over each scratch and bruise in turn, placing a tender kiss as she went and listened while Zeke started his story.

"I was mad. Mad doesn't really describe how I was feeling. I was mad when I heard them threaten you. After they tried to harm you, I was enraged. Last night I acted on that rage. What I did was stupid. It was irrational, and it was risky. I charged in blindly, thinking about nothing but revenge. I wanted them to pay for what they had done. I didn't care who they were or how high they were in the pecking order. If they stood between me and their leader, then I fought my way through them. I wasn't fighting to injure either. I fought to kill.

"They weren't innocent. They all knew what they were doing there. I wasn't innocent either. Last night was far from the first time I have taken a life. I have never taken an innocent life, but when I started out in this, I was hoping to give them every chance possible to change their ways. I knew the higher ups, the more evil ones, wouldn't, but maybe the lower level lackeys might have. Last night... I wasn't thinking of second chances."

"You killed them all?" Roxie finally asked in a shaky voice.

"No, some ran."

Roxie took a deep breath. This was a violent life that she was not at all accustomed. "Maybe the ones who ran, will leave for good. Maybe they will change. Maybe... maybe you made a difference."

Zeke wrapped Roxie in his arms and took a rugged breath. It was like he was fighting back his own tears. Roxie knew instinctively that he was not holding her to offer her security this time. He was holding on to her for his own security.

She wrapped her arms around his waist and hugged him tight. His whole body was tense. "Zeke? What will you do now?" she breathed against his chest.

"I don't know. I guess I'll have to start over again, but I won't give them time to recoup."

"What does that mean? Start over what, like intel?"

"I'll have to reassess the situation and decide from there what the best plan of action will be to shut them down with the least amount of violence."

"Least amount of violence?" Roxie asked with a sly smile. It was cruel, and she knew it. She had no idea what had come over her, but she couldn't help herself. She never would have guessed in a million years that she could have handled something of this magnitude this calmly, yet here she was handling it with a smile.

Zeke gave her a shocked look, shocked no doubt that she would tease and throw it back in his face like that. "Yes, baby, the least amount of violence. You are never going to let me live this down, are you?"

Roxie bit her bottom lip, gave Zeke a mischievous grin, and shook her head. Zeke struck back quick and unexpectedly. Before Roxie could figure out what was happening, she was flying through the air. Then she was free falling. She squeaked out a quiet shriek as she hit the couch and realized that Zeke had not only picked her up but crossed the room and dumped her on the couch as well. As the reality of the situation hit her, she was pinned to the couch underneath Zeke's heavy body.

"You're fast," she panted.

"I am."

"You're heavy too," Roxie accused while giving Zeke a playful shove on the chest.

"You're not trying too hard." Zeke leaned in even closer and kissed her silly. When he eventually stopped kissing her, Roxie laid still underneath him while she caught her breath, and Zeke impatiently nibbled at her neck while she caught her breath.

"You didn't answer the question," Roxie finally reminded him. "What does you'll start over mean? What will you do? Are you going tonight, and if so what are you going to do?"

Zeke buried his face in the crook of Roxie's neck and groaned. "Do you really want to know? Did you ever ask Kris what he was doing overseas? Would you ask him now? War is war, Red, no matter where it is fought or on how grand a scale. It's hard. It's gory. It's not the kind of thing that you go home at the end of the day and share with your loved ones."

"You don't want to tell me." She hadn't meant it as a question or even a statement. It was meant as an accusation, and he knew it.

Zeke pulled up to look at her, his eyes hard. "No, Red, I don't want to tell you. What I'm doing is terrible. I'm sorry I have to do it, but there it is. I don't want you haunted by those things too."

"But I am!" Roxie protested. "I am haunted by what you're doing! The only difference is I don't know what you're doing, so I laid in bed last night and imagined all sorts of horrible things. I imagined you getting shot... cut up... beaten and left for dead... I imagined you in some dark, dank, grotesque place in pain and dying alone calling out for help, and I had no idea where you were."

"Oh, Red, baby, don't." Zeke nuzzled her neck. "Please, don't worry yourself like that. I'm harder to kill than you think. I'm a good fighter in either form; I was trained for it. The only advantage they have are their numbers, and after last night, those numbers are seriously depleted. Even outnumbered, I can still outsmart them. I admit that last night was not real smart, but that won't happen again, ok? I'm going to be more careful, and you have nothing to worry about." He kissed his way up her neck, across her cheekbone, and to her lips.

"Yeah, but can't you just tell me... something. I'm not asking for all the gory details. Just give me an idea what you're doing, so that I'm not up all night worrying."

"After last night, they'll need a new base of operations. Tonight I'm going to do some sniffing around, search them out. When I find them, I want to get an idea of how many are still around. I don't know how many I killed last night and how many were smart enough to get out while they still could, so I'll be doing recon each night until I know what I'm up against, where they are, and what's the best way to hit them... Is that good enough?"

"So, you'll be... spying?"

"Yes," Zeke sighed.

"Ok, that doesn't sound too bad," Roxie answered carefully. "Can we go back to the kissing part now?" Zeke gave her a smile that was part relief part excitement and kissed her with exuberance.

Chapter Twenty-One

They spent the rest of the afternoon kissing. After an early dinner, Zeke left out to do a little recon. He offered to come back after he finished, but Red insisted that she was fine. She kept telling him to take his time and be careful. She also made him keep the spare key with him just in case he needed it sometime in the future. The truth was she was ready to take that next step, which wasn't such a bad idea. Maybe he would get her a key to the house too, but he could worry about that later. Right now he needed to focus on the task at hand.

He strapped the belt to his bare torso again. He promised Red he wouldn't go anywhere without his phone, so it looked like he would be wearing a belt in wolf form for the foreseeable future. It wasn't necessarily comfortable, but it wasn't real awful, not as cumbersome as he had expected. It could have been worse, and this way he could shift back and get in touch with Red immediately if he needed to.

Zeke went back to the scene of the crime, his crime. The bodies had all been disposed of, but nothing else had been cleaned up. Blood was still everywhere. Its smell was repugnantly strong. Zeke closed his eyes and took deep breaths in through his nose. Slowly he began distinguishing between smells. Blood was still the strongest by far, but now he could pick out the underlining smells he needed. Like sweat, and other distinguishing scents like fear. It might have sounded odd to anyone without an animalistic nose, but Zeke could most certainly smell fear. It didn't smell the same on everyone. Everyone's fear has a distinguishing scent, and it made them easy to track and easy to control.

There was a lot of residual fear left lingering around this warehouse. It wasn't likely that Zeke could follow the scent of fear all the way to the gang's new location, but maybe if he followed it long enough, he could pick up on some more familiar scents.

The fear took him nearly five miles. Zeke smiled to himself to think that he had made grown men run in fear for almost five miles. Perhaps that wasn't something to be proud of, but in this situation, with these men, Zeke felt anything but sorry.

Finally Zeke picked up on a couple of familiar scents. They began back tracking and eventually met up again with a few more scents a little less familiar to Zeke. All together seven of the separate scents lead to the same empty store front. The glass front had been painted black, but Zeke could hear men inside. They really were making this too easy. He wouldn't do anything tonight, but Zeke knew one of the first things he wanted to do was break out their front windows a couple times. It was childish, yes, but he couldn't resist getting a little payback for Isabella's family.

Zeke poked around for a while, went around back. There were no windows in back, not that he had really expected there to be. This was going to be more complicated than he thought, but he wasn't giving up. He would find a way. He would know how many were left and what they were going to do now.

◆◆◆

Zeke had not been gone three minutes when Kris called Roxie's cell. She wondered idly as she answered if Zeke had told Kris he was going out and to keep an eye on her. "Hey, Kris."

"Hey, is Zeke there?"

"No, he just left."

"Ok, I'll be there in two minutes... We need to talk."

"Ok."

Kris was not here for a friendly visit. The look on his face was serious, grim. Roxie was almost afraid to ask, "What's up?"

"Are you expecting Zeke back soon?"

"No, I convinced him that I would be ok until morning, why?"

"I want to talk to you about Zeke... I don't want you to take this the wrong way. Zeke is a great guy. He'll be good to you. I just have some... suspicions, but even with all my suspicions I'm still glad to see you together. I'm just saying don't let what I'm going to say scare you off."

"If it's not important enough to scare me off, why are you telling me?"

"I... Honestly I thought I was crazy at first, but... anyway. I wouldn't tell you-I wasn't going to tell you, but maybe in light of recent events I should."

"Kris, I love Zeke. I really don't think-"

"I know you do. I'm not trying to change that. Heck, I love him too, not the way you do obviously, but you get close in the middle of a war zone. He was my best friend out there, still is, but with this wolf that keeps hanging around you... we should talk."

"Kris-"

"Don't say anything. Just hear me out. This is going to sound insane, but... There were times when Zeke would just disappear. There was no pattern to his disappearances. At first I thought maybe he was up to something that could get him into serious trouble. It was something he kept from all of us, something he kept from me. Back then we didn't keep anything from our brothers in arms, so I assumed it had to be bad. What else would he keep from us? I didn't say anything, because, you know, it was Zeke. I didn't want to get him in trouble, get him caught.

"I followed him a few times. I figured that if I knew what he was doing, I could talk him out of it. Maybe I could offer him some help. I always lost him though. Eventually I gave up. He stayed out of trouble, and I was the only one who ever noticed his odd disappearances. Then I began to notice other things.

"He could smell things long before any of the rest of us. Sometimes he could sniff things out that none of us could. When the circumstances got the roughest and most of us began to weaken, Zeke was still as strong as ever. It didn't make sense. He didn't dehydrate as quickly as the rest of us. The hot, blazing sun didn't effect him the way it did the rest of us. Even when we didn't get to work out regularly, he never faltered. He didn't fatigue like the rest of us either.

"I didn't understand. Steroids wouldn't even do that to a man. There is no enhancer known to man that could cause the things I had started to notice from Zeke. It was like he was superman or something. I might have started to believe he was an alien from a different planet if I hadn't seen him get shot with my own eyes.

"That was another thing. I saw him get shot. He bled just like the rest of us, but he didn't heal like the rest of us. He healed at warp speed. I mean it. A bullet went all the way through him. Don't hold your breath like that. It didn't hit anything vital, and obviously he's ok. Anyway, it went all the way through him, and in two days all that was left was the scar. No one heals that fast. It's inhuman.

"I still didn't say anything, because he was my friend. I know him better than a lot of people. He may not have been human, but he is one of the best men I know. I tried to ignore it, to be as blissfully unaware as everyone else, but curiosity started getting the better of me.

"I should have let it go, but I started following him again. Then one day I lost him, as always, and on my way back I stumbled across his clothes hanging on a tree next to a lake. I looked across the lake expecting to see him skinny dipping or something like that, but there was nothing out there on that lake but a huge-butt wolf playing out in the water. A couple other times I found nothing but his clothes and a wolf nearby.

"The more it happened, the more I started to wonder. I started paying attention to the wolf, distinguishing marks and stuff, you know. It was the same wolf each time. After that, my imagination began to run wild. I imagined Zeke as a werewolf running amuck. It was crazy, right? I mean it wasn't always at night that I would lose Zeke and find that wolf. It didn't correlate with the full moon or anything else equated with that myth. I wrote it off to the heat and stress playing tricks on my mind.

"But then... early one morning we started taking fire from some unknown shooter. We took cover and shot back in the vicinity, but we could not get a visual on the shooter. Zeke ran out in the direction of the shooter. The next thing we know, we heard these horrible gurgling screams, and the shooting stopped. When Zeke came back, his clothes were hanging on his body shredded. Later we found the shooter's body where it had been mangled by some wild animal."

"Kris, do you have a point?" Roxie asked anxiously. This whole talk was making her nervous. How had Zeke never noticed that Kris was getting suspicious? What did she do now? Did she warn Zeke? What would he do?

"I never saw him change into a wolf, but Red, I swear it was him. He saved our lives that day. You can think I'm crazy if you want, but I seriously do believe that Zeke is a werewolf. It doesn't change who he is. Like I said before, he is a great man, and there is no one I trust more with my baby sister. It's just... First there was that wolf at the first attack. Then you swear you saw the same wolf at the campground where Zeke just happened to be with us, and now the wolf stopped another attack... I'm starting to think maybe you did see what you think you saw, but maybe it was Zeke the whole time. I'm telling you this because I think you should know; I'm not telling you to scare you. This is Zeke we're talking about. We had each other's back, and he saved my life over there more times than I can count. If I'm right, he's saved your life twice now too."

"Kris, Zeke was with me during the second attack," Roxie pointed out hoping to throw Kris off the trail.

"I know, but you were pretty shook up. I saw you afterwards. You were unresponsive. I don't think you know what you saw, or maybe you saw Zeke change and it scared you enough that you repressed it. Who knows?"

"Kris, you were right about one thing. You sound crazy."

"Ha, ha. I know how it sounds, but now you know. I'll sleep better knowing that I told you, and I do sleep better knowing that Zeke is looking out for you now too."

"Ok, well, as long as you feel better."

"I do. I love you, Red. You need anything else while I'm here?"

"Nah, thanks."

"Ok, good night, kid."

"Good night, Kris."

Roxie locked the door behind Kris and watched as her hands shook. She didn't know what it meant that Kris had put two and two together, but she wanted Zeke here to tell her that everything was ok for all of them. She got her phone and dialed up Zeke.

"Red, are you ok!?"

"Yes, I'm fine. Kris came by to see me."

"Did something happen?"

"No, nothing happened. I just changed my mind. Would you come back here when you get done tonight?"

"I'm on my way right now. I'll be there in two minutes."

"Zeke, don't rush. I told you everything is fine." Roxie wasn't sure if Zeke heard her before he hung up or not.

A couple minutes later, Roxie heard the door knob rattling. Before she could get over there to check the peep hole, the door swung open. Zeke gathered her up in his arms and hugged her tight. "I'm here. What happened?"

"I told you nothing happened."

Zeke pulled back a step. He held Roxie's head between his hands and quickly swept his gaze up and down her body. "Are you hurt?"

"No, I'm not hurt. Nothing happened. Would you close the door and come in here already?"

Zeke kicked the door shut as he crashed into Roxie with a smothering kiss. It was a sizzling hot kiss that Roxie had no objections about. "Don't you ever scare me like that again," he barked out, and that was the part that Roxie objected to.

"I can't help it if you are too paranoid to trust me. I told you that I was fine and that nothing happened. I even tried to tell you not to rush, but you wouldn't listen to me."

"I'm sorry. I was just so scared."

"Well, you were being silly."

"What did you call me back for?"

"I didn't call you so that you would come running back this instant. I just wanted you to come back here when you got finished... Kris came by, and he said some things. He sort of made me nervous. I wanted to talk to you about it."

Zeke took a deep breath and let it out as his face finally relaxed. He reached down and wound his arms around Roxie's thighs and lifted her off the ground. Roxie wrapped her legs around Zeke's waist while he carried her to the couch. He sat down with Roxie still wrapped snuggly around him. "Ok, I'm here now. Tell me what Kris said that made you so nervous."

Roxie told Zeke about Kris's visit down to every last word.

"Wow, I don't know how I missed that. There were times I'd smell Kris on my clothes stronger than others, but my clothes smelt like all the guys in our unit. We were living in close quarters," Zeke mumbled. "I knew Kris was a good friend, but... wow."

"What are you going to do?" Roxie asked in a trembling voice.

Zeke looked at Roxie, and dawning washed over his face like he was noticing Roxie for the first time since she started her recount of what had been said. "Red, relax, it's not like I go around killing anyone who figures out my secret. Besides, Kris is a friend. Did you really think I would hurt him?"

Now that Zeke put it that way, she felt horrible for ever fretting in the first place. "I didn't know what to expect," Roxie admitted.

"Oh, baby, no wonder you called me to come back. You must have been worried out of your mind." Zeke pulled Roxie into a crushing, possessive hug. "Thank you for trusting me enough to tell me."

"I feel like an idiot."

"No, this is all very new to you, and you are doing very well with the adjustment. You're not an idiot. Know, though, that Kris really is the best friend I've got, besides you. That in itself is enough that I would never purposely hurt Kris. Then you add to it that he is your brother. I could never hurt you; it would literally hurt me to hurt you, and I know how close you are to your family. Even if Kris and I were not friends at all, I could never hurt him, because it would hurt you."

"I know that now. I just wish I had stopped to think. I can't believe you're being so understanding about this."

Zeke kissed the top of her head and said, "This whole mate thing is new to both of us. We're both learning as we go. I've known about shifters and mates all my life, but for you this is the first you've ever heard of any of it. I'm trying to see things from your point of view to make the transition as easy as possible. That's not to say that I'll always do everything right. I'm going to make mistakes. We both will. Just promise me that we will work though it all together?"

Roxie nodded her head against Zeke's chest. Now that they had talked it out. She felt foolish and drained.

"I'll talk with Kris tomorrow," Zeke said more to himself.

"How did tonight go?" Roxie asked.

"It went well. I found them again. I only smell seven of them. I don't want to go on that alone, and I can't see inside. The front windows are blacked out, and there is only a brick wall around back. I don't know what I'm going to do yet, but I'll figure something out."

"Mmm," Roxie hummed. She wasn't really paying much attention any more. She was barely awake. It sounded like a terrible sleeping position wrapped around Zeke's torso the way she was, but she was utterly comfortable and relaxed unable to keep herself awake a minute more.

Zeke gave Kris a call the next morning. "Hey, Kris, I was thinking about taking Red over to my house today and throwing some steaks on the grill for lunch. You interested?"

"Sure, man. I'll let Mom know not to expect me for lunch. See you then."

"Yeah."

Kris knew something was up with the invite. His tone was suspicious, and he knew better than even ask if anyone else was coming. Zeke knew that Kris knew, but at least he had agreed to come.

Red was inside making potato salad and some kind of pea salad when Kris pulled into the driveway. Zeke was sitting on the front porch waiting for him, his stomach twisted in knots.

"What's up?" Kris greeted.

"Can we talk?" Zeke didn't waste any time. There was no sense in beating around the bush. They both knew what this was about.

Kris sighed and said, "Red told you, huh?"

"Yeah, she was more than a little nervous after you came to see her."

"She knew?"

"Yeah... you called it right. I shifted in front of her the other night. That guy was holding a gun aimed at her, and I just lost it. I didn't think. All I did was react... I wish I knew you knew. I'm pretty sure that seeing me shift is what threw her into shock. If not, it was at the very least the final straw. You knew just what to do, though."

"Naw, not really. I was just trying the first thing I could think of. It was dumb luck that it worked."

There was a moment of uncomfortable silence before Zeke said, "I told her all about it, and told her I'd answer any questions she has. So far she hasn't had many... She's my mate, Kris."

"Man, I don't want to hear that about my sister. I don't know exactly what that means, but I'm sure I don't want to know about any of it."

Zeke laughed. "It means she's it for me."

"Yeah, I've already figured that one out for myself. The way you look at her, you've never been one to wear your emotions on your sleeve, but I don't know what took the two of you so long."

"You... and Michael, mostly you."

"Me?"

"Yeah, Red, didn't want to affect our friendship. She was afraid dating me would ruin what we have," Zeke said motioning between

Kris and himself. "It wasn't easy convincing her that we were close enough that it wouldn't hurt our friendship. She didn't want us fighting. She also didn't want me to lose my job with Michael, but I think she was still more concerned about our friendship."

"Guess, I had that coming. I've never let any of the past creeps get near my baby sister. I like you though; I approve."

"Even though you believed I might be a werewolf?"

"Even then. You're one of the best men I know. She could do worse. She might could do better, but you'll do," Kris said with a smirk.

"Very funny."

"Nah, seriously, I couldn't think of someone I trust more to take care of my baby sister. I must be a good judge of character too if you were willing to out your secret to save my sister."

"Yeah, it was only a matter of time. I couldn't hide the fact from my mate forever, but I had never dreamed I'd have to tell her so soon or spring it on her like that."

Kris nodded thoughtfully. "Can I ask you something?"

"Sure."

"Those hunters you asked me to take care of, were they looking for you?"

"Yeah, they were."

"I figured. I kept praying that you would stay inside until they cleared out. I couldn't get things moving fast enough."

"You got them out of there a lot faster than I expected. Thank you for that. It's nice knowing that someone like you has my back."

"Always."

"It's also nice to have a friend who really knows me," Zeke added tentatively.

"You can trust me. You're my best friend, and I've got your back no matter what you are."

"About that, we don't call ourselves werewolves. That old myth is a myth. The full moon has no control over us, and it isn't contagious."

"Yeah, I'd figured that out about the moon. It's good to know it's not contagious. I didn't want to even think about you biting my sister; that is too much information, dude."

Zeke gave Kris a hard shove out of the chair he had sat down in. "You want a piece of me, Miller?" Kris threatened playfully.

"Alright you two," Red came outside interrupting the fun, "Those steaks aren't going to grill themselves."

"Yeah, yeah," Zeke relented as he started through the house to the backyard.

"Whipped," Kris coughed pointedly into his hand.

"Big talk from the big guy who comes running every time she calls your name."

"Yeah, yeah. So, now that we are all on the same page, Werewolf, are you going to tell me what's going on?" Kris asked.

"Kris," Red scolded.

Zeke smiled at his innocent mate. She was going to have a time getting used to his and Kris's good natured ribbing. "I don't know. It's intense. You think you can handle it, Gardner."

"I can handle anything you can, more even."

"We'll see."

"Does it involve Red?" Kris asked seriously.

"Yeah... yeah, it does now. It's my fault. I'll tell you all about it over lunch."

"Kay."

Red had gone overboard on all the fixings, much like her mother. She had made potato salad, pea salad, squash casserole, and cut up a watermelon. She sat next to Zeke at the patio table, and Kris sat across from them. Red sat and ate quietly as Zeke filled Kris in on everything that had been going on. Kris asked a few questions here and there to further understand the situation, but Red sat still. Zeke was sure that she was taking it all in, both what he had already told her and all the little tidbits that she had not heard yet.

"So, what's our next move?" Kris asked after Zeke finished filling him in.

"Our?" Zeke questioned.

"Yes, what's our next move? We've always worked as a team. This is important to you. It involves Red, and she's important to me. There's two good reasons that I need to give you a hand, and if that's not enough for you, I've already told you... I've always got your back, so what's our next move."

Zeke smiled across the table at Kris. Kris returned his smile with a mischievous smile of his own. "I need more intel," Zeke admitted.

Kris nodded, and Zeke could almost see the wheels turning in his head. "There has to be a way... Maybe a wolf can't get in, but two ex-marines might."

"No, absolutely not. I don't want the two of you just walking in there," Red spoke up for the first time.

"Chill out, Red, we've been in more dangerous situations than this. All you've got here are a handful of thugs. They don't even compare with a platoon of terrorist," Kris pointed out.

Zeke wrapped his hand around Red's and leaned in close to her neck. He kissed her earlobe and whispered. "We'll be careful."

Kris slid back in his chair and shook his head. "Red, you've already got him so whipped. The poor boy never stood a chance."

"Shut up, Kris," Red retorted.

Zeke knew how Kris would take that, whipped and letting a girl fight his battles. The teasing would never end, but all Zeke could do was smile. It was all worth it to have Red by his side.

"You know you should have told me all this before. We could have gone in there together, and maybe there wouldn't be anyone left to be a problem," Kris boasted. Zeke knew better than that; it was all talk. Kris was a tough guy. He was a strong fighter, and he could handle doing what had to be done. This wasn't a war zone. Until it felt like a war zone to him, it would feel like cold blooded murder, and no matter what Kris said, he wasn't capable of that.

Chapter Twenty-Two

That night Kris and Zeke went together to do a little investigating. It was nice to be working like that with Kris again. Zeke had not realized until that night how much he hated working alone. Wolves are pack animals; he was never meant to work alone like that, but for years he had been doing what he had to do. Now he had finally found his mate, and his closest friend is as good as family.

"So, you gonna' go all wolf on me?" Kris asked as they got out of the car.

"Why? You trying to get me down to my birthday suit?"

"You know it. Take it all off, baby!" Kris joked. Zeke couldn't help but laugh at the ridiculous look on Kris's face. Kris had never been one plagued with insecurities.

"I don't think your sister would like that."

"Yeah, yeah, don't think I don't see that smirk on your face. She doesn't ever have to know."

"Shut up, perv." Zeke said punching Kris on the arm.

"Awe, am I making the little wolfie uncomfortable?"

297

Zeke quirked an eyebrow at Kris and questioned, "Little?"

"I could take you, come on. Any time you're ready, Mills."

Zeke smiled and shook his head. He loved this camaraderie. Kris brought a sense of relaxation to an otherwise tense situation.

"That's it, two blocks up, the one with the blacked out windows," Zeke pointed out their destination.

Kris automatically swapped over from his playfulness to all business. "Someone's home; the lights are on... Who owns that property?"

"Not sure. You thinking it could be one of them?"

"It's possible, but if this gang is as new as you make them sound, they're still getting themselves established. I doubt any of them have that kind of dough. I'll look into it. It may be that there is an owner somewhere who would be willing to press charges. It won't solve anything, but it will keep them on the move, keep them from getting settled and causing optimum trouble."

"In the mean time I want to find a way in there."

"Yeah, the question is how."

"We have infiltrated terrorist organizations. Why should some small time thugs be so problematic?" Zeke mumbled.

"Why don't we just walk up and knock on the door?" Kris grinned.

Zeke smiled. "I like the way you think, but we promised your sister we'd be careful."

"No, dude, you promised my sister we'd be careful. I didn't promise jack." With that, and one wicked grin, Kris grabbed a discarded beer bottle from the ground and gave it a good shake to dislodge the dirt and grime. Then he proceeded to walk up and bang on the door. Zeke heard everything inside get deathly silent, but no one answered the door. "Hey, open up. We want to parrrtaay!" Kris yelled out with a purposeful slur, like he was drunk off his butt.

A guy considerably shorter than Kris opened the door and barked, "Get out of here. No one is going to be partying here."

"Ain't this the address that Steph gave us for that rave thingy? Dude," Kris beseeched looking over to Zeke, "she said the blacked-out windows on Second Street."

"That's what she said," Zeke giggled like a fool as he clung to the side of the building like he couldn't stay on his feet without help.

"This is Fifth Street," the guy said with a roll of his eyes.

"Fifth Street!" Zeke burst out laughing. He threw himself on the door pretending to have fallen forward. Taken off guard, the guy at the door lost his grip on the door, and it was forced wide open. "Help me up. Help me up. Help me up," he slurred at Kris, who sloppily pretended to pick his friend up off the ground and start back towards Second Street.

As soon as they were out of sight of the building, Kris and Zeke let go of the act. "Seven men," Kris confirmed. "Small guys, not a one of them is in real good shape, but everyone was armed to the tooth."

"Still, I like our odds," Zeke interjected.

"They were sitting in a makeshift circle, too hard to tell where the head sat."

"What were they doing?"

"Nothing, they were all watching the interchange at the door with suspicious eyes. They may be stupid, but they're wary. Every one of them got a good look at us. We won't get away with something like that again."

"We won't need to next time."

"I don't understand how a handful of thugs like them got all those hunters out and about in the middle of a business district," Kris voiced.

"Paranoia is easy to spread with a few well placed whispers. Virtually anybody can start a panic."

"Yeah, I guess so."

"So, that was easy enough for one night's work."

"Yep, and you didn't even have to get all furry. Let's face it; you needed me."

"Alright big mouth, don't stand there and act like I've been sitting around doing nothing until you showed up."

"Oh sure, you've been working, but things are faster and easier now that I'm around."

"Not to mention crazier, you drunken fool. Red's not going to like that."

"So don't tell her," Kris stated like it was that easy.

"I'm through keeping secrets from your sister. If she asks, I'm going to tell her the truth, and believe me she'll ask."

"There are some things that Red is better off not knowing."

"Yeah, things like the stunt I pulled the other night, charging in like a raging bull."

"So why'd you tell her?"

"She asked."

"That simple? She asked, you told her? You're whipped."

"Shut up, I am whipped. Yeah, I can own that. Wait till you find the one, man. You'll be falling over yourself to be as whipped as I am right now."

"If I ever get that bad, I want you to shoot me. You just going to keep telling her this crap, dude?"

"Yeah, for now. Eventually it will get to be too much, and she'll quit asking for anymore specifics."

"So, you're going to keep telling my baby sister about all the gory details until she can't take anymore?" Kris asked with an accusatory tone.

"Kris, I love her. You're just going to have to trust that I would never do anything to hurt her."

Kris took a deep breath and let it out on a sigh. "Yeah, but I still don't like it."

"I lied to her about what I am. That's a big deal, Kris. She's trying to relearn how to trust me. We're walking a thin line right now, and trust is not something I'm willing to gamble with. When she gets to a point that she doesn't feel like she needs to hear all the details, she'll quit asking. Until then..."

"Yeah, ok. Hopefully this won't drag on much longer now that you're not on your own. The sooner we take care of this, the sooner we can put it all behind us."

"Thanks, Kris, I owe you one."

"You don't owe me," Kris said shaking his head. "We're a team. We have each other's back. That's just how we roll. Give me a call later and we'll plan our next move."

"Sure, see ya."

◆◆◆

Roxie hated that she didn't know what Kris and Zeke were going to do when they left her apartment, and she hated even more that Zeke was going back to his place afterwards. She had gotten used to him coming back to her apartment and holding her while she slept. She felt secure that way. Without him here, she was alone... and vulnerable.

She knew, though, that it wasn't right. She couldn't ask Zeke to keep staying over like that. People would talk even though nothing was going on except actual sleep. It was probably driving Zeke up a wall sleeping there every night with nothing more than sleep going on. It wasn't fair to him.

So, resigned not to give in and call Zeke, Roxie went to bed alone. She didn't sleep well. Every noise, every creek, every drip made her jump. She was still scared, but life didn't stop because she had been through so much. She had to go back to work come Monday. A week off was going to be hard enough to catch up from, and Michael was probably ready for Zeke to get back to work as well.

Roxie closed her eyes and took a few deep breaths trying to clear her mind, but it was useless. Her thoughts went straight back to Zeke and Kris. She wondered what they were doing right then and if they were safe. She was glad they were together if nothing else. She knew Zeke felt better knowing that Kris knew his secret. He needed someone who he could talk to, someone who he didn't have to keep secrets from. Of course he had her, but he needed another guy, a friend. Kris was the closest friend Zeke had, and he was the closest friend that Kris had. It was good that they didn't have that wedged between them any longer.

Roxie's thoughts were interrupted by her phone buzzing on the night stand. She picked it up to see a text from Zeke: I'm home. How are you doing? She texted back a real quick: Much better knowing you're home safe. She still didn't sleep soundly, but that was one less weight off her shoulders.

<h1 style="text-align:center">Chapter Twenty-Three</h1>

Time flew by in an exhausting blur. Monday morning came, and Zeke insisted in walking Roxie into the office and coming to walk her back to her car at the end of the work day. She felt much like a kindergartener being walked in for the first day of class. Still, she wouldn't ever admit it to Zeke, but she did feel better knowing that she wouldn't have to make that walk alone.

As soon as she stepped foot inside the office, Lucy latched onto Roxie in a crushing hug. "Oh, Roxie, are you ok? I've been so worried. I can't believe that happened to you twice! You are so brave; I don't think I would come out of hiding if it were me. Did they catch the creep who did it? Was it the same one as last time?"

"Slow down," Roxie instructed with an appreciative smile. "I don't think the first guy had the money to make bail. It wasn't him at any rate. They didn't have to catch this one; he didn't survive."

"What do you mean he didn't survive?"

"It was the wolf. The same wolf as last time attacked the attacker. This time there was no doubt about it. The attacker was dead before the police were even called."

304

"You're kidding! Honey, are you ok?"

"Yeah, I am. That wolf saved my life twice."

"Oh, I've been so scared," Lucy cried as she pulled Roxie back into another hug. "I know your text said that you were fine, but I was still so scared. How could something like that happen?"

"It's ok, Lucy. I'm fine. See? Look at me, not a scratch on me, and Zeke walked me into the building this morning. He's coming back to walk me back to the car."

"Well, good. I don't want you going anywhere alone for a long time, like ever, and wherever that wolf is I'd like to give him a whole truck load of dog treats or maybe steaks or both." Roxie laughed, and Lucy rebuked her, "No, I mean it. Wolf or not, he's my favorite canine in the world right now."

"Yeah, I kind of like him myself."

"Kind of like him? Girl, you need to take that wolf home. Offer him a good, loving home and a full time job."

"I'll try to keep that in mind. So, what all have I missed?"

"You won't believe it! Everyone around here felt so horrible about all you've been through, they've all pulled together to keep things going around here. The company president is even offering to pay you for your time off last week without cutting into your vacation time. I think he's afraid you'll sue the company or something."

"You're right. I don't believe it."

"Check your inbox. You'll see for yourself."

Roxie walked into the inner office and glanced at her inbox. Sure enough, it was not nearly as full as it should have been after missing nearly a week. There was still a nice sized pile that needed her attention, and there was sure to be much more waiting on her computer for her attention. There would be a lot of catching up to do, but it looked that it could have been much, much worse.

"Of course, there is still a lot that needed your personal signature or that no one else was sure how to go about, but they did as much as they could to help out," Lucy said.

"No, it's tremendous," Roxie insisted.

"Yeah, it is, isn't it," Lucy said dreamily. "I've never seen this field or this company specifically pull together and rally behind their own like that. I know you'll still be crazy busy to get caught up, but it was so encouraging to see the way everyone came together." Lucy's voice was beginning to wobble. Roxie looked up to see tears rolling freely down Lucy's face.

"Oh, Luc," Roxie said sympathetically. She pulled Lucy into a hug and laid Lucy's head on her shoulder. "It's ok. I'm fine, honest, and I'm back now. Everything is going to be fine."

"I know. I was just so scared," Lucy sniveled. "You know Jerry from PR? He came by everyday just to check on me, to see how I was holding up and ask for any updates on you."

"Well, that's good. Why are you still crying?"

"He was so great to me while I was so scared. I've had so many extreme emotions over the last week. I think they are just catching up with me."

"It's ok, Luc. It's ok. Let it out." Roxie stayed right there, standing in the middle of the office with Lucy's head on her shoulder. She rubbed Lucy's back and let her cry onto her shoulder until she got it all out.

"I'm sorry, Rox. You were the one who was attacked, twice, and I'm the one blubbering on your shoulder."

"Don't worry about it. Trust me I've already done my share of blubbering onto Zeke's shoulder. I cried myself to sleep that first night."

"I can understand that."

Lucy was nearly three states away from any of her family. She was single, and Roxie was her best friend. Roxie felt horrible that she had not thought about Lucy dealing with all this completely on her own until that moment. "Yeah, I had Zeke. You've been here on your own. It's no wonder that you are upset."

Lucy gave Roxie another hug and said, "I'm ok now. Thank you. Now, back to work." Roxie gave Lucy a reassuring smile before getting started on what was sure to prove to be a very long, busy week.

Lucy slipped into Roxie's office about twelve-ten and shut the door behind her. "Roxie," she said in hushed, excited tones, "Jerry asked me if I wanted to go to lunch, but I told him there was so much to do here that I didn't think either one of us would be taking a lunch break today." Roxie was about to tell her to go ahead and go to lunch with him when Lucy rushed on. "He got a lunch and brought it back here... to the office... for both of us. Roxie, please, take a break, and let's eat with him," Lucy begged.

Roxie could not believe how affected her friend was by Jerry's kind gesture, and it was very kind. Lucy was flushed, and she obviously had developed a bit of a crush over the last week. There was no way that Roxie could deny her. Not to mention, Roxie did not remember much about Jerry, and she couldn't wait to find more out about the man who had meant so much to her best friend.

"Yeah, come on," Roxie was now as excited as Lucy, her excitement infectious. "Luc!"

"What?"

"Take a deep breath."

Lucy complied, taking a deep breath and smiling ear to ear. Then she turned and rushed out the door with Roxie close behind. Roxie wanted to tell Lucy to slow down and play it cool, but it was no use at this point. Lucy's excitement was too far gone.

Jerry smiled at Lucy. He didn't even notice Roxie until Lucy turned to look back at her. "Oh, hi, Roxie, right?" he greeted, sticking his hand out to shake hands with Roxie. Roxie took his hand and shook. He had a nice, firm handshake.

"Yes, hi, Jerry. I wanted to thank you for everything you did while I was gone."

"I didn't do much," Jerry said with a blush. "There wasn't much I knew how to do."

"I hear you were very supportive when Lucy needed it the most."

"I certainly hope so," he said giving Lucy a shy smile. The smile had still not left her face as she beamed at Jerry. "Oh, I brought lunch," he said shoving a bag at Roxie. "Lucy said that you wouldn't have time to go get anything today. I thought I could save you the time."

"Thank you, that was very thoughtful."

"It's not much."

Roxie glanced at Lucy, who was still staring at Jerry with a big goofy grin on her face. Lucy was usually an outgoing, bubbly person, yet here she stood silent in a trance like stance. "Well, shall we?" Roxie asked pulling a couple extra chairs to sit around Lucy's desk.

"Oh, here, let me help," Jerry offered. Jerry took the chairs from Roxie, and she moved to grab Lucy's chair and pulled it around next to Jerry's.

They started eating as an uncomfortable silence fell into place, thick and smothering. "Um, I heard that security is going to be beefed up in light of what happened. There is going to be a night guard in the lobby after hours, and they are adding more lighting to the parking deck and the walk to the deck," Jerry said.

Roxie smiled politely and said, "No offence, but I don't think any of that is going to make much of a difference. Both times I was attacked in the parking deck within reach of my car. A security guard tucked safely in the lobby would not have even heard the disturbance. Lighting was not a problem. I saw the attackers very clearly as they could me. It's a nice thought that the company is trying to do something to prevent more violence, but I think that the problem is more that these guys are getting bolder."

"Is it true that the second guy was looking specifically for you?"

Lucy came back to reality with a gasp. "Jerry," she said disapprovingly.

"Oh, I'm sorry."

"No, it's fine," Roxie assured them both. "Yes, he was. My boyfriend was with me, and the attacker kept saying that if I'd give myself up, that my boyfriend didn't have to die too. The police think that he may have had ties somehow to the first guy somehow." That was a lie she didn't know what the police thought, but she knew that Zeke knew for sure.

"Oh Roxie!" Lucy cried.

"Lucy, it's ok. He didn't hurt either one of us," Roxie rushed to reassure.

"I heard that there was a wolf or something that came out of nowhere to protect you both times," Jerry interjected.

"That's true."

"Wow, it seems all the rumors are turning out to be true. How often does that happen?"

"This whole thing has been so fantastical, there is really no need to fluff it up."

"I'll say." Jerry looked back to Lucy and must have seen the same thing that Roxie did. Lucy's bottom lip was trembling, and she looked like she was fighting back tears. Jerry grabbed her hand and soothed, "It'll be ok. I'll make sure that you girls always have someone to walk you out. We won't let anything like that happen again."

Roxie was not at all sure that Jerry could do much to prevent a very determined and armed attacker, but she didn't want to upset Lucy further by saying so. Besides having Jerry to walk her out was better than having no one at all. "My boyfriend has actually made plans to start walking me both in and out each day, but Lucy and I don't always leave at the same time every day. I would feel better knowing that you were walking with her."

"Of course." Jerry gave Lucy's hand a squeeze. It was obvious at this point that he only had eyes for her.

Roxie finished up her lunch quickly and excused herself. "Well, I hate to eat and run, but I really do have a lot of work to catch up on. You two take your time and enjoy your lunch. I'm just going to get back to work. Thank you again, Jerry, for lunch and everything you've done for Lucy."

They barely took notice of Roxie as she retreated into her office leaving them alone.

Lucy knocked on the door as she pushed it open almost an hour later. She shut the door and came to sit across from Roxie on the other side of the desk. "Isn't Jerry wonderful?"

"Yes, he seemed very nice," Roxie chuckled. "Not too hard on the eyes either." In truth, Roxie had not given him much thought in the looks department. It was more important to her how he treated her best friend, but thinking back Jerry had not been bad looking. He was not as tall or good looking as Zeke, but he was certainly no dog, she thought with a smile. He was roughly Lucy's height with sandy blonde hair that was combed and neatly styled. He was not overly muscular, yet he filled out his designer suit nicely. He had a kind face and eyes. His eyes were green, maybe, Roxie thought.

"I know! He's cute and caring. He's sweet and a real hard worker, makes good money too. He makes me laugh."

"He makes you turn to goo too, huh?" Roxie asked with a smirk.

"What? Yes, I mean what?"

"You got awful quiet out there. I noticed you couldn't keep your eyes off him either."

"Am I that obvious?"

"I don't think he noticed. He was too busy doing the same."

"You think so?"

"Yeah, definitely."

"He's coming at five to walk me out to my car. Do you think we'll be through by then?"

"You go on and walk with him. I wouldn't think of making you miss that opportunity. Besides, Zeke is coming to get me. I'm sure he'll wait with me. No problem."

"Are you sure?"

"Of course!"

"Thanks, maybe I'm just swept up in everything, because he was there for me during a hard time. I really like him, though."

"I think that's great! Enjoy this time together. It's about time you found someone who you are so fond of."

"Yeah," Lucy said dreamily as she floated back out to her own desk.

They didn't talk again throughout their busy afternoon until nearly five o'clock when Lucy stuck her head in the office door. "Tall, dark, and handsome is here, and Jerry just called; he's on his way up. Are you sure you don't need anything else."

"No, thank you, Lucy. Will you send Zeke in here, and talk to Jerry for heaven's sake."

"I'll try. I just get so tongue tied around him, and I don't know what to say."

Roxie was still laughing as Lucy stepped out and Zeke walked in. "Hey, beautiful," he greeted.

"Hey!"

"Working late?"

"I'm sorry," Roxie apologized realizing that she never called to let him know.

"Nah, I figured," Zeke said pulling up a chair and making himself comfortable. "I remember how it is."

"Hey, that's right. I always wondered how your story all checked out, how you had time in your lifetime to do all that you've claimed. I guess it makes better sense now."

"Yeah, I'll have to start paying more attention to the small details like that in my story. So, what's got her so giddy," Zeke asked gesturing back to the outer office.

"Jerry from PR. Apparently he has been checking on Lucy while she was worrying about me. Oh, and he's dreamy," Roxie sing-songed.

"Is that so?" Zeke asked with narrowed eyes.

"Don't act like that. He's not my type."

Zeke's face relaxed back into neutral expression. "So, is this a good thing? Do we like Jerry?"

"Yeah, he seems like a nice enough guy. He brought us lunch today, and we all ate at Lucy's desk. He maybe a little nervous, but then Lucy barely said two words while he was here."

"Lucy? Are we talking about the same Lucy?"

"I know. Lucy never stops, and I've never known her to have a shy bone in her body. She clams up, though, and just stares at him like some lovesick puppy when he's around."

"Wow."

"I know, right? He tried to make small talk at lunch, but he doesn't really know me. It was sort of uncomfortable. I inhaled my lunch so that I could get back to work and leave them some alone time. I haven't really gotten to talk much to Lucy today. I hope they talked about something when I left. They seemed content enough to sit and watch each other."

"I could sit and watch you all day."

"It's not the same, though. We talk to each other. They just sit and stare."

"I'd be content to sit and stare if that's what you wanted."

"You can't seriously think that is what Lucy wants."

"I don't know her that well, but no, I was not given that impression. They'll get there. It just takes time."

"Yeah, in the meantime it's just weird to see Lucy so hushed... Zeke, what kind of business were you in before?"

"Oh, I um, I was interested in electricity when it was first discovered. I got in with the General Electric company when they were first getting off the ground. I rose pretty quickly through the ranks before I was forced to quit. I couldn't risk anyone noticing that I didn't seem to age. It turned out that business came easy to me, so I dabbled in the stock market for some time after that. Although I understand the inner workings of business and the stock market, I never enjoyed it as much as you. It didn't make me happy."

"What does make you happy, Zeke?"

"You," he answered with a lift of his brows.

"You know what I meant."

"Yeah, I know what you meant. I liked military, but like anything else, I could only do that for so long before people started getting suspicious."

"I'm sorry... What you're doing now because of that gang, is it sort of like your military career?"

"In a way, I guess so. It utilizes a lot of the same skills at least. It's better now that I have Kris helping out."

"You don't like working alone, do you?"

"I don't like to do much of anything by myself. Wolves are pack animals by nature."

"It must get lonely living in that big house by yourself," Roxie said thoughtfully.

"It does. It's not the same as it once was. It used to be so full of life... Maybe soon it will be full of life again."

Roxie looked up at him quizzically, but Zeke just watched her as if his meaning should be apparent. "What do you mean?" she finally asked.

"Maybe we'll have a family soon."

"Oh." She wasn't sure what else to say to that. She hadn't thought much about it. Did she want a family of her own, children? Yes, but she had not thought of that so soon. She especially had not thought of starting a family with all the unrest surrounding them right now.

"I see your mind spinning. What is it?"

Roxie shrugged, not sure that she wanted to talk about it right now.

"Is it the house?"

"What?"

"I never asked you if you would want to move into the house. I just assumed. Do you not like the house?"

"No, it's not that! I love your house. It's beautiful. Really, I'd be honored if you wanted to share your family home with me, and I never could dream of asking you to leave your family home."

"I don't want you to feel like you have to. I want you to be happy, but once we're married, of course, you will be family. It wouldn't be a matter of sharing my home; it would be just as much yours."

"Zeke, it's really not the house."

"What is it then?"

"You just surprised me talking about having kids, that's all."

"You don't want kids?" Zeke asked carefully, obviously trying to mask his hurt.

"I-I do. I want to have kids. I just... I hadn't thought about it yet. We're moving so quickly, it blows my mind sometimes."

"Should we slow down," he asked apprehensively.

"No, I don't want that! I have trouble keeping up sometimes, but I don't want us to slow down. I'll catch up. I think the talk of kids so soon took me off guard because of everything going on as well."

Zeke nodded, but didn't say anything else for a few minutes. "Kris called earlier today. He wanted to know if he could come by later tonight. I told him that I was almost positive you'd be working late but that I would give him a call after I talked to you."

"That sounds fine. I'm about done here for tonight, if you want to shoot him a text or something."

Zeke picked up pizza on his way to Red's after walking her to her car. Kris was going to meet them at her apartment. He said that he had something that he wanted to talk about, but he had not hinted at what. Zeke was leery about leaving Red alone to walk up to her apartment from her car. It was a bit obsessive, but if they ever figured out where she lived...

Zeke cut that thought short not wanting to give life to the thought. He would only be a few minutes behind her, and Kris was on his way already. She wouldn't be alone for long, if at all with the way Kris drove.

Kris was already there when Zeke got to the apartment. "Finally, I'm starved, man," he said taking the pizza from Zeke's hand. Zeke leaned in to kiss Red. "Hey, what is up with this veggie mess?" Kris demanded.

"It's for Red. The other is a large meat lovers."

"Thank you," Red cooed as she wound her arms around Zeke's neck and kissed him again, this time a deeper more lingering kiss.

"Come on. Cut that mess out!" Kris complained. "You're going to make me lose my appetite."

"You said you had something to talk about?" Zeke pushed.

"Yeah, I got some info on that building our thugs are hiding out in. It was foreclosed on last year. The bank still owns it, hadn't sold yet," Kris said around a big bite of pizza. Zeke and Red helped themselves to some pizza while they listened to Kris. "So, I was thinking we might can kill two birds with one stone. I've got a little money put back. You've got that background in business."

"Yeah, so?" Zeke nudged when Kris paused.

"Well, I've been thinking about opening up a gym for a while. There's really nothing around here for the guys who are really hard core. That building would be perfect. I was wondering if you would want to go in with me. I know you don't want to work for Michael forever. Once the building is ours, it would be easier to go in and clean house. I know it can get expensive when you're first starting out, but I'm sure we could get like a small business loan or something like that."

"Money won't be a problem."

"Whoa, listen to him," Kris said to Red. "Money won't be a problem. You Mr. Money bags all of the sudden?"

"My family has money. We won't need the loan. I like the idea, though. Yeah, a gym sounds like fun."

"Not one of those sissy gyms either, put up or shut up."

Zeke smiled at Kris's enthusiasm that was quickly infecting him. "Yeah, and it's something I could stick with too. I wouldn't have to worry about the aging thing."

"What aging thing?" Kris asked.

"I usually have to move on before long to keep people from noticing."

"You don't age?"

"Slowly."

"Yeah, so what do you think?"

"I love it. Red?" Zeke looked to Red for her thoughts on the idea.

"Mmm," she mumbled caught off guard. She swallowed the bite she had been chewing and said, "I will agree with whatever you say. We were talking about that earlier. You need to find something that makes you happy. If not military... maybe a gym?"

"Yeah, I think I could be very happy running a gym with Kris," Zeke replied feeling his spirits lift.

"So, you're in?"

"I'm in."

"Perfect."

Kris stayed late into the night until Red declared that she had to get some sleep before work the next day. Zeke kissed Red good night, then walked out with Kris.

"So, you're still staying at your house?" Kris asked uncomfortably.

"Yeah, I stayed here a couple nights until she was comfortable to stay on her own, but no, we have not moved in together."

Kris nodded thoughtfully then turned his face away from Zeke. He asked even more uncomfortably, if that was possible, "Are you sleeping with my sister?"

"If I am, I don't think your sister would appreciate us talking about it."

"I don't think Red would appreciate us talking about it either way, but she's my baby sister. I have to ask."

"As a friend, I can respect that, but if you ever tell Red we talked about it this I will deny it and beat you... No, I'm not sleeping with your sister, but I'm going to marry your sister... soon, so you better get used to the idea."

"Yeah, I know, and when that happens I'm going to pretend that you are the only celibate married couple on Earth. Until then, it's my job to protect my baby sister... and her virtues, you know?"

"Yeah, I know," Zeke agreed, trapping Kris in a head lock. "You make a pretty good big brother, but you don't need to worry." Kris twisted around out of Zeke's grip, and they commenced horsing around.

"Get in your car and go home, numbskull, before one of Red's neighbors look out the window and call the police to come save your tired butt," Kris taunted.

"Don't count on someone breaking this up. You've got to finish it on your own unless you're too out of shape and need to call a mercy rule."

"You wish."

"We will finish this later," Zeke threatened as he fell back.

"I'm counting on it. I'll swing by when I get all the paper work together."

"Sure, I think this will be good."

"I know it will. See ya'!" Kris called climbing into his truck.

Chapter Twenty-Four

The rest of the week was blissfully uneventful. Red worked late everyday to catch up on everything missed. Zeke swung by the building, where the gang was holed up and where he and Kris would open a gym, each night on his way home from Red's. Nothing changed.

Plans were made for Red and Zeke to eat at her Mom's on Saturday, and Zeke made plans for him and Red to go out Friday night. All he told her was that they were going out for dinner and that she should dress comfortably. He had already talked to her Mom as well as Kris and Michael, so they all knew what was going on. More importantly, they all approved of what was going on.

"Where are we going?" Red asked again. She must know that there wasn't much out this far, and she was getting suspicious.

"Zeke, what are we doing? I thought you said we were going out for dinner tonight? I skipped lunch today. I worked through lunch thinking we would have a big meal tonight. What are you up to?"

Zeke appeared to be thinking it over. If he didn't tell her what was going on soon, she was going to go crazy. Finally he glanced at her with a wide smile and said, "We're going for a picnic."

"A picnic? Really? At night?" Roxie was surprised to say the least, but she was also excited. She had never been on a moonlit picnic. The idea had never even crossed her mind before. Moonlight meant so much more to her now in light of all she had learned about Zeke. Yes, she knew that the moon had no control over him, but she still couldn't sever the connection between them in her mind. The moon wasn't quite full tonight, but it was precariously close, and it was large and bright. The further out they drove, more stars showed up sprinkling the sky with their twinkle.

Roxie leaned back in her seat and tried to relax. However, it was useless. She was far too anxious to relax before; now she was far too excited to relax. "Is it much farther?"

"Not too much," Zeke answered with an amused smile. He was clearly enjoying himself. Let him. If keeping his little secrets was enjoyable for him, he could enjoy himself all he wanted, because she was certainly enjoying the anticipation of a moonlit picnic.

"Where we are going, will we have a clear view of the sky?"

"Yes."

"This was a good idea."

Zeke smiled, but didn't have anything to add. He continued to drive for another five minutes while Roxie tried to keep her excitement reeled in. They were out in the middle of nowhere by that point. They had not passed any signs of civilization for miles. All there was to see were trees. Zeke turned off the road onto a small dirt path. Roxie hoped there was not anyone else out tonight since the path they were on was most definitely one way.

"Ok, we get out and walk from here," Zeke said putting the car into park on the dirt path. Roxie looked at him skeptically but followed him out of the car and around to the trunk where he pulled out a large picnic basket that she recognized at once.

"You borrowed Mom's basket?"

"Yes," Zeke answered holding the basket in his left hand and taking Roxie's hand with his right. He pulled her behind him as he continued, "She packed it for us too."

"Well, that is reassuring. I was scared to think what you might have packed," Roxie teased, but Zeke did not rise to her bait. "Do we have far to walk?"

"Not far, it's just up this hill." Roxie had not been paying attention to much of anything except Zeke. She had not even noticed that they were indeed walking uphill.

"What's just up this hill?"

"The perfect picnic spot."

"What makes it so perfect?" Roxie asked with genuine curiosity.

"The view is fantastic, and it's a completely private, secluded area."

"Secluded, like the perfect place to leave a body?" Roxie asked with an almost evil grin.

"Red," Zeke said disapprovingly.

"What? I'm just joking."

"You're not funny. Look."

Roxie stopped dead in her tracks when she realized they had topped the hill. She could see for what must have been miles in the daylight. In the dark, it looked like tall tree silhouettes painted onto the most beautiful back drop she had ever seen. She turned around taking it all in. It was amazing. It gave her the illusion that she and Zeke were the only two people left on Earth. She looked up and gasped at the clarity of the stars above. She thought that she could see the stars from her mom's house, yet there were so many more from here. There must have been millions of stars speckling the sky out here tonight. She looked back to Zeke who was already laying a blanket out on the ground. She was taken by the way the moonlight shown down. It was like a moonbeam was narrowly shinning directly on Zeke singling him out.

"Zeke!" she shrieked and ran into his arms. He lifted her up easily onto his waist laughing at her excitement. "You were right. It is absolutely perfect." She crushed her lips against him in a mind numbing kiss. She continued to kiss him until his legs actually fell out from under him.

Zeke fell to his knees on the blanket and lowered Roxie carefully onto her back. She clung to him as he hovered over her with her legs still wrapped tightly around his waist. "I love you," Roxie whispered.

"I love you too," Zeke said. He kissed her lips then moved to her chin. He kissed up her jaw and down her neck. She could feel him inhale deeply as he went.

"Are you smelling me?"

Zeke smiled. "I like the way you smell." Roxie looked at him incredulously, but he didn't let that wipe the smile off his face. "Come on. Even normal humans associate smells with certain people, and my nose is somewhat more sensitive."

"Like you have an enhanced sense of smell?"

"Yes."

"Anything else I should know about?"

"My hearing is sharper," Zeke mumbled against the skin of her neck as he continued licking, kissing, and nibbling.

Roxie giggled and asked, "Are we going to eat, or are planning on eating me?"

"Is that an option?" Zeke asked as he dove for Roxie's lips again. As he devoured her mouth he eased her legs away from his waist. Roxie moaned when Zeke sat up pulling away from her. Even though it was a warm night she felt chilled to the bone without the warmth of his body next to her own.

Roxie sat up pouting while Zeke unloaded the picnic basket. Zeke looked over at Roxie and smiled despite himself. He reached up and ran his thumb along her bottom lip, which was jutted out slightly. "Your mom worked hard on this meal. It would be very rude of us if we never even unpacked it." He gave her another quick peck and went back to unpacking.

"When did you talk to Mom about all this?"

"I still have a few tricks up my sleeve," Zeke replied still refusing to give anything away.

"When did you have time to pick this up?"

"Michael gave me the day off," he answered with a shrug as if it was no big deal.

"Wait. Michael gave you the whole day off just so you could pick up a picnic basket?"

"I ran some other errands as well."

Roxie looked at Zeke skeptically and inquisitively studied him. "You are up to something Patrick Zeke Miller, and I'm going to find out what it is... later," she added straddling his legs and sitting herself comfortably in his lap. Wrapping her arms around his neck she started kissing him hungrily. Although Zeke was kissing her back, he was preoccupied still fiddling with the stuff from the basket behind her back. "Zeke, leave that stuff alone and put your arms back around my waist," she whined.

Suddenly Roxie stopped and took a big whiff of the air around them. "Is that lasagna?"

"Your mother said it was your favorite," Zeke said in answer.

Roxie slid out of Zeke's lap and made a move for the lasagna. "And, she packed it for a picnic?" Taking in the food spread in front of them for the first time, Roxie realized that there was not only lasagna. There was salad, garlic bread, and even wine. "Zeke, what have you done that you felt you needed to involve my mother?" Roxie asked cautiously sure that she was about to receive some sort of bad news.

"I haven't done anything. Can't you just enjoy the romantic gesture without the accusations?"

Roxie couldn't tell if he was hurt or not by her accusation. "I'm sorry. It is very romantic. You thought of this on your own?"

"More accusations."

"I didn't mean..."

"I did have help here and there. Your mother suggested the lasagna and cooked. Michael chose the wine. Did you know he considers himself a coinsure?"

"Only in his mind... Was everyone in on this?"

"In a way?" Zeke answered carefully.

"What does that mean?"

Zeke gave an noncommital grunt. "Enjoy your lasagna while it is still warm."

"Wait, wait, wait!" Roxie leaned over and gave Zeke another deep, longing filled kiss.

"What was that for?" he asked.

"I wanted one more kiss before we both have garlic breath."

Zeke laughed and started eating.

Once they had finished their delicious meal, Zeke admitted, "Red, there is something I wanted to talk to you about tonight."

She knew it. Roxie took a deep breath and prepared herself for the onslaught. "Ok, what is it?"

Zeke reached into his jeans pocked and took something out. Roxie could not tell in the shadows what he had removed until he held it out in front of her and asked, "Roxie, would you marry me?"

The ring was gorgeous. The gold band had diamonds circling all the way around and in the center sat a dark, red ruby. Roxie couldn't find her voice. She couldn't catch her breath. Somehow she managed to nod her head, and Zeke eagerly slid the ring on her finger.

"It fits perfectly," he whispered.

"Oh my gracious, Zeke," Roxie managed to cry looking at the ring on her finger. "This must have cost you a fortune."

"It didn't cost me a dime, but it is very valuable. It's more valuable to me than any price a jeweler could put on it... That was my grandmother's ring."

Roxie gasped then repeated, "Your grandmother's ring!"

Zeke reached up and rubbed his thumb across her cheek. "Red, why are you crying?"

"I'm crying?" She had not realized before that she had started crying, but now that he brought it to her attention, she could feel big fat tears rolling down her cheeks. "I'm just so happy."

Zeke leaned down and softly kissed her lips as he continued to wipe tears from her face.

It was late when they got back to the apartment and even later when Zeke eventually left for his house, yet Roxie was up with the sun the next morning, bubbling over with excited energy and ready to get to Mom's for lunch. By the time Zeke got to her apartment so that they could leave for Mom's, Roxie had been baking for hours.

"Mmm, it smells good in here," Zeke commented as he walked through the door.

Roxie skipped to the doorway to greet him with a kiss and then told him, "That's the mint you're smelling. I made chocolate mint brownies, but I made some lemon squares too."

"The mint and lemon make a delicious smelling combination."

"I don't even smell the lemon."

Zeke tapped his nose, then Roxie's and reminded her, "Stronger nose."

"That's not the only thing that's stronger," Roxie commented as she returned to the kitchen to get the dessert dishes. "Are you ready to go?"

"Sure, are you in a hurry?" Zeke asked as he took the desserts from her.

"I can't wait to see Mom!" Roxie was aware that she was almost singing as she spoke, but she couldn't seem to settle down no matter how hard she tried. Zeke shook his head with an amused smile, but he didn't say anything.

Mom, Michael, and Kris were all waiting outside when Zeke pulled into the drive and parked the car. Roxie was out the door and running in their direction. Mom held out her arms and embraced Roxie in a bone crushing hug.

"You're certainly in a good mood. I guess that means you told the lug nut yes," Kris smirked.

"Did everyone know before me?" Roxie asked with the best pout she could manage in her good mood.

"Yeah," Kris retorted.

"Zeke asked each of us individually for permission to ask for your hand in marriage. Since your dad wasn't here, he wanted to do the next best thing," Mom supplied.

"We all had something to add to the proposal too," Michael added in a kind, brotherly tone.

Zeke walked up behind Roxie and wrapped his arms around her waist. She noticed that Kris now was holding the desserts and was peeking in at what they had brought. Zeke spoke softly in her ear. "I gave everyone an idea of what I had planned for your proposal. Your mom said lasagna was your favorite meal and packed the picnic basket. Michael gave me the day off and chose a wine based on the meal and your past preferences, and Kris helped me scout out the area to find the perfect spot."

"Yeah, yeah, it was all soooo romantic. Are we going to stand out here and talk mush day, or are we going to eat?" Kris asked. His words were sarcastic and dismissive, but Roxie was sure that as he turned away she could see moisture in his eyes.

Mom oooh'ed and ahh'ed over the engagement ring, while the only thing that her brothers oooh'ed and ahh'ed over were the desserts. Michael fell asleep shortly after lunch while Mom and Roxie huddled in a corner of the den talking about wedding plans and Kris and Zeke disappeared to who knows where.

"You did good, I guess. I think you made this the happiest day of Red's and Mom's life. You know they are just going to get worse the closer to the wedding we get. Can you imagine them?" Kris said.

"Yeah, did I see you getting a little misty eyed yourself earlier?" Zeke teased.

"Fat chance. Just because you've gotten soft, doesn't mean we all have."

"Soft?"

"Whipped," Kris coughed into his elbow.

"Whatever, don't you have some paperwork you needed me to fill out?"

"It's highlighted everywhere you need to sign," Kris said handing Zeke a large stack of papers. "So, how do you want to handle the clean out? We can bring in the police and wait for them to get everything squared away, or we can go in ourselves and make a clean sweep."

"Oh, I think this is something we can handle on our own, don't you?"

"Most definitely," Kris said with a satisfied grin. "I say we move in today. No time like the present."

"That wouldn't have anything to do with your eagerness to start the gym, would it?"

"A little, but it has to do with Red's safety too. You know that."

"Yeah, I know that."

"So, you have a plan to..." Kris pushed.

"No, but it sounds like you do."

"When we get through here, we make a trip to check on our new investment. We find some undesirables waiting there. We politely inform them that the building has been sold and ask them nicely to leave. Of course they refuse, so we drop by again late tonight with an offer they can't refuse."

"So, that's your plan. We go in and remove the problem. Are you sure you're ready for that?"

"Look, I don't like it. I can admit that, but they crossed a line. They threatened my baby sister, and to protect her, I'll do anything. So yeah, I'm ready for that. Are you ready for that?"

"I'm ready. What about the gym?" With the matter being taken care of, Zeke changed the subject.

"Yeah, so, I've been checking out some equipment online. Let's go open up the lap top and get your input."

Chapter Twenty-Five

Kris and Zeke spent the next two hours looking at varying types of gym equipment and discussing the best practices for a practical gym. They even ordered a couple pieces that they both indubitably agreed upon at once.

"Mom, I'm headed out with Zeke and Red. We're going to check out the building for the gym," Kris told his mom.

Zeke wrapped his arms around Red in an attempt to hide the way her whole body stiffened with the announcement. Then he gave her a reassuring squeeze before saying their goodbyes and dragging Red out to the car. Kris followed them to the apartment.

"Are you really going to check out the building?" Red asked as soon as they pulled out of the drive with Kris's truck behind.

"Yes."

"Zeke," she said in a stern voice as if she honestly believed that would stop him.

"Red, what good will it have been to buy the building if we let some two bit thugs keep us out of it?"

"I don't want the two of you going in there and getting hurt."

331

"Baby, we have a plan. We are both trained professionals. Not to mention we have the element of surprise on our side as well as a few special abilities no one will see coming."

"I know, but..."

"It will be fine. I wish you wouldn't worry about this. We can handle it; it will be a breeze. I don't like thinking that you will be at your apartment worrying yourself like this. I need for you to trust us."

"I'll try."

When they got the apartment, Red was still jittery, but she was keeping it quiet. "Red, go on up. We'll watch you up before we leave. We'll be back in no time and fill you in." Zeke kissed Red goodbye then climbed into Kris's truck.

Kris waited until Red was safely behind closed doors before backing out and heading back towards the future gym site. "Just like old times," he mumbled as much to himself as to Zeke.

Kris put the key into the door, unlocked it, and swung it wide for Zeke to walk right in. Zeke walked in and was immediately stopped by three men in his face. "Whoa, whoa, whoa!"

"Hey, fellas... what's going on here?" Kris asked.

"We should be asking you the same thing," one of the men responded.

"We just finished signing all the papers to buy this place. No one said anything about anyone still evacuating the building," Zeke said.

"That's because no one is evacuating."

"Yes, you are. This place is ours. You'll need to vacate the premises immediately," Kris enlightened them.

Kris and Zeke turned their back on the three men and left without another word. They were both pumped up as they hit the road again.

"I love good cop, bad cop," Kris exclaimed, "and I can't wait to see their faces when the good cop becomes their worst nightmare. You think they'll all be there tonight?"

"Definitely. Those three are on the phone right now calling the others to get down there so that they can plan out what to do about us."

"It's going to be like shooting fish in a barrel."

"Except these fish will be armed."

"We've seen worse odds. You thinking this could go south?"

"I'm trying not to get too laxed, but honestly, I don't think I'll even have to shift to take care of those punks."

"Maybe not, but it sure would be fun to watch their faces."

Zeke smiled sadistically. Having Kris know his secret was not only a weight off his shoulders, it was fun. It had been so long since Zeke had let go and actually enjoyed embracing what he was. The constant secrets and loneliness had made what he was feel more like a burden and a curse since the deaths of his family. Kris was not disturbed by what Zeke was or even scared. He accepted it as a part of his friend, his best friend, and thought of it as a part of Zeke's artillery. "Are you armed?" Zeke asked suddenly curious.

"Not a chance. That would tip the scales in our favor, and they already don't stand a chance. That would just be cruel. Besides, I want to draw as little attention as possible."

"You know everyone of them are armed. The area is pretty deserted this time of night, especially on the weekends, but there is always that possibility. They might draw attention."

"All taken care of. In fact it will just corroborate our story."

"Which is what exactly? I was wondering what we were going to do with the bodies. It's not as easy as it used to be. That, and I've never had to dispose of bodies that weren't in wolf form."

"If you die in wolf form, your body will stay like that?"

"We can't exactly shift from the dead," Zeke answered with a role of his eyes. "Try to focus. Have you already got a plan of action for disposal?"

"Sure, let the police do it. It's their job to clean the streets of crime anyway, right? All we have to do is call and report that we heard shooting. We had gotten there a good while earlier but were sitting in the truck arguing about gym equipment. We were about to go in but heard the shots before we made it that far. The obvious thugs must have gotten into a dispute and resorted to violence. Thank goodness we had not walked in there yet." All this Kris recited with a straight face. No doubt he would play the part for the police to perfection.

"You are a disturbingly good liar."

"I was trained for this mess. The government shouldn't have taught me so well if they didn't want me to use the knowledge."

"Do you think we'd get flank for a move like this... or called heroes as everyone looked the other way?"

Kris gave Zeke a sly smile and asked in a too innocent voice, "A move like what?"

"Yeah, you're right. No one would ever know anything about it except us lowly soldiers, and who would rat out a fellow marine?"

"Sounds like you're the one who isn't ready, dude," Kris accused solemnly.

"No, for me this started out a turf war. Wolves are territorial. War is war. But now... now it's personal. They threatened Red. A man has a right to protect himself and his family. Self defense."

"I think you may be pushing it with the self defense plea, but I'm with you. I've got your back all the way."

"What we're headed into now may be the hardest part?"

Kris gave Zeke a quizzical look and questioned, "What are you talking about?"

"I told Red we'd fill her in when we got back."

"Why do you keep doing crap like that, Miller?"

"I promised her honesty. Wait until you find someone. She'll take your heart by surprise, and you'll do anything."

"Yeah, we'll see about that."

Kris refused to have anything to do with the explanation to Red. He sat back on the couch and chowed down on chips while Zeke did all the work.

"Are you sure that's the best way?" Red asked concern evident in her voice.

"It's going to be fine. We know what we're doing. We wouldn't go in like that if we were not sure," Zeke tried again to soothe her to no avail.

"What if the police don't believe you?"

"It's not likely. They're not going to believe that we called it in ourselves if we were responsible. Not to mention the fact that it would be hard for them to believe that we would go in there and take on seven armed men." Red opened to mouth to start another argument, but Zeke put a hand up to hold her off. "On top of all that, we were both model soldiers. There's not a mark on our records to indicate that we were trouble makers. It will be much more believable that a conflict broke out in the middle of a gang meeting between gang members."

"If it is so hard to believe that you would take on seven men by yourselves, why are you?" Red looked like she was almost in tears. Zeke pulled her over into his lap and rested his forehead against hers, their breath mingling.

"Red, baby, I know this is hard for you, but try to see it from where we are coming from. Those policemen, who will have a hard time believing it, most were not military at all. None of them were Special Forces. Kris and I were Special Forces marines. We were trained to be elite fighters, whether armed or not. Some of the situations we have gone into and aced, make tonight look like child's play. In some ways, Kris and I are better equipped to handle this than the cops. This is what we do. This is what we're good at. All I'm asking you to do is have faith in our abilities and let us do our thing."

Red took a deep breath and relaxed on a sigh. "Zeke?" she said in a low moan.

"Hmm?"

"I love you." Red pressed her lips to Zeke's in a passionate and expressive kiss that lingered and lead to more. Zeke wrapped one arm around Red's waist and the other went to support the back of her head, and he pulled her tight against him, as close as he could get her.

After a few minutes of kissing, Kris cleared his throat loudly, but Zeke and Red both ignored him. Next, Kris resorted to throwing chips at the couple intertwined together. "Break it up! I gave you your moment, but that's just nasty. Get off of him; Zeke let my sister go!"

Zeke pulled back for just a second, grabbed a nearby pillow and, lobed it in Kris's general direction.

Red gave Zeke one more kiss and said, "Promise me you'll be careful?"

"I promise."

"Both of you," Red demanded turning her stern eyes on Kris.

"Yeah, yeah, I promise too. Just quit sucking face over there. There is only so much I can take."

"Oh, guess what!" Red exclaimed with a quick change of subject. "Lucy called while you were gone. Apparently Jerry worked up the nerve to ask her out yesterday when he was walking her to her car. She waited to call, because she knew we were having lunch at Mom's. They're going out tonight. I hated to shadow her good news with an engagement, but she would have killed me if I didn't say anything. I hope it goes well for her."

That night Kris and Zeke synchronized their watches before going in. Kris went around back while Zeke went in the front door. The gang had still been discussing what to do about someone buying their building. Zeke could hear them discussing different ways of "taking care" of the two meddlers. The discussion had started to get heated. Zeke watched his watch for the designated time, then charged in without hesitation.

The first guy within Zeke's reach went down easily. Everyone started screaming and firing their weapons haphazardly. The shots were all off target. The thugs were panicking, which would only work in Kris and Zeke's favor.

One of the guys got a gun pointed at Zeke not two feet in front of his face. Zeke swung his arm up and around effectively breaking the arm holding the gun. He was careful not to touch the gun, not wanting to leave behind any prints to confuse the police. Once the guy was clutching at his broken arm, he was another easy take down.

Another one of the thugs got hit by flying bullets. He staggered backwards until he hit a wall. He slid down the wall into a crumpled heap in the floor where he sat and bled out of his chest cavity.

Zeke turned to see one man lying limp on the floor. A second was going at Kris with a knife while a second was charging Kris from behind with a knife. Kris ducked down and out to the right leaving the two men to collide together effectively stabbing one another.

Kris stood and scanned the area. "Now how do you like that? They took out each other. I was fairly useless, taking out only one man. You?"

Zeke chuckled at Kris's every playful attitude. "Two."

Zeke and Kris re-scanned the area. The man who had been shot was starting to gurgle. Shot through the lungs, he wouldn't make it more than another minute or two. The two with knife wounds had both gotten in a direct hit to the heart, too bad for them it was on their own buddy.

"Well, shall we go call the authorities like good citizens?" Kris asked.

"It certainly appears there has been a gang scuffle in here."

Kris and Zeke walked back halfway to the truck and called 911. "I heard shots... I'm on Fifth Street... yeah, that's it..." Kris reported.

"That was short and sweet," Zeke observed after Kris hung up.

"Yeah, they pulled the location off the cell. I guess we wait here."

"Guess so."

Less than five minutes later sirens blared and two police cars pulled down the road.

"Hey, are you the ones who reported hearing shots."

"Yeah, they were that direction," Kris pointed out to one cop.

While Kris pointed the first cop in the right direction, Zeke started explaining the situation to a second. "We just bought that building right up there and were coming to check out what we had to work with. We're going to open a gym. We got out of the car and were about there," he said pointing down the sidewalk, "when we heard shots fired. Sounded like several guns. It reminded me of being deployed in hostile areas. It went for a few minutes then stopped just as sudden as it started. My friend called it in, and we hung back here until someone else got here. Is there anything we can do to help?"

"No, the best way for you to help right now is to wait right here. We'll check it out then come back if we need anything else."

Kris walked over to Zeke. "Well, hurry up and wait."

It took hours for the cops to finish getting Kris and Zeke's story before they were satisfied enough to let them go. Kris headed home, and Zeke went straight back to the apartment.

"Red?" he called as he walked in the door.

"Zeke!" Red squealed and came running from the back of the apartment. She launched herself at Zeke and was kissing him before he even got his arms around her. "Are you ok? Put me down, so I can check on you."

"I'm fine," Zeke told her, but put her down anyway and submitted to her appraisal.

"So, everything went well?" she asked once she was satisfied that Zeke was ok.

"Yes, not a scratch on either of us. Kris is on his way home now."

"Is it all over?"

"Yes, it is all over."

Chapter Twenty-Six

One year later...

"Zeke, your baby mama's here," Kris called across the gym.

Zeke looked up and saw Red waddling in the door with both arms wrapped around her rounded belly. "Red," he jumped up and started running toward her, "are you ok?"

"I'm fine. Calm down."

"What are you doing here?"

"Jerry is taking Lucy out to see her family this weekend. I told you about that and that he has been dropping some pretty big hints that he is going to pop the question. Anyway, she still hasn't packed yet, so I told her to take a half day. You know Luc. She wouldn't leave me there on my own in my condition. I knew the only way I was going to get her to take off was if we both took off, so I asked her to drop me off here," she explained quickly before taking a breath and kissing Zeke.

"You can't hang out here all day," Kris butted in. "I'm serious. This is no place for a pregnant woman, and I don't want to have to take down a client for bumping into my pregnant sister."

"I'm almost done. I've got one more appointment today. Go have a seat at the front desk, and I'll take you home after I get through," Zeke said.

"Great, two sissy girls in the gym," Kris gripped.

"What's wrong with women in the gym, Kris?" Maggie called from one of the weight machines. Maggie was a tall blonde about Kris's height and tough as nails.

"Nothing, nothing... It's just sissy girls that don't belong in here. I'd say the same thing about guys," Kris quickly backtracked.

Zeke looked at Kris and pantomimed a whip being cracked. Giving Kris grief about his relationship with Maggie never got old. They had only been dating for two months, but Kris was already effectively caught in her web, head over heels.

"You want something, Miller? The ring's open, and you've got thirty minutes before your next appointment," Kris challenged.

Red made eye contact with Maggie and laughed as the two boys made their way over to the fighting ring.

About the Author

Elizabeth Lee Sorrell is an Alabama native. A gifted teacher, she has worked with babies and preschoolers, from her teens all the way to today. She is a teacher in the Federal Head Start program. She has her Associate's Degree in Early Childhood Development, her Bachelor's in Early Childhood Education and Elementary Education, and her Master's in Early Childhood Education.

When not teaching, or leading as the Nursery Coordinator of her church, she is with her family and dear friends, probably reading or writing a book. She loves to spend time with her nieces. Elizabeth is a Christian. She cheers for the Auburn Tigers, and the Atlanta Braves. As a big baseball fan, she has, more than once, written stories in the world of MLB, and watches as many games as she is able.

She enjoys pairing up with Sandra JS Coleman for her covers and illustrations. Sandra, Elizabeth's sister, is a graphic designer and an illustrator.

Learn more at www.ElizabethLeeSorrell.com

Colophon

Cover Design, Cover Photography, and interior
layout designed by Sandra JS Coleman using
Adobe CC software. She is the graphic designer and
illustrator for Yarbrough House Publishing Inc. Sandra lives in
North Alabama with her husband and daughter.

The typefaces used on the cover and interior are
Sketchnote Square, Garamond Premier Pro, and Beyouty Script.

Sketchnote Square was designed by Mike Rohde in partnership
with Delve Withrington. Beyouty Script was designed by Ian Irwan
Wismoyo in Indonesia. He is a graphic designer turned illustrator,
turned type designer. Garamond Premier Pro is an established
typeface designed by Robert Slimbach in 2005 and even more
originally, Claude Garamond in 1499-1561.

The book was printed in the United States of America, on 50lb white
paper, perfect bound, with a gloss color cover.